MW00412605

7|20

NEARLY DEAD
Anglesey Murders Edition; book 3

CONRAD JONES

'You had a gun in your sock and a vest on,' Kim pushed. She raised her eyebrows.

'I always carry that thirty-eight. You have been spying on me for fourteen months, Inspector, you know what kind of people I have to deal with. It's a risky business sometimes.' Lloyd shrugged.

'We arrested Brian Selby two days ago,' Alan said, changing tack. It was Lloyd's turn to look shocked.

'Fat Brian?' Lloyd shrugged. 'What did he do to get himself arrested?'

'He was coming out of Berwyn woods late at night.'

'And?' Lloyd said, composing himself. He glanced at Jacob, who had leaned forwards with a concerned expression on his face.

'We found the body of Stuart Radcliffe buried in the woods.' Kim moved closer to the bed. She watched his expression change. 'Would you know anything about that?'

Jacob shook his head.

'No, nothing at all. What happened to him?' Lloyd asked, feigning surprise.

'Brain Selby said that you shot him,' Alan said, watching his reaction.

'Me? Brian said that?' Lloyd sounded disappointed. 'Stuart and I were friends for years. Why would I kill my friend?'

'You found out that he was an informer,' Alan said, flatly.

'I am shocked that Brian has blamed me. I can't say that I'm surprised if I am honest. He's a strange character.'

'Granted,' Alan agreed. 'Strange or not, he has made a statement that you killed Stuart Radcliffe with a spade.'

Lloyd's eyes opened wide. He looked at Jacob and laughed. 'I thought fat Brian said that I shot Stuart.' Lloyd looked genuinely shocked. 'As for killing someone with a spade, I haven't got a clue what you're talking about!'

'I just want to clarify something,' Jacob interrupted. 'You said he had been shot?'

'He was shot but our witness claims that Radcliffe came around while he was being buried and you stabbed him three times with an entrenching tool.'

'An entrenching tool?' Lloyd asked. 'What the fuck is that?'

'A folding spade,' Alan replied, calmly.

'I bet you that if you look through fat Brian's finances, he'll have bought one of those.' Lloyd looked around the room and studied their faces. 'He's a geek. If anyone owns one of them, it's him. I don't have a lot of folding spades. I've been trying to give them up,' Lloyd said, laughing sourly. 'Are there prints on the handle?'

'We're not at liberty to say,' Kim replied.

'I promise you, lady,' Lloyd said, sitting forward and smiling. 'You will

not find my prints on that spade. Your witness is a liar.'

'Do you have proof that my client was there?' Jacob asked, frowning. 'I'm not hearing anything concrete here.'

'Apart from an eyewitness?' Kim snapped.

'I should have seen this coming really,' Lloyd said, shaking his head. 'Those two never got on from the day Brain approached me with his idea for smuggling gear over the wall into the prison.'

'Brian Selby approached you?' Alan snorted. 'I've heard it all now.'

'You can ask his work colleague. He'll verify what I'm saying. His name is Luke Davis. The drone idea was Brian's. He needed the money to pay for his mother's carers. He looks after her but needed some help when he was at work.'

'Are you serious?' Kim scoffed.

'Deadly serious,' Lloyd answered. 'He's a very clever man. He builds those drones himself; you know?'

'We know,' Alan said.

'Have you seen his website?' Lloyd asked. He could tell by the expression on their faces that they hadn't. 'It's amazing. He flies his drones all over the place and films it and uploads it onto his website. It's well worth a look.'

'We'll do that.'

'He comes over as a geek but he has the mind of a criminal. Some of the ideas he had for using his drones were amazing. Don't fall for the fat child routine,' he added, wagging his finger at them. 'Stuart didn't trust him. He had his number straight away.'

'What do you mean?' Kim asked. She had seen both sides of Brian Selby and she was beginning to have her doubts about just how stupid he was. Lloyd's version was messing with her mind.

'Stuart hated Brian,' Lloyd sighed. 'From the very first time that they met. I should have known that things might get out of hand.'

'What are you talking about?' Kim asked, her tone full of frustration.

'They didn't get on at all,' Lloyd explained. 'There was an argument about the drone and they had a fight.' He paused as if to recall the memories. 'They took some separating I can tell you. Stuart cut Brian's face with a knife. He needed stitches.'

'Brian said that you cut his face,' Alan said, in a matter of fact tone. Lloyd looked annoyed but didn't react.

'I suppose it would back up his story if he said that I'd cut him but it isn't the truth. Stuart cut him. Brian was very angry about it. I've never seen him become violent like that. He's a big unit. Brian said that he was going to kill Stuart but Stuart just laughed at him. He said that he wouldn't know when or where it would happen but he would kill him. I didn't think that he meant it though, but looking back, there was something in his eyes when he

said it, you know what I mean, don't you?'

Alan looked at Kim and shook his head. It was obvious that either Lloyd Jones had been working out his answers very carefully with Jacob Graff or Selby was leading them wherever he wanted to. One of them was lying.

'You're saying that you weren't there?' Alan asked for clarity. Lloyd was about to answer but Jacob raised his hand.

'You don't need to answer that. Are you going to charge my client with the murder of Stuart Radcliffe?' Jacob interjected.

'Not right now,' Kim said, looking at Alan. He agreed. 'We have enough with all the surveillance evidence to keep him here while we decide exactly what to charge him with. There's so much, we'll just pick the really bad stuff,' she said, with a straight face.

'My office is working on exactly what is admissible so I wouldn't be counting your chickens just yet, detectives,' Jacob said, with a lizard smile. 'Your informers were involved in criminal activity themselves while they were gathering evidence. I think we can class the majority of what you have as illegally obtained evidence. Hence it will be thrown out and a jury will never hear most of it.'

'Bullshit,' Alan sighed, tiring of Graff. 'There's enough admissible evidence there to convict the pope. He's in it way above his head.'

'I don't think so but I think that we should proceed with 'no comment' for now, while you decide how credible your witness is or if he will even testify,' Jacob said, with a half-smile. He shrugged his shoulders. 'You know what witnesses are like in this kind of case, very unreliable.'

'I think the forensics will back it up,' Kim said.

'If you had forensics, you would be charging my client right now.'

'Most of it is still being processed,' Kim snapped. 'You know what you said about counting chickens.'

'Brian also told us about your abattoir and the Wicks brothers,' Alan said, throwing a grenade into the conversation. He wanted to unnerve the smug bastard. Lloyd shot a worried glance at Jacob. The confident mask dropped for a few seconds but soon returned.

'No comment.'

'We've made initial enquiries about the Wicks brothers, David and Graham,' Kim added. 'They're listed as missing.' Lloyd grinned but it looked more like a grimace. 'Did you know them?'

'No comment.'

'But you do have an abattoir?' she pushed. Lloyd looked at Jacob and nodded.

'My client had a legitimate business interest in Caergeiliog a few years ago,' Jacob interrupted. 'It consisted of an abattoir; a processing plant; and a working farm shop where the public and trade people could buy meat and

produce in bulk at a huge discount. The abattoir and animal pens have since been demolished and sold on as real estate.' Jacob looked at Lloyd for support. What Jacob had told them was the truth but even Jacob didn't know about the illegal meat site a few miles away. Lloyd nodded that he was correct. 'A housing association made an offer that my client and his partners couldn't refuse. The shop still runs well. All the paperwork is legitimate, they have regular inspections and the business is thriving and well respected.' He paused to look at the detectives, his face stern. 'The farm shop won several awards last year for the quality of its produce. I have no idea what your witness is referring to but any slanderous comments aimed at the business will be defended rigorously. As for your missing brothers, charge him with murder or move on.'

'We don't need to charge him with anything else until we're ready,' Alan said, trying hard to remain calm. 'Possession of a firearm and theft will do for now.' He paused and looked at Lloyd in the eyes.

'Sorry it's been a wasted journey for you,' Lloyd said, smiling.

'Talking to you in handcuffs is never a waste of time, Lloyd,' Alan said, coldly. 'We heard from one of our CI's yesterday that there's a contract out on you,' Alan said, gauging the reaction in his eyes. He decided that Lloyd already knew. 'He said the Karpovs are offering big money for you to be wacked.' Lloyd didn't speak but his face flushed purple. There was anger in his eyes. 'The doctor said that you'll be moved onto the wings from tomorrow. You'll be like a fish in a barrel out there.' Lloyd's expression darkened. Alan smiled thinly. 'I think we'll leave it for now.' He looked at Kim and she agreed, a half-smile on the corners of her lips. 'You sleep tight,' Alan added as they headed for the door. Jacob Graff folded his arms and smiled. It wasn't a confident smile.

They made their way back through security and headed for Alan's BMW. It was a dull morning and dark moody clouds were rolling across the sky, threatening to empty their load on the city. Both detectives were weighing up the situation in their mind.

'What do you make of that?' Kim spoke first, putting on her seatbelt.

'He didn't just muddy the water, he took a great big dump in it,' Alan said, starting the engine. 'We need to get to Derrick Makin fast and we need to clarify what the CPS is going to allow from the surveillance. As it stands, there is so much doubt in the case that it is way beyond reasonable doubt. I couldn't convict on what we have and I know that he did it so a jury would have no chance. The CPS will throw it back in our faces.'

Alan's mobile rang. The screen showed it was Dr Graham Martin from the forensic lab.

'Dr Martin,' Alan answered. The call was on loudspeaker. 'Any good news for us?'

'No,' Dr Martin said. 'The thirty-eight-calibre gun that you found on

Jones is not the weapon that killed either of your victims. It is clean, I'm afraid.'

'What type of weapon are we looking for, Doctor?' Kim asked.

'The ammunition was nine-millimetre parabellum, probably a Glock, possibly something older like a Beretta.'

'Doctor, about the Radcliffe killing in the woods,' Alan said, rubbing his palm over the stubble on his chin. 'Do we have a definite cause of death yet?'

'Well, he was shot first, as you know and then we have the three deep lacerations to the face and neck, which were inflicted while he was buried. The killer blow was to the throat. The larynx was smashed and the carotid artery was severed causing massive blood loss and cardiac arrest.' He paused. 'Does that help?'

'Not unless you can tell us who was holding the spade at the time,' Alan said, shaking his head.

'I can't do that but I can confirm that the prints on the handle belong to Brian Selby.' Alan and Kim exchanged glances. 'I'm still waiting for the DNA to come back. That could be another week, not that it is going to help much is it?'

'It would be enough to put Jones at the scene but I'm not holding my breath. Thanks, Doctor,' Alan sighed. The line went dead. They sat in silence for a few minutes.

'Brian Selby killed Radcliffe?' Kim said, sourly. 'I can't see that man shooting anyone, can you?'

'I don't see it,' Alan agreed. He switched the headlights on as the rain intensified. 'But the spade will be his. I'm sure of that and his prints are on it.'

'His prints are on it because it is his spade,' Kim said, trying to find an explanation. 'What if Jones was there but had gloves on. He shot Radcliffe, buried him but he starts to struggle because he isn't dead, so, he stabs him through the dirt, just like Selby said.'

Alan glanced at her. She looked stressed. He could see that she was trying to work out a way to lay the blame with Lloyd Jones, twisting things in her mind to make them fit.

'What if he wasn't there?'

'He was there. I know he was there and I know he shot Radcliffe. The rest of what happened is a cluster-fuck and it could jeopardise us proving Jones had anything to do with it. Something about Selby's version isn't sitting right with me.'

'Classic one man's word against another. We don't have any proof to put Jones there but we do have Selby's prints on the spade. It's not looking good for him right now.'

'Lloyd Jones is behind all of this,' Kim said, playing with the hair at her

temple, curling around her finger. 'Do you know what I hope for?' Kim said, looking out of the window as the rain began to pour. The windscreen wipers squeaked into action. Alan turned the heating up and looked at her without answering. He could see in her eyes what she meant before she said it. 'I hope someone gets to him in there and saves us a massive pain in the arse.'

CHAPTER 20

Jack Howarth opened the industrial washing machine and dragged the wet clothing out onto a trolley. The smell of detergent filled the air but it didn't mask the odour of stale sweat that came from the huge piles of dirty laundry; clothes; bedding and towels. He reached inside the drum and grabbed the socks that were stuck to the metal. There were always socks stuck to the metal. Touching them made him nauseous even when they were clean but they were not as bad as handling skid-marked boxer shorts. They were the worst. He wore gloves nowadays and didn't look at the dirty laundry anymore; he just grabbed it and looked the other way. He had been working in the laundry for two years, six hours a day, six days a week. There were three shifts working around the clock with a two-hour shut down of the machines in between each shift change for the clean laundry to be separated and distributed around the prison and for the dirty laundry to be collected and sorted into loads. As far as jobs inside prison went, it was decent enough. Not as good as working in the kitchen though. The prisoners working in the kitchen got to eat more and never went hungry. They could steal from the stores and make cash on what they could sneak back onto the wings. Working in the laundry had its own perks but they were not as lucrative as the kitchen. Some prisoners would pay for extra socks and clean underwear but most of them didn't give a shit. Stinking of body odour and having skid marks in your undies made it less likely that a predator would single you out as a potential bitch. Rape was uncommon in British jails but the threat was part of the environment. The prison officers knew that it went on occasionally and they also knew that they could never stop it completely. If you lock up hundreds of males together with no females to fuck, they will end up doing each other whether it is consensual or not. One cell mate had tried to fuck Jack once and nearly succeeded. He had waited for lights-out and then attacked him. Jack was a small man, skinny and unable to fight off his much bigger attacker. He had punched him senseless and held him down over a bunk but Jack had remembered what an older boy had told him at the orphanage where he had spent his younger years. If you can't get away, shit your pants. No one wants to see or smell that up close. He had been right. Jack had squeezed as hard as he could and managed to fill his pants which had the desired effect. His cellmate let him go and didn't bother him again that night. It was a frightening flashback to his childhood where the catholic priests had abused him. Painful memories flooded back to him, memories that shaped who he

had become as an adult, a serial abuser.

The day after the incident in his cell, Jack looked battered and bruised and when asked what had happened, he didn't grass. The other prisoners put two and two together and figured that his cellmate was a nonce. Everyone knew that Jack had been jailed for grooming a teenage girl but being held down and buggered in your cell wasn't tolerated on the wings. The prison officers made the same conclusions and they moved Jack to a single cell that afternoon. Unfortunately, a new intake arrived unexpectedly. One of the new prisoners was a nineteen-year old shoplifter who had been sentenced to fourteen days for repeat offending. He was put in the only bunk available, which was beneath the nonce. That night he was attacked and buggered so severely that he saw out his sentence in a hospital bed. The entire wing was incensed and the nonce was sent to the block for a month with privileges removed. When he returned to the wing, the prisoners had planned a reception for him that he wouldn't forget. The nonce went to take a shower the next day and the officers turned a blind eye while six men went into the showers and slashed him to ribbons with razorblades that had been melted onto toothbrushes. They set the blades a centimetre apart so that it was difficult to stitch and infections would slow the healing process, making it as painful as possible. He had required over three-hundred stitches. Jack remembered the incident like it was yesterday. His good fortune had led to a young man being brutalised in his place. Just like the orphanage. That was prison. If you put humans in a cage – they revert to being animals sometimes. Jack had made a point of trusting nobody since then.

Jack whistled an old Elvis tune as he pushed the trolley from the washer to the driers. There were four huge tumblers in a line, turning twenty-four seven. They were never dormant, even during shift changeover. They sucked the moisture from the air and made it uncomfortable to breath. He opened the door and grabbed an armful of laundry, bundling it inside and pushing it to the back of the drum. When the trolley was empty, he moved to the next drier and opened the door. It stopped rumbling and slowed to a halt. The laundry inside was bone dry and needed to be moved. Jack looked around for the other inmates that worked with him.

'This load needs taking out, you lazy bastards!' he shouted. Silence answered him. He waited a few moments for an abusive reply but none came. 'Ellis, you lazy twat, where are you?'

Nothing. Only the drone of the machines turning came to him.

'Ellis?' Jack shouted. 'Cooper?'

Nothing.

'Ellis?'

The machines turned and the gurgling sound of a washing machine emptying made him jump. His co-workers had vanished. That wasn't good.

He backed up towards the washers, his eyes fixed to the exit. There was a wooden paddle near the washing machines. They used it to push laundry into the driers when they were hot. It was thick and heavy. If a predator thought they could attack him, they would have to chew on wood first. Ellis and Cooper were sex offenders too. No one else would work with them. He would give Ellis and Cooper a smack for fucking off and leaving him to face them alone. Cowards. The machines rumbled on. Sweat formed on his skin and he felt it trickling down his back. He listened intently and watched the exit for movement. All seemed quiet. He racked his brain for the answers to what was going on.

'Jack Howarth!' a voice shouted in his ear. He turned to face whoever had sneaked up on him and twisted straight into an uppercut, which connected with his jaw with concussive power. His glasses flew across the room and clattered along the floor and settled under the washing machines. A second blow landed on the solar plexus, forcing the breath from his lungs. His knees buckled and he felt white lightning flash across his brain. He would have collapsed but strong hands gripped his arms and held him fast. Black faces crowded in on him and he felt himself being carried across the laundry.

'Listen to me, Jack Howarth!' a deep voice growled. He recognised it. It belonged to AJ. His heart began to beat so fast that he thought he was going into cardiac arrest. He felt a sharp slap to his face and his vision began to clear. They stood him upright near the driers. The air was scorched and his throat was parched from the heat and the fear. 'Are you listening to me?'

'What have I done, AJ?' Jack gasped. He couldn't fathom why one of the prison's senior hierarchy would be pissed off with him. He kept himself to himself and worked hard at avoiding the gangs, especially AJ's outfit. 'What have I done?' he repeated.

'You have been a sneaky bastard, Howarth, you little nonce,' AJ said, wagging his index finger in his face. 'And I don't like sneaky bastards on my wing. It makes me feel uneasy when there are nonces on my wing, messes with my karma, you know what I mean?' AJ towered above him, so big that he seemed to block out the light. His black skin seemed even darker in the fluorescent light of the laundry. 'So, what am I going to do with you, Jack?'

'Nothing, AJ!' Jack blurted. 'You don't need to do anything with me. Why am I a sneaky bastard, what have I done?'

'Oh, I think you know what you have done.'

'I haven't got a clue, AJ, honestly I haven't!'

'You have been running errands for Lloyd Jones on my wing,' AJ chided. 'Now I don't like Lloyd Jones and I don't like his little rats running errands on my wing. I won't have nonces running around doing errands for Jones.' AJ tilted his head to one side. 'Do you know what we do with

nonces?'

'No, AJ,' Jack bumbled. 'And I don't want to know. I don't know what you're talking about. I haven't done anything for Lloyd Jones. I hardly know the guy.'

'Now that is a huge mistake, Jack,' AJ said, shaking his head. 'I'm very disappointed.'

'What?' Jack looked at the men. 'What mistake?' he rambled. 'What did I do?'

'You lied to me, Jack.' AJ grimaced. He gestured to the drier with his head. One of his men opened the door; the drum was empty. 'I know for a fact that you know him.'

'No!' Jack knew what was coming. He had seen it happen to other prisoners who were sex offenders. One of them broke his neck and never walked again. 'No, AJ! Don't do this to me, please!'

The other men lifted Jack up and shoved him into the drum headfirst. He clawed at the edges with his fingers, desperately trying to grip the door. One of the men smashed his fingers with his fist. 'Don't, please!'

'You can have a minute to yourself while you think about lying to me again.' He nodded and his men closed the door and twisted the dial to a minute. Jack's screams were muffled and incoherent. The drum clunked and rattled as he tumbled around against the drum. AJ watched the dial turn slowly. When it reached thirty seconds, he nodded and his men opened the drier. Jack was whimpering like an injured dog; his eyes were wide with panic. His nose was bleeding and he was covered in his own vomit. They dragged him out and he crumpled onto the floor. He curled up into a ball. 'Do you want to go back in, Jack?'

'No!'

'Lloyd Jones?'

'Okay, okay,' Jack said, his voice breaking. He spat a broken tooth onto the floor. 'I hate Lloyd Jones, let's get that straight.' He pushed himself up to his knees. A bruise was forming above his right eye and a blister was rising on his cheek. The skin on his head and face was red as if he had been scalded. 'He threatened my daughter. She's vulnerable,' Jack lied.

'Vulnerable how?'

'She is easy to find, exposed a lot of the time.'

'What do you mean?'

'She works on the streets.'

'She's on the game?' AJ sneered. Jack looked frightened. 'I knew that.' Jack looked at the floor. 'What, you don't think we do our homework?'

'She's an addict,' Jack said, nodding, going along with his story. 'She works the streets to buy her drugs and she's vulnerable.'

'I get the picture.'

106

'Jones said that he had men watching her and if I didn't do what he said, they would throw her into a van and …' Jack choked on his words. 'You know what he said he would do to her, he's sick!' Jack looked for sympathy but there none there. 'He wanted Officer Clough's fingerprints on some coin bags. I didn't see the harm in stitching up a screw so I went along with it. I was only looking out for my daughter.' He looked at AJ, hoping that his lie wasn't obvious. He had done it for money and nothing else. 'I didn't mean to piss you off, AJ. I didn't know you were enemies, honest.'

'Where are the packets?' AJ asked. He folded his arms. 'I need them.'

'What about my daughter?'

'Do you think Jones is the only one with men on the streets?'

'No.'

'I need those packets, right now.'

'They are in the filter on the far washing machine.'

'Good man,' AJ said. One of his men moved to retrieve the parcel. They were all over six feet tall, more reminiscent of a basketball team than a prison gang. He pulled open the drawer and pulled out the watertight package. He held it up for the others to see. 'Carry on with your work, Howarth. Not a word about this, understand?'

'Of course,' Jack said, nodding. 'I'm not a grass.' AJ and his men walked away without a word. 'AJ, you won't tell anyone that I gave them up, will you?'

'What, anyone like Jones?' AJ said, turning back to look at him. Jack nodded silently. 'You can tell him yourself tomorrow. I've heard he's on the hospital wing.'

'What?' Jack said, his voice a whisper. 'He'll kill me.'

'You need to tool up, Jack,' AJ said, grinning. 'Carry something sharp and if he comes near you, stick it in his eye.' He paused and winked. 'Don't worry too much, I've heard there's a mark on him. Fifty-grand, I've heard. I think he'll be busy watching his own back. Keep your head down and stay out of his way, you'll be fine.' Jack nodded and wiped congealing blood from his nose.

AJ and his men walked out of the laundry. A few minutes later, Ellis and Cooper walked back in, sheepishly. 'Are you okay, Jack?' Ellis asked.

'Get fucked,' Jack replied, quietly. He stood up and pushed past them. 'There's a load in that drier that needs shifting.' He walked towards the exit.

'Where are you going?' Cooper asked.

'To change my clothes if that's okay with you,' Jack said, sourly. 'I've shit myself,' he added as he left.

CHAPTER 21

Matt Freeman was sitting in his car at the top of the Great Orme, looking down over Puffin Island and across to Anglesey. The wind was making the car shake and he watched the waves crashing against the mainland at Penmaenmawr; foam from the sea covered the coast road. He sipped coffee from a McDonalds cup and looked at his watch. She was thirty-minutes late. She was always late. She had been late for every date they had ever been on and she was late for their wedding. Not fashionably late, twenty--minutes late. Everyone thought she had changed her mind, including him. She had no concept of punctuality. Even now, when he was on the run, she couldn't turn up on time. The police had been to his house three times since Chris had thrown himself out of the car. He hadn't heard from any of the outfit but he had heard that Lloyd had been shot and banged up in prison. That took the pressure off him a little. With the ringleader locked up, the police wouldn't be as bothered about his minions. That was his take on it, anyway. It might give him the time and space to leave the country.

The sound of an engine approaching snapped him from his thoughts. She was here. Her white VW Golf appeared over the hill and entered the little car park. She waved a hand and smiled. Her smile made him melt. It was her sad smile. She had two, one happy, one sad. The happy one made him glow but the sad one always sent him into a spin. They had been teenage sweethearts. He still loved her very much. When she hurt, he hurt twice as much.

She parked next to him and turned off her lights. The daylight was fading fast. Matt leaned over to open the passenger door. His wife, Sandra climbed out of the Golf and ran the short distance to his Range Rover. She climbed up and hugged him tightly. The smell of her perfume made him feel safe. She was his everything, wife, lover, friend, mother to his children, advisor, and the one person he trusted. Probably the only person he trusted, if the truth be told.

'Sandra,' he whispered in her ear. She held him tighter. 'I've missed you.' He pulled away from her a little and looked into her eyes. They kissed gently. 'Are the kids alright?' he asked as they parted.

'No, they're missing their dad,' she said, shaking her head. 'The police were around again last night. They turned the place upside down again, even went up into the loft. The kids are asking questions and I don't know what to tell them, Matt. Shelby keeps waking up in the night crying and asking for her dad. They don't understand why you're not coming home.'

'Tell them I'll be home soon,' he said, touching her face. 'We'll be together soon. I've got a plan.'

'No, Matt,' she said, frowning. 'I'm not lying to them. If I tell them you're coming home and the police grab you, what then?' Matt pulled away completely and looked out of the window. 'How long do I tell them you will be? A year? Five years?' she said, turning his face back to hers. 'Could it be ten years? I can't lie to them. That is cruel. It would make things worse.'

'I don't know what to say, San,' he said with a shrug. 'I'm not going to let them lock me up. That's why I needed to see you face to face.' He looked into her eyes and smiled. 'I've arranged for a boat to take us to Ireland. We can go tomorrow.' He looked deep into her eyes and saw confusion. They filled with tears and one fell onto her cheek. 'Don't cry, San.' He touched her cheek with the back of his hand and wiped the tear away. 'Everything will be alright if we got to Ireland, you'll see. We need to get away from here.'

'What are you talking about Ireland for?' she snapped. 'Are you mad?'

'No. I've been giving a lot of thought,' Matt said, calmly. 'You me and the kids could get the boat to Ireland. I've got a friend who can sail us across. We'll be safe in the south. I've got enough money put by to buy somewhere and to keep us going for a few years. The kids would love it over there.'

Sandra flicked her blond hair behind her ears and shook her head. She sighed loudly.

'What makes you think that the kids would love it there?' she asked, incredulously. 'All their friends are here, their schools are here, their grandparents are here, their cousins are here, and I am here!' She began to lose her temper. 'What the fuck is there in Ireland that they would love? You are living in cloud cuckoo land.'

'They would adjust,' Matt replied, keeping his cool. 'They're young. It's the only way I can stay out of jail.'

'What about my mum and dad, Matt?' she held up her hands and shrugged. 'What do I tell them? "You won't be able to see me or the kids again because Matt is on the run from the police." Have you lost your marbles? Our lives are here.'

'I'm trying to keep the family together, San,' Matt pleaded. 'I don't know what else to do. Come on, I'm struggling here, San.'

'You should have thought about that before you got mixed up with Lloyd Jones,' she said, wiping another tear from her eye. 'I warned you what a bastard he is. Look at what happened to Stuart and Chris.' She stopped to compose herself when her voice broke slightly. Matt held her for a moment but she felt distant. 'I cannot believe Rachel and Claire are dead. That poor woman. What must she have been thinking in that car? All because of Lloyd Jones.' Her lip quivered. 'I know Chris was a grass and he's caused all

this shit but he didn't deserve what happened to him. None of them did. An entire family wiped out because you lot wanted to play gangsters.' She shook her head and took a deep breath. 'Well, it's blown up in your face hasn't it and you expect me to uproot my children and take them away from their home, their friends, and their family?' she shook her head again and looked into his eyes. 'Not a chance, Matt. That is not happening. You're going to have to front this up. You need to swallow the medicine, not your kids, only you can do it.'

'What can I do, San?'

'Turn yourself in, Matt.'

'What?'

'You heard me. Turn yourself in,' she said, touching his face. 'Do your time and I'll be here when you get out. So will the kids. I'm not taking them from their home, Matt.'

'We're not talking a few months here; I'll get years, San!' he banged the steering wheel. 'I'm not going away for years, watching my kids grow up from a prison cell, talking to them in a visiting room.' He shook his head vehemently. 'No way.'

'How selfish are you?'

'What?'

'You know if you get convicted and don't cooperate that they can take the house from us?' she said, glaring at him. 'It's called the proceeds of crime act. They can confiscate everything, even my home. They will take the lot, Matt.'

'Who told you that?'

'They did.'

'Who are they?'

'Matrix and the Drug Squad. Two DI's came to our home and told me that they were going to make sure that it won't be our home for much longer.'

'When was this?'

'Last night!'

'They're trying to frighten you.'

'They are frightening me!' she said, another tear rolled from her eye. 'We have to cooperate with them, Matt or we'll lose everything and you will end up in jail anyway.' She checked her watch. 'There is no other way.'

'What are you talking about, cooperate?' Matt said, nervously. 'Why are you checking your watch? What the fuck have you done, San?'

Three police cars screeched into the car park. One stopped directly behind the Range Rover; the others stopped at an angle either side.

'I'm sorry, Matt,' San whispered. 'I can't let them put me and the kids on the street.'

'What the fuck have you done?' Matt said, looking around as armed

police deployed from their vehicles. 'Did you grass me up, San?' the driver's door opened and the wind rushed in. A nine-millimetre Glock was pointed at his face. He could see the officer's lips moving as he read him his rights but he couldn't hear what he was saying. He felt his hands being forced behind his back, felt them pulling him from the seat and handcuffing him. He couldn't take his eyes from Sandra's. Tears streamed down her face, streaking her skin with mascara. 'Did you turn me in, you of all people?' he blurted.

'I'm sorry, Matt. They said if I didn't, we would lose everything. I was thinking of the kids…'

They pulled him away from his vehicle and the wind took her words away. He couldn't hear what she was saying anymore. *Sandra turned me in, he thought over and over. The only person I ever trusted …*

CHAPTER 22

Justin leaned against a wet brick wall and watched the shop doorway across the street. The window was steamed up with condensation. He was hidden from the relentless rain in an alleyway, waiting for the shop owner to return. Vince Barker owned a string of betting shops across the island. He made a lot of money from the people who could least afford to gamble. His secondary business was selling cocaine, again to the people who could least afford it. He was at the top of Lloyd's debt list and Justin was determined to collect at least some of the debt that night. If he was going on the run, he needed money, a lot of money, and he was having a bit of a dry patch financially. Collecting the Vince Barker debt would increase his chances of getting out of the country. It would guarantee him a decent lifestyle somewhere in the sun. He fancied the Canary Islands. They were cheap and accessible and sunny. He fingered the switchblade in his pocket. It was cool to the touch. Vince Barker had a reputation for being difficult about paying his debts. Justin didn't have the time to negotiate. Vince was his ticket out of the country whether he liked it or not.

A dark green Jaguar pulled up outside the shop; surface water sprayed up from the asphalt. Vince Barker climbed out of the driver's seat, locked the door and jogged through the rain to the betting shop, his head bowed. Justin watched him as he went inside and closed the door behind him. It was near closing time. The diehard punters would be thrown out in the next few minutes. Justin walked across the road and waited near the door. Rain ran from the peak of his baseball cap in a constant stream. He could hear the voice of a commentator listing the horses that were running in the last race from Chepstow. There were only a few minutes left. The betting would be halted as the horses approached the stalls, the race would be run and that would be goodnight to all the punters until the following day.

Justin pushed the door open and walked in. The heating was on and the contrast between inside and out was startling. It was warm and welcoming to encourage the customers to stay. His collar was up and he kept his shoulders hunched as he picked up a betting slip and filled it out. A five-pound win on number six at the odds of five to one. He took it to the counter and placed the bet. Vince was standing in the doorway of an office to the rear of the shop. His black hair was too dark for a man of his years and he had developed a paunch but he had the nose and swagger of a man who had fought and won many battles with his fists. A clear plastic screen

protected the staff behind the counter from the punters. Despite not reaching the ceiling, it acted as a deterrent. Tempers could flare when punters lost money, especially if they were coming down from drugs or alcohol or both. The doors were fitted with security locks and CCTV recorded every transaction. Vince Barker was a shrewd businessman.

Justin took his betting slip and moved away from the counter. He sat on a high stool and watched the horses line up. They were off and running within seconds. He looked around at the other punters. They were sallow-faced men with a lost look in their eyes. It was as if all hope had been sucked from their bodies, each race a drain, each bet sapping their lifeforce. They were sitting glued to the screen, their watery eyes not blinking as their last chance of a win that day played out. There were no cheers of celebration as the horses crossed the line. Two of the men screwed up their betting slips and tossed them into the waste basket with expert aim. A third studied his accumulator wondering where it all went wrong. The more he looked at it, the more the harsh certainty was etched into his expression. Not a single bet had come in. He wouldn't even get his stake back. The men put their coats on, drifted towards the door, muttering about how unlucky they had been and that tomorrow was another day. Justin screwed up his own betting slip and tossed it onto the floor, his horse had come in last. The lights flickered and dimmed as the staff prepared to lock up. One of the women put her coat on and joked with Vince as she made her way to the security door and punched a code in. It clicked and opened.

Justin waited as she stepped into the customer area. She looked shocked when she came face to face with him. He looked into her eyes and smiled. She relaxed a little.

'Is Vince about?' he asked, politely.

She looked over her shoulder and pointed.

'Vince!' she called. He poked his head around the doorframe. 'This man is asking for you,' she called, and then looked back again. 'What's your name, love?'

'Justin.'

'His name is Justin.'

'Justin who?' Vince tried to get a better look at him.

'Justin who?' she repeated.

'I work for Lloyd Jones,' Justin said, loudly. Vince frowned and went back into the office. He reappeared a few seconds later.

'You ladies get yourselves home,' Vince said to his staff. 'Go home and put your feet up, you've worked hard today,' he said, smiling. His eyes flicked nervously to Justin every few seconds, watching his every move.

'He's such a charmer. The best boss I've ever had,' one of them said to Justin. 'Hey, is that what your girlfriend calls you, just-in?' she nudged him with her elbow. 'Do you get it, just-in?'

'Funny, never heard that one before,' Justin said, sarcastically. The woman laughed at her own joke and nudged him again. He grinned to humour her.

The second woman cackled a little too loudly. They walked towards the front door laughing and readied their umbrellas for the deluge outside. 'Do you want me to lock this door, Vince?'

'No, leave it open. We won't be long.' The women closed the door to as they left. Vince turned to face Justin, the safety glass between them. 'So, you're one of Lloyd's men?'

'I am.'

'Have some respect and take the hat off when you're talking to me, son,' Vince said, in a patronising tone. Justin removed it without argument. 'That's better. What can I do for you?'

'Lloyd sent me to collect your debt. You owe him one hundred large,' Justin said, calmly. 'He needs it tonight.'

'Does he?' Vince said, flatly. 'I need a lot of things but that doesn't mean I'll be getting them.' Vince grinned but Justin remained deadpan. 'Why have you turned up out of the blue? He normally calls ahead when a payment is due.'

'He's busy.'

'He's busy, is he?' Vince looked into Justin's eyes. His expression showed the distaste that he felt for the younger man. 'Let's not fuck about,' Vince said, smiling coldly. He looked at the CCTV camera and nodded with his head. 'We need to be careful what we say here. We're on camera. Let's not mention what the money is for.' Justin glanced up and nodded. 'Lloyd Jones isn't busy, son so don't treat me like a mug. No one is too busy to collect their money.' He paused. 'I heard he got shot outside the Paradise club.'

'He did. The debt stands and he has asked me to collect everything that he is owed before morning. You're top of the list.'

Vince put his hands deep into his pockets and pursed his lips, a thoughtful expression on his face. His hair, the dark suit and overcoat made him look like a throwback to a Kray twins' documentary. He checked his watch and then looked at the clock on the wall. Correct as usual.

'You got to be somewhere?' Justin asked, sarcastically.

'A bookies clock has to be correct,' Vince explained. He looked back at Justin. 'I've also heard that Lloyd was lifted by Matrix at the hospital and is banged up at Her Majesty's pleasure.' He nodded and shrugged. 'He will be away for a long time from what I've been told. Might even be a life stretch, I heard.'

'I don't care what you've heard,' Justin said, with a shrug. His eyes narrowed, snake-like. 'Like I said, the debt stands and I'm here to collect.'

Vince walked closer to the screen and stared into Justin's eyes. Both

men were testing the other. Vince shook his head and sighed.

'Do you really think that I keep that kind of cash around and even if I did, that I would just hand it over to one of his monkeys?' He shook his head again. 'I don't even know who you are.'

'I've been here twice before to collect,' Justin said, offended.

'You have?'

'Twice.'

'There you go, you see. I have met you twice but I don't remember you. That says a lot about the measure of a man. Were you here with Lloyd?'

'Both times.'

'That is why I don't remember you. Lloyd is a man who deserves respect from other men. You, however, are a different kettle of fish.'

'I'll still be needing that money.'

'Protocol you see,' Vince said, raising a finger. 'We have developed a protocol that suits us both. He either calls ahead or comes himself. That is what we old school businessmen call respect.'

'Extenuating circumstances I'm afraid. I need that money.' Justin took the switchblade from his pocket and activated the blade. The knife glinted in the dull light. He jumped up onto the counter and cocked one of his legs over the screen, straddling it. 'You should have had this fitted to the ceiling.' He waved the blade from side to side. 'Don't make me come down there and carve you up, old man. I know you haven't got it all but I'll take whatever you have got.'

'I'm too old for this shit. I see how this is going to go,' Vince said, nodding, unperturbed. He shrugged, his hands still in his pockets, not bothered in the slightest. 'I don't want any trouble, son. I'll see what I can do. Wait there.' Vince turned and walked into the office out of sight. 'You'll have to bear with me while I open the safe. I have so many shops nowadays that I can't remember the codes and obviously, I can't write them down. Memory is something that young people don't appreciate enough. I often walk into a room and forget what I was doing. It's my age.'

'Take all the time you need, just do it quickly!' Justin called after him. He watched the front door nervously, wishing that he had locked it before making his move. 'Hurry up in there!'

'Calm down. I'm going as fast as I can. Less haste, more speed, my old man used to say,' Vince said, calmly from the other room. Justin heard the door creak open. 'Now then, how much is in here. There's a lot of coins. I don't suppose you want coins, do you?'

'No. I don't want coins!'

'Let me see what I can do.'

There was a long pause. Justin was getting edgy. Sweat was running from his head at the temples. He thought about jumping down from the counter but decided against it. Men like Vince were wily. He could have a

tool in the office and be waiting behind the door for him to walk in.

'I've only got a few grand here. The girls must have done a bank run,' Vince said, from the other room. 'I don't keep much cash around these days. Everything is digital nowadays.' Justin could hear him but he couldn't see him. 'I have punters coming in here putting a quid each way on a debit card. madness. It saves me a fortune on banking charges but when I need to get my hands on a big sum of cash, it creates problems. You understand, I'm sure.'

The sound of bags of coins being moved around came from the office. Justin looked at the clock.

'And as for the taxman, well that's a whole other story. You can't hide fuck all anymore. No cash transactions, you see. The world has gone digital and the taxman knows everything you have taken nowadays. I used to have two sets of books but not anymore, oh no.' Vince went quiet for a moment. 'You know what I was thinking then?'

'What?' Justin called.

'One of the reasons I got fucked on my divorce was the cashless world.'

'Oh, for fuck's sake!' Justin muttered. 'Hurry up, Vince!'

'She was bitch you know. Much younger than me but she'd been around. She had a fanny like a yawning donkey. I should have known better but sometimes our brains are in our trousers. When I first met her, I was blown away. She was a stunner. One of my pals tried to warn me. He said she had had more fingers up her than Sooty and Sweep put together.' There was another pause. 'Still, we don't listen were women are concerned. You know what I mean, don't you?'

'Yes, yes, just hurry up.' Justin checked his watch. The minutes were ticking by. 'What are you doing, printing the stuff?'

'I can do five grand,' Vince called. 'I've got six in here but I need a grand to operate tomorrow.'

'Five grand?' Justin shouted. He rolled his eyes towards the heavens. Five grand wouldn't last long. 'Are you fucking with me?'

'Like I said, I don't keep cash lying around, can't afford to these days. Do you want it in an envelope?'

'Are you taking the piss?' Justin said, watching the office door for Vince to come back. He appeared in the doorway and leaned against the frame. His hands were still in his pockets. He winked at Justin and smiled, checking his watch.

'Where's the money?' Justin shouted.

'In the safe where it's staying,' Vince said, casually. He gestured towards the window with his head. 'Your taxi will be here in a minute.' A blue light began to strobe on the ceiling, followed closely by another. 'You are a real amateur, son,' Vince said, shaking his head. 'Haven't you heard of silent alarms?' Justin's jaw dropped. Anger flashed in his eyes but he knew he had

fucked up. 'I triggered it as soon as you said you worked for Lloyd Jones. I'd put that knife down before you get yourself shot.' Vince chuckled to himself. 'Fucking idiot,' he muttered, as the police burst in. Justin dropped the switchblade and put his hands in the air.

CHAPTER 23

Brian was sitting at the table, nervously biting his nails. There wasn't much left to bite. He had been chewing them constantly all his life but his habit had intensified since his arrest. His regular brief couldn't make the interview on such short notice and had sent Thomas, a junior from the practice, in his place. He was younger than Brian, scruffy and smelled of alcohol. It was obvious that he had been out on the town until the early hours. His eyes were bloodshot and bleary. Brian wasn't impressed with his pre-interview briefing, which had consisted of Thomas glancing through the file, yawning every few minutes and texting between yawning. When he had finished, he said, 'Don't worry. It should be a walk in the park. They haven't got anything.' Brian wasn't convinced that he was right about that. There was something niggling at him, something that he couldn't put his finger on. He had spoken to his mother the night before and she was very distressed that he was locked up and that had rattled him further. Looking after her had been his primary function for as long as he could remember. Listening to her crying had broken his heart. He had to get out and go home. What had happened had no sense of reality to it. It was all like a bad dream. He wanted to wake up at home in his bed with the smell of coffee and toast in the air. The stink of custody was choking him. He had decided that he would tell them whatever they wanted to know to get out.

The door opened and DI Kim Davies stepped in. Her dark business suit touched her curves subtly. Alan was a few steps behind her. They looked stern as they took their seats and went through the legalities. Brian had the feeling that there had been a paradigm shift in his situation.

'I want you to take us through what happened in the woods when you were with Lloyd Jones and Stuart Radcliffe,' Kim opened. Brian was about to object but she held up her hand to silence him. 'You need to think very carefully about the sequence of events and exactly how things happened. Take your time and tell the truth, Brian.'

'My client has answered this several times,' Thomas interrupted. 'Why are we going over this again?'

'Because the evidence tells us that Brian is telling lies and this is his last opportunity to tell the truth,' Alan said, leaning forward. His forehead was creased with deep lines. 'I would suggest that rather than being obstructive, you advise your client to tell the truth.'

Thomas opened his mouth to speak and then decided not to. He

looked at Brian and nodded. Brian had no idea what he meant by that. He shook his head and frowned. The atmosphere was oppressive. He felt like he was being suffocated. The desire to be outside in the fresh air, free to walk around was crushing. He pulled at the neck of the grey sweatshirt that he was wearing.

'Brian?' Kim pushed.

'I've told you everything.'

'We don't think that you have.'

'Do we have to do this again?'

'Yes. We do.'

'Where do you want me to start?' Brian said, sighing. His chin was down, making him appear to have no neck.

'Start from when you were digging up the drone,' Kim encouraged.

'Okay. I dug up the bag and showed them what was inside.' He began. 'I thought that would be enough but Lloyd took out a gun and told me to keep digging. Stuart kept shouting at me. He hit me a couple of times and scratched my neck. I thought that they were going to kill me and bury me and I was pleading with Lloyd not to kill me.' He looked up and tried to gauge how the detectives were reacting. 'Then Lloyd started asking how much the Drug Squad had paid for information. I didn't know what he was talking about.' He paused and looked down at the table. 'Then he turned on Stuart and shot him twice in the chest.'

'And then?' Alan asked.

'Then he made me help him drag Stuart into the hole and we started to bury him,' Brian said. He nodded to reinforce his words. The detectives remained silent, waiting. 'We covered him with soil but then he tried to get out of the hole. He wasn't dead.' Brian looked from Kim to Alan. They looked back at him, their eyes boring into his brain, searching for the truth. 'Lloyd picked up the spade and stabbed it three times into the ground, one, two, three,' he explained. 'Then Stuart was really dead. Lloyd covered him and then he told me to fill in the grave so no one could tell anyone had been there. He said he had to be somewhere so he left and I did what he told me to do. When I was finished, I left the woods and the police arrested me.' He sat back and took a deep breath, relieved that he had finished without being put under pressure. He steepled his fingers on the table. 'Now can I go home to see my mum, please. She's very upset by all this.'

'I'm afraid not, Brian,' Alan said, with a shake of his head. 'You won't be leaving for a while, I'm afraid.'

'Why not? I've told you everything!'

'There's a problem with your version, Brian,' Alan said, calmly. Brian blushed but didn't answer. 'You see, we didn't find any evidence to prove that Lloyd Jones touched that entrenching tool.' Brian felt his heartbeat quicken. 'There are no prints and no epithelial tissue on the handle.' He

paused. 'If someone had held that handle tightly and stabbed it into the ground with force, there would be skin cells sheered from the hands. The only epithelial tissue on the handle is yours.'

'Oh, come on, detective,' Thomas interjected. 'Jones was wearing gloves!'

'Who said he was?' Kim countered. Her stare turned him to stone. 'Brian never mentioned gloves.' She looked at Brian. 'Was Lloyd wearing gloves?'

'Yes,' Brian said, swallowing hard. His face flushed again. Beads of sweat appeared on his lip.

'What type of gloves were they?' Alan asked.

'What?'

'What type of gloves were they?'

'I don't remember.'

'Leather or wool?'

'I don't remember.'

'But you do remember him wearing gloves?'

'Detective,' Thomas objected at the repeated question.

'There was no fibre or leather trace on the spade,' Alan said, shrugging. 'How do you explain that?'

'I can't,' Brian mumbled. His eyes filled with tears. He swallowed hard again.

'You said that Stuart Radcliffe scratched you,' Alan changed tack.

'Yes,' Brian said, touching his neck instinctively. 'He was a bully.'

'You were standing up when he scratched you?'

'What do you mean?'

'It is a simple question. Were you standing up when he scratched you?'

'Yes,' Brian mumbled, confused.

'You had deep scratches on your ankle, Brian,' Alan said. His face turned purple. Brian sensed what was coming. 'How did he scratch your ankle if you were standing up?'

'I...' Brian stuttered. 'I scratched myself walking through the woods, on some brambles.'

'The scratches on your ankle were made by a human hand, Brian. Our experts can testify to that beyond questioning.' Alan watched his face. He broke eye contact and wiped his lips with his sleeve. 'Which would suggest that you were standing over him or kneeling above him when he scratched you.' He paused. 'Which was it?'

Brian looked at his brief for help. His brief offered none. He seemed to be intrigued by the evidence.

'Do you know what else we found?'

Brian shrugged. A bead of sweat trickled down his cheek.

'Your blood and skin under his nails.'

'I told you that he scratched me.'

'You did but you said that you were standing up.'

'I was.'

'So, was he?'

'Yes.'

'The thing is, Brian,' Alan said, lowering his voice. 'There is soil under his nails too.' Brian stared at the table. 'But the soil is beneath your DNA. Which suggests that he forced his hand upward through the soil to scratch your ankle. Your skin is above the soil. He was in the ground when he scratched your ankle.' Alan paused another moment for effect. Brian glanced at his brief again but he wasn't game to challenge the evidence. 'Stuart Radcliffe wasn't dead when you buried him. He tried to fight his way from the grave and he scratched you and you stabbed him three times and you killed him. You did it, not Lloyd Jones.' Alan pointed his index finger in a stabbing motion towards his face. 'You killed Stuart Radcliffe. Lloyd Jones may have shot him but you struck the blows that killed him.'

'Lloyd said he would hurt my mum if I didn't do what he said,' Brian whimpered and put his head in his hands. 'Lloyd shot him twice. I thought he was dead. I was so shocked and scared and I didn't know what to do! I thought he was dead.'

'But he wasn't. He wasn't dead, Brian, and when he tried to fight his way out, he clearly wasn't dead, was he?' Alan pushed. 'That was your opportunity to help him but you didn't, did you?'

'No, but I panicked.'

'You could have phoned for an ambulance and Stuart Radcliffe might still be alive,' Kim said, sharply. 'You killed him, Brian. We're going to charge you with his murder.'

'Can we talk about a deal?' Thomas said, quickly realising that they had just called checkmate on his client.

'A deal for a cold-blooded murder?' Kim asked, laughing. 'We don't do deals with murderers. Especially when they try to pass the blame. I'm afraid this is on Brian. We're still trying to put Lloyd Jones at the scene but Brian removed the only evidence that there was. We can't prove anything in front a jury. This is all on Brian.'

'Surely there was gunshot residue on his hands?'

Alan and Kim exchanged glances.

'Jones had been shot when he was taken to hospital and he had tried to protect himself by raising his hands. He was rushed into surgery before any swabs could be taken. Obviously, his skin was cleaned before they could remove the shotgun pellets. There is no trace evidence.'

'My client will testify that Jones was there and that he shot Radcliffe.'

'Your client is a liar and he's going to jail. I'm not sure how much credence a jury would give to his evidence.'

'What do you mean, going to jail?' Brian said, astounded. 'What about my mum?' Brian gasped. 'I need to go home!'

'You won't be going home for a very long time,' Kim said, shaking her head. 'Get used to the idea.'

CHAPTER 24

Lloyd Jones pulled on a pair of green denim prison jeans and a grey sweatshirt; standard issue in HMP Berwyn. The stench of incarcerated men filled his senses. The smell of the wings intensified as he neared the landings. He could hear the prisoners shouting abuse at each other and at the PO's from behind their cell doors. The prison was still locked down. Someone was banging something hard against their door; the noise echoed along the wings. The smells and sounds of incarceration were familiar to him. They held no fear for him. Fear wasn't something that he endured. He had no fear of being locked up and no fear of any other man. One to one, he was a monster with no empathy or sympathy. If an opponent dared to take him on then he had better be prepared to die. Lloyd would not stop beating an opponent until he was pulled off or they stopped breathing. He believed that letting an opponent live was creating a serious problem for further down the line. Most opponents in his world lived or died on their reputation. Take a hiding and you lose more than your dignity. Your street credibility would be seriously impacted and the lesser animals would see you in a different light, as weak and vulnerable. Lloyd was neither weak nor vulnerable in his own eyes. There were others that thought differently.

They approached the sterile area and he was handed his washing kit. The landings quietened for a moment as whispers passed from cell to cell that a new intake was being brought onto the wing. He was being admitted to B Wing, where category B prisoners were housed. This was where the dangerous inmates were kept. Security was tighter than the other wings and the PO's were tougher. Discipline was harsh. He had walked those landings before and they held no anguish for him. It was part and parcel of the job.

They proceeded through a series of buffer gates to the final entry point. The prisoners in the cells nearest to the gate began shouting excitedly as they caught sight of him.

'Fuck me, it's Lloyd Jones!'

His name bounced off the walls up to the top tiers and back down again. The wing exploded in a maelstrom of noise. A cacophony of excited welcomes mingled with vile abuse and threats. Some were pleased to see his arrival, others not so much. He listened to the voices, trying to identify allies and narrow down where his enemies were positioned. It was an impossible task. Their voices reverberated from the iron landings and steel

staircases.

'I hear you're a dead man walking, Jones. You horrible bastard!' One voice kept repeating. It was like a stuck record, the voice excited and full of hate.

'Fifty-grand for whoever kills your fat arse, Jones!' another voice called from further along the landings. Raucous laughter rolled along the landings.

'Fifty-grand for that soft shite?' a voice from his left shouted. 'I could do him without putting my brew down! Wanker, Jones!'

'Fifty-grand? I'll do that bastard for nothing!' Another one shouted from his right.

'We've got your back, Lloyd!' A friendly voice pierced to deafening racket.

'Take no notice, Lloyd boy. They are all shithouses on this wing,' a deep voice growled. 'Fucking window-warriors the lot of them!' he added, referring to how brave some of the inmates were when they were safely locked in their cells. 'We'll see how brave they are later!'

The insult resulted in another deafening wave of abuse crashing along the landings. This time the noise didn't subside for five long minutes. Even Lloyd was surprised at the vehement polarity his arrival had caused.

'It sounds to me like you've made a good impression already,' a familiar voice said. Lloyd looked through the bars. Peter Clough was on the landing. 'I think you're going to fit right in on B Wing.' The officer winked and smiled wryly.

'Officer Clough,' Lloyd said, grinning. 'What a nice surprise to see you here. I needed to see a friendly face!'

'I think they're going to be in short supply somehow,' Peter said, straight-faced. 'In fact, I'd go so far as to say, you'll be lucky to see a friendly face in the mirror!'

The officer escorting him opened the final gate and ushered him through. He handed a paper bag to the officers on the landing.

'That's his medication,' he explained. 'All the dosages are on the bottles. The doctor said that he can't work for a few weeks until the bruising has gone down. The governor wants him on the top tier out of the way.'

'A third-floor penthouse, eh, Jones,' Peter scoffed. 'The top tier with all the nonces and paedophiles. Sounds about right to me. Like I said, you'll fit right in here!'

Lloyd stopped grinning. His eyes fixed on Peter.

'You should be careful, Officer Clough,' he said, leaning closer. 'That nasty mouth could get you into trouble.'

'I don't think so somehow,' Peter said, shaking his head. He gestured with his hand. 'Get this piece of shit off my landing.' Lloyd looked both confused and slightly amused. 'Enjoy your stay, Jones,' he added with a

smile. 'The only way you're leaving here is horizontally.'

'Fuck you, Clough,' Lloyd snapped. 'You had better remember who you're talking to.' The PO's dragged him away towards the stairs. As he came into view of all three landings, the noise level increased again. Lloyd looked around at the cells, cages for humans. Why didn't they just call them cages? That always puzzled him. A bear was put in a cage but a man is put into a cell. Same thing but a different name, why?

He studied the faces, some were friendly, most were not. Some of the prisoners just stared, impassively, unaware of who he was and why his arrival was causing such a stir. He made a mental note of who was shouting abuse, remembering their faces. He smiled coldly, as one man realised that he had made eye contact midsentence. Lloyd Jones had heard what he shouted and seen his face. The man withdrew from the bars but he was too late. He would be on the list of enemies. Lloyd would remember his face and he would punish him brutally. He could try to avoid him but there was nowhere to hide in prison and Lloyd had years to wait. There would be an opportunity sometime in the future. There always was.

As he reached the middle landing, he caught the eye of a familiar face. His smile faded as the black face looked at him with interest. He was expressionless, uninterested. Anthony John stared at him; his face impassive. Lloyd nodded a silent greeting and AJ returned the gesture. Keeping an uneasy peace with the other top dogs would narrow down his potential enemies. There would be plenty of them when there was fifty-grand on his head. It would not be personal. Del Makin was a personal issue. Killing Lloyd for fifty-grand would appeal to a lot of people who had no axe to grind with him. Business was business and fifty-grand was a lot of money. Lloyd had put out hits on dealers for fifty-pounds and a gram of coke; fifty-grand was another level. Life was cheap in the big prison especially in the drug world. The rewards were huge, the risks equally so.

Lloyd looked away from AJ and climbed the staircase slowly. The PO's wanted him to move faster so that the wing would settle down but Lloyd was taking his time purposely. His huge frame couldn't be moved anywhere that it didn't want to go without a mammoth effort. The officers didn't want to end up rolling around on the landings with Lloyd and he knew it. He played the power game with the PO's and inmates alike. They could see that he was dragging his feet, making eye contact with as many caged men as possible on the journey just to let them know that he did not fear them in fact, quite the opposite. He was showing them that they should fear him.

The procession climbed to the second landing. The noise didn't abate. They walked past a cell and Lloyd eyed the occupant. The man was squat and solid, as wide as he was tall. A scar ran from his forehead down his nose to his chin. Someone had opened his face from top to bottom,

splitting the nose in half. Whoever had stitched him back together would never win surgeon of the year. Stitch marks crisscrossed the scar, making it look like a pink ladder that climbed his face. His left eye had a turn in it. He grinned widely, making him look crazed.

'What the fuck are you looking at?'

'I'm deciding what you do on the outside, bet you're a model aren't you?' Lloyd said, sarcastically.

'You're one funny man.'

'You're one ugly bastard!'

'My boss sends his regards, Jones,' the man growled. His accent was guttural, as if he had phlegm in his throat. 'I'm looking forward to meeting you properly,' he said, grinning like a lunatic. He ran his finger across his throat in a cutting motion. 'You're already dead.'

'Shut it, Volkov!' one of the PO's shouted. 'You'll be put on report!'

'Fuck you!' Volkov snarled. He turned back to Lloyd and smiled again. He blew a kiss. 'I'll see you soon.'

Lloyd blew a kiss back to him. The Russian stopped grinning and glared at him.

'When they open the doors, I'm going to come and see you. We'll see how tough you are then, Jones.'

'I'm looking forward to it,' Lloyd said, nodding his head. Lloyd cleared his throat and spat in his face. A thick globule of saliva and phlegm splattered on his cheek. He stepped backwards, in disgust and wiped at it with his sleeve. The Russian flipped and clawed at the bars.

'I'll kill you!' he snarled.

'Get in the queue, Drago!' someone shouted from below.

They walked on quickly and climbed up the stairs.

'You shouldn't have done that,' a PO said.

'Is he one of the Karpovs?' Lloyd asked.

'There's no fooling you is there, Jones?' one of them answered, sarcastically.

'How many of them are there in here?'

'There's four of them on the wing and another half a dozen across the other wings. If I had it my way, I'd deport the bastards. This place is like the Hilton compared to a Russian gulag. They're trouble. You'll need to watch your back.'

'That's the impression that I'm getting too,' Lloyd joked, dryly. 'There's nothing like a warm welcome, and that was absolutely nothing like a warm welcome!'

They reached the top tier and the din from below lessened a little. The inmates on the third floor knew better than to join in with the abuse. They were rapists and paedophiles and sexual deviants of all descriptions. Their offences made them less than human in the prison ecosystem. Attracting

attention wasn't advisable. They tiptoed around trying to be as invisible as possible. None of them were about to hurl abuse at Lloyd Jones. He scanned the landing and looked at the faces of the men who had come to take a look. They were all unfamiliar except for one.

Jack Howarth made eye contact but showed no signs of recognition. He didn't want anyone in the prison to know that he had run errands for Lloyd. AJ and his crew already knew and that was bad enough. Making allies with the hierarchy meant making enemies elsewhere. On B Wing, Jack was just another nonce and he wanted to keep it that way, although something told him that it wouldn't be that simple. Lloyd would come asking for his packets to control that screw, Clough and when he did, he would have to tell him that AJ took them from him. That would set AJ off and officer Clough already had it in for him; all he needed now was a lunatic like Lloyd on his case too. Things were going to turn nasty, quickly, and there was nowhere to run.

CHAPTER 25

Del Makin waited at the bus stop in Bangor, watching the taxi rank across the street. It was pouring down and shoppers scurried along beneath a rainbow of umbrellas. Office workers and the city's retail employees moved quickly through the crowds with a practised expertise. A double-decker pulled up and the doors hissed open. Commuters jostled onto the bus, leaving Del alone. The driver looked at him to see if he was going to climb aboard but Del was busy watching. Watching and waiting.

Black cabs pulled into the rank opposite and picked up their fares from the front of a queue that stretched along the pavement and around the corner. It never seemed to diminish when it was raining. A taxi left with a customer and another customer joined the queue. He waited patiently. Hours went by and the rain stopped. The sun went down. All the people had gone home and the line of black cabs grew longer than the queue of customers. Then he saw the taxi that he wanted.

He pulled up his hood, crossed the road, and lingered near the back of the queue. He counted how many customers there were and how many taxis were in front of the one that he wanted, when they matched, he joined the queue. The customers shuffled forward as each cab left, leaving a wake of spray behind them. The stink of diesel tainted the air and oil floated on the rainwater puddles; the colours like the iridescent hues of a pigeon's neck. Someone walked past eating chips from a white paper parcel, the aroma made him feel hungry. The penultimate cab trundled away and he stepped towards the one that he wanted. He opened the door and climbed it. The heaters were on full blast and the windows were steamed up.

'Where to, mate?' the Asian driver asked, a hint of Welsh in his accent.

'The White Eagle, please,' Del said, chirpily. 'The entrance on the Rhoscolyn side will do fine.'

'I know it,' the driver said, indicating and pulling into the traffic cautiously. 'Nice part of the island. Do you live there?'

'No. Just visiting friends.' Del put his head back onto the seat and closed his eyes. The driver got the hint that he wasn't much of a talker and wanted to chill out. He slid the glass window closed, muffling the noise from the city streets. The traffic was stop-start through Bangor but thinned out as they drove away towards the island. As they turned off onto the bridge, Del took a sawn-off shotgun from his jacket. He moved to the seat

behind the driver and tapped on the window with it, holding it up so that the driver could see it in the rear-view mirror. 'Pull over nice and slowly and don't do anything stupid unless you want to see your brains all over the windscreen.

'My money is under the seat, mate. I don't want any troubles,' the driver rambled as he brought the vehicle to a stop. The stretch of road was dark and unlit for a few hundred yards. 'Take my money and leave me alone.'

'Shut up,' Del said, opening the window between them. He pushed the barrels hard into the back of his head. 'I don't want your money!'

'What do you want?' the driver said, his eyes squeezed tightly closed.

'You gave a statement to the police outside of the Paradise club in town. Any day now, you will be asked to go to the police station about the shooting,' he said, pressing the gun harder still. 'You should have kept your big nose out of it and your big mouth shut but you didn't!'

'I'm very sorry for that. I didn't think.'

'Too late to retract now. You will be asked to give a formal statement and to identify the shooter in an identity parade, understand me?'

The driver opened his eyes and looked at him in the mirror. Recognition twinkled in them.

'I know you know,' he said, nodding. 'You don't know me and you certainly won't recognise me in the line-up and if you decide that you do recognise me then someone will get into your cab one night and blow your head off. Do you understand me?'

'I've never seen you before in my life,' the driver said, swallowing hard. 'I won't go. I won't tell them anything.'

'Listen to me,' Del said, calmly. 'I'm only going to say this once so listen hard. You will go to the police station and you will do the line-up but you will not identify me. You will identify someone else, understand?'

'Perfectly.'

'Good man,' Del said. He passed a crumpled ten-pound note through the window. 'Keep the change,' he said, sliding the shotgun into his jacket. He opened the door and climbed out, jogging into the darkness of the night. He was gone within seconds.

CHAPTER 26

Alan pulled up in his driveway and his heart sank a little when he saw it in darkness yet again. The bungalow looked bleak silhouetted against the light of a half-moon. Its gardens were spotted with mature trees and bushes, which were different shades of black in the darkness. Kim had been working late more and more and her social life was hectic and rarely included him. He had broached the subject a few months earlier and she launched a broadside at him that he would never forget as long as he lived. She told him in no uncertain terms that for years, she had built her own life around her because he was hardly ever in it. Sometimes they were on and sometimes they were off. More off than on. When he mentioned taking the relationship to the next level, usually after a few whiskies, she pointed out that his hours as a senior detective were unsustainable for any relationship to survive and yet she had remained with him all that time when most women would have been gone. He was shocked when she told him the number of times that she had nearly walked away because of the loneliness. He couldn't believe that she had felt lonely for most of their time together. She was in a relationship yet she felt alone; it was all part of their careers. If he had to stay late on a shift, her evenings were spent watching the clock, trying to keep food warm without ruining it. Invariably, when he did get home, he would be so exhausted that he would fall asleep in front of the television and she would cover him up with a quilt. She spent more nights alone in her own bed than most single women did.

Alan turned the engine off and climbed out of the BMW. He closed the door; the indicator lights flashed twice and then he walked towards the house. A movement to his left caught his eye. He stopped and turned around. A hooded figure emerged from the bushes; his gun glinted in the dim moonlight. Alan thought about running but didn't think he would make it far. There was too much distance between him and the gunman to try to disarm him.

'We believe that you have surveillance tapes that might incriminate several of our mutual acquaintances,' the man said, his accent local.

'What tapes would they be?' Alan asked, studying the man's demeanour. He was ice cold, no nerves at all. This was a pro. 'There are a lot of surveillance tapes in my world.'

'Not that incriminate the Karpovs there aren't.'

'Ah, those tapes,' Alan said, nodding. 'What about them?'

'I would think you've got teams of detectives ploughing through hours and hours of mundane shite, looking for something on the Karpovs haven't you?'

'That's about the size of it,' Alan agreed. Despite the gun, he didn't feel threatened. 'What is it to you?'

'A friend of mine asked me to give you a message.'

'Okay.'

'He said look for anything that was recorded in the second week of February this year. Especially over the weekend. It will have been filmed in London.'

'How would your friend know what is on the tapes?'

'He doesn't.'

'I'm not following you.'

'He doesn't know what is on the tapes but he was there on the trip to London.' The man paused. A rustling in the bushes made him jumpy. 'He was in London that weekend and so were the Karpovs. It might be just what you're looking for.' The man backed away slowly. He glanced behind him before ducking into the bushes and scampering away.

'Tell your friend that I said thank you,' Alan muttered to no one. He waited until he could no longer hear the man's footsteps. When he was sure that he was gone, he took out his phone and called Kim. The information could save hundreds of man hours and produce a conviction. It rang a couple of times as he put the key in the door. He stepped inside and closed it behind him. Kim answered as he switched on the lights. 'Hello.'

'I was just about to call you,' Kim said, excitedly. 'Uniform have arrested Derek Makin outside his house. They're bringing him in now.'

'I'm on my way,' Alan said, turning the lights off again. He opened the door and stepped outside.

'What did you call me for?' Kim asked.

'I'll tell you on the way in,' Alan said, locking the front door. He looked back at the house in darkness and thought that it hadn't felt like a home for a long time; especially since the boys had left.

CHAPTER 27

Del Makin was sitting in the cells after being processed and arrested for the attempted murder of Lloyd Jones. He hadn't tried to put up a struggle when they came for him and he had made sure that the girls were at their nana's house so that they didn't have to watch him being taken away in handcuffs. Once he found out that Jones had survived, he knew that it was only a matter of time before they came for him. His wife, Lucy had agreed with the plan. Unlike some cocaine-dealer's wives, Lucy Makin knew every move that Del made. They were partners. He bought one kilo every week on a Thursday and by Sunday morning, the lot was gone and Del was fifty-grand richer. They never sold to anyone outside of the circle, absolutely never and no matter how big the demand, they never bought more than one kilo a week. They never cut their product and they never used their product themselves.

Del's business had made them millionaires but they portrayed their lives as just comfortable. Lucy worked to make their situation look normal and realistic and their two beautiful daughters went to a good school but not the best one. They didn't flaunt their wealth. Lucy was smart. When Del came home one day with a blinged-up Range Rover, she made him take it straight back and made him swap it for a Lexus.

'*You might as well have a tattoo on your forehead saying I sell cocaine!*'

He listened to Lucy. It was her influence and support that had got him over his encounter with Lloyd Jones at the abattoir two years earlier. He had arrived home that night a bloody mess and a nervous wreck. It took him nearly an hour to stop crying enough to be able to tell Lucy what had happened, while she cleaned the blood from his cuts and bruises. The injuries were superficial but the video of the Wicks brothers being minced was on replay in his mind and he couldn't erase it. He was adamant that he was getting out of the business. Lucy had remained calm all the way through as he recounted the episode. His hands were shaking when he sipped his whisky from a crystal glass, his lips still swollen. When he told her that Jones had threatened to hurt their daughters an extraordinary thing happened. She slapped his face, once and very hard and then stood up in front of him, legs apart, hands on hips. Her long auburn hair hung over one shoulder nestling at her breast. There was a sparkle in her green eyes.

Del had been open mouthed in shock, not quite sure what he had done wrong but aware that she wasn't happy about something. She had told him to get a grip. *Get a grip of yourself straightaway!* Her mind worked at warp

speed to protect her family. She loved Del but he needed to toughen up to survive.

'I'm getting out, Lucy,' he whined. 'It's getting too dangerous. We have to think about the girls.'

'Get a grip, Derek!' she snapped. Her eyes were narrowed, her face stone. 'Do you think this man will let you just stop and walk away after what you have seen?' Del hadn't thought of that. 'Of course, he won't.' A thought occurred to her. 'Why did he kill the Wicks brothers?'

'I'm not one hundred percent sure but I think they were becoming too big for their boots,' Del had mused. 'I had heard rumblings that they were spreading themselves thin and moving into areas that belonged to some dangerous people.'

'Greed, Del. That's how they all get caught in the end. Greed.' She had dabbed at the cut above his eye. 'You're not a greedy man, Derek Makin and we will not make the same mistakes as they did. We need to stay calm and look at the options.'

'I still think we should get out and move away, Lucy.'

'And go where?'

'I don't know.'

'And do what?'

'I don't know.'

'That's because you're not thinking straight. You've had a nasty shock. We need to think this through and stay calm.'

'Okay.'

'This Jones character wants to keep supplying us on a regular business just like before, right?'

'Right.'

'And you won't have to deal with him directly?'

'No. I am to arrange the exchange on a Wednesday night each week with a guy called Matt.'

'Then I don't see an immediate threat.' She had walked to the window and looked out at the landscaped garden. They had invested too much into their home to walk away from a bully, even he was a dangerous one. 'We continue on the same track. As long as the product remains a consistent quality, then we'll never have to deal with the man again.'

'And what if it doesn't?' Del argued. 'What if they start cutting it?'

'People won't tolerate shit product, Del.'

'Who is going to complain to a psycho like Jones?'

'No one.'

'Exactly.'

'That is why we need to kill him,' she said, shrugging. She played with her hair as she spoke, rubbing it between her fingers. 'If he starts playing games and tries to cut the product or push us around, then we take him out.

You will take him out.'

'Just kill him?'

'Just kill him,' she said, nodding slowly. 'He threatened my children and from what you have told me tonight and judging by the state of your face, he will carry out his threats. We will carry on as normal for now but that man will not hold us to ransom by threatening my children. No one threatens my children. Whatever happens, we kill the bastard, sooner rather than later.'

They hadn't looked back. Over the following two years, their attitude to the business became more clinical. Del slipped into the role well, joined a gym, injected some nandrolone, cut his hair and had boxing lessons. He did what Lucy wanted him to do. He toughened up. The product arrived regularly as promised and business stayed constant and smooth. Until recently, that is, when their clients started complaining that the gear was cut. It was inevitable really; greed reared its ugly head. They made the decision to remove him. Lloyd Jones had to go at the first opportunity and Del was now sitting in a cell.

Del heard footsteps approaching and then a key being inserted in the lock. The door opened and two uniformed officers stepped in. One of them smiled and gestured for him to stand up.

'Interview time,' he said, taking his arm. They walked a short distance through the custody suite to the interview rooms. Alan and Kim were already sitting down. Del had his brief attending, a Jewish man from a Rhoscolyn firm called Goodstone and Goodstone. They dispensed with the legalities and Del played the answers over and over in his head. If he got this right, he would walk.

'Can you tell me where you were on the night of the twenty-seventh, Derek?' Alan began.

'Call me Del, please,' Del began in a relaxed tone. 'I was in Bangor at the Paradise club doing some business with an associate of mine, Jazz. His real name is Walter Ricks.' Del answered confidently. He held eye contact with Alan. 'And I didn't shoot him if that is your next question. He was alive when I left his office.'

'Tell me about that.'

'We were concluding our business when Lloyd Jones turned up. It was late so I shook their hands, said goodnight and left.'

'This was in the office not on the stairs?' Kim asked.

'Nope. It was in the office. When I left, both men were in the office and very much alive.'

'What exactly was your business there that night?' Kim asked.

'Walter wanted to move into the champagne market, you know, go a bit upmarket. The fizziest thing his punters drink is a Jägerbombs! I told him he was flogging a dead horse but he wouldn't listen.'

'And?'

'I offered to supply him with some bubbly on the cheap.'

'That's it?'

'That's it.'

'Lloyd Jones has made a statement that you were leaving as he arrived and that when he reached the office, Walter Ricks was already dead.' Alan paused. 'He said that he heard three silenced shots before you came down the stairs. That you shook hands and you ran from the scene in a hurry.'

'Your witness is lying. That would suggest that he knew the gun that killed Mr Ricks had a silencer fixed to it and there's only one way that he could know that,' Goodstone said. 'Do your forensic results confirm that?'

'Yes.'

'I didn't kill Walter,' Del said, flatly. 'Lloyd Jones killed him.'

'Why would you say that?' Alan asked.

'He was in the office when I left. It makes sense,' Del said, shrugging. 'I've heard there's a contract out on Jones. A contract taken by our Russian associates and we all know that they had a hold on Jazz, don't we.' He looked from Alan to Kim. They nodded. 'The Karpovs set Jazz up in business and they could have knocked him down just as easily. If they told him to jump, he jumped and didn't stop jumping until they told him to.'

'Do you think that's why he went to see Ricks so late?' Alan asked. 'Because of the contract?'

'You're asking my client to speculate,' Goodstone intervened, without looking up.

'I'm just asking his opinion.'

'He doesn't have one in here.'

'I'll answer that,' Del said, calmly. 'If you want my opinion, I think that he found out that you lot had acquired informers on his crew, didn't he?'

'We can't talk about that,' Kim said.

'That might have pushed him over the edge.'

'What makes you think that?'

'The entire island knows that there was a contract on him and where it had come from. He would have been in a panic; anyone would. Good news travels fast.'

'Good news?' Alan frowned.

'Look, Lloyd Jones shot my friend. If there's a contract out on him, happy days. I'm not going to lose any sleep over him.'

'He says that you tried to kill him outside the club.' Alan didn't soften the blow.

'Does he?' Del said, straight-faced. 'And why would I want to do that?'

'You obviously dislike the man,' Kim pointed out.

'I don't like a lot of people but that doesn't mean I run around the island shooting them.'

'We have a witness who says he saw you pull the trigger,' Alan said. He watched Del's face. It showed no reaction. That worried him.

'Oh, you do, do you?' Del said, shaking his head.

'Yes, we do. Are you prepared to do a line-up?' Alan asked. Del looked at his brief and whispered in his ear.

'My client is prepared to take part in your identification parade providing it is noted that he has cooperated throughout your investigation.'

'It will be noted,' Alan said. He was disturbed at how easily Makin had agreed to take part.

'I'll give you another little tip,' Del said. He leaned forward. 'I've heard that Jones carries a Beretta. A nine-millimetre. That's what Walter was shot with isn't it?'

'It was a nine-millimetre, yes.'

'There was no gun at the scene?' Goodstone asked.

'We found a gun on Jones but it wasn't the murder weapon.'

'Was it a silver thirty-eight?' Del asked.

'Yes,' Alan answered, intrigued. 'How do you know that?'

'Jazz, I mean Walter, had that old thing for twenty-years. He kept it locked up in his desk, only took it out when he was blind drunk, showing off. I don't think it was ever fired.' Del shook his head. 'Jones took that gun from the desk. I'm telling you that for nothing.' He leaned forward and lowered his voice. 'And another thing. Have you lot found the Wicks brothers yet?' Alan and Kim exchanged glances. They didn't answer, waiting for Del to speak. 'They have been missing for years now and you won't find them but I'll tell you this, I've heard there's a video knocking about somewhere, that shows what happened to them.' He nodded to make the point. 'I heard the place was an abattoir in Caergeiliog, demolished now but there's no way a narcissist like Jones would ever delete something like that. He would keep it to show people what a hard man he is. That's the way his mind works. You have a little dig beneath the surface and you might be surprised at what you find.'

'You seem to know a lot about Jones suddenly,' Alan said, eyebrows raised.

'People like him are always cut from the same mould.' He stopped talking and clapped his hands together. 'Anyway, let's get this line-up organised so that I can go home to my kids.'

'Interview terminated,' Kim said, for the tape. 'We can have it done in the morning. If you need a few hours with your brief, you can stay here if you like.' Del nodded that that was acceptable. Alan and Kim left the room and a uniformed officer stepped inside.

'What do you think?' Kim asked.

'I don't think he shot Ricks. I don't know if he shot Jones but if he did, we can't prove it yet.' He stopped and looked at her. 'Makin said that

Jones is known to carry a Beretta.'

'So?'

'If he shot Ricks with it, then he must have disposed of it somewhere between the nightclub and where he was shot, right?'

'Right,' Kim agreed. 'I'll get a search team back over there now.'

CHAPTER 28

Lloyd didn't sleep very well on his first night on the third landing. His brain was whirring away all night, figuring out his next move. The options were limited and each risk had to be a calculated one. If he made a mistake, he would be killed. He needed allies and he needed power. Money created power inside and out. Drugs created money. First off, he needed a supply of drugs very quickly. There wasn't time to arrange a delivery although that would happen quickly. There were already plenty of drugs on the wing, he just needed to find them and take them. He could hear the PO's moving methodically along the landings, opening the cells so the inmates could go and collect breakfast, three at a time, then he could hear them being locked up again. He could hear abuse being hurled from below and it echoed off the walls. He lay on his bunk with his eyes closed until his cell door was opened. The PO called him out. He stepped out onto the landing and looked around. A short fat nonce was outside the cell to his left. Jack Howarth was to the man's left, two cells away. Jack didn't look at Lloyd but he could feel Lloyd's eyes burning a hole in his head. Lloyd always glared at him as if he was something vile on the bottom of his shoes. Lloyd Jones was no better than him. He just thought he was.

The PO's ordered them down the stairs and they moved quickly and quietly. Lloyd pushed past the other man and nudged Jack with his elbow. He towered above him and Jack had to look up to make eye contact.

'Are you not talking, Jack?'

'Okay, Lloyd,' he answered, nervously.

'I need those packets.'

'I haven't got them.'

'You what?'

'They were taken from me.'

'By who?'

'I can't really say.'

'I suggest that you do say, Jack or I'm going to pick you up by your feet and smash your skull open on the wall.'

They reached the second landing where Volkov was waiting to give Lloyd some abuse. He was about to speak when Lloyd spat in his face for the second time. The expression on the Russian's face was priceless. He couldn't believe it, wiping at the green goo with his sleeve like a demented man possessed. He let off a tirade of foul-mouthed abuse, half Russian, half

English although it was difficult to distinguish. Lloyd didn't give him a second thought. His focus was on Jack. 'I'm warning you, Howarth. Don't fuck me around. Where are those packets?'

They were descending the first staircase as Lloyd pressed for an answer. He looked across the landing and made eye contact with AJ. Jack blushed and Lloyd knew the answer immediately.

'You're blushing, Jack,' Lloyd said.

'Am I?'

'Has that lanky streak of piss got my packets?'

'No,' Jack said, looking straight ahead, never once taking his eyes from the stairs. 'He took them from me but I don't think he has them anymore.'

'Officer Clough?'

'I think so. I'm very sorry, Lloyd. They put me in a tumble drier and turned it on. That's why my face is a mess. I can't fight against men like them,' he said, apologetically.

'Did he know that those packets were mine?'

'Yes.'

'Right, well that makes my next move very simple. Now he knows that I know he stole my property, if I don't respond then I might as well hang myself. That lanky bastard will be sorry he ever heard of me.'

'You're not going to hurt me, are you?' Jack asked, looking at him for the first time.

'AJ moves most of the gear on the wing, doesn't he?' Lloyd asked, ignoring his question. They joined a queue of three other inmates and waited patiently to get their food tray. Lloyd saw toast and cereal. The toast was cold and the cereal was soggy but it was better than nothing. Being fussy in prison would leave you hungry and make you weak. He couldn't afford to be weak.

'Most of it,' Jack mumbled.

'Where does he keep his stash?'

'How the fuck would I know that, Lloyd?'

'Because you're sneaky little nonce, now don't fuck me around, where does he keep it?'

They collected their trays and headed back to the stairs. Lloyd glared at AJ, hardly concealing his anger. AJ remained impassive. He had seen it all before. The big hard men walking into prison like they owned the place. Most of them were chewed up and spat out within a week. It was the smart men who made it to the top of the ladder not the angry ones. Anger burns a man out in prison.

'They spread it out around the wing apparently,' Jack said, from the corner of his mouth. 'They stash it in the back of their radios, only in the double cells and then there's always one man watching the gear.' He saw AJ watching him and trotted up the stairs quickly. 'I've said too much already.

Now leave me alone please.'

They walked up to the second landing and Volkov had prepared himself for when Lloyd returned. He scratched at the door like a singed hound trying to escape a fire. His voice was almost demonic and he screamed at Lloyd. Lloyd paused to watch for a second, almost fascinated by his madness. Lloyd's presence was driving the Russian into a frenzy. Lloyd took a bite of toast and chewed, sipped his tea and put a spoonful of cereal into his mouth too and then he walked up his door and spat it all into Volkov's face. The Russian fell back onto the cell floor and hammered at the concrete with his fists. He howled like a banshee; his frustration echoed from the walls. Laughter spread from the landings as the incident was spread from cell to cell by those who had watched it. Even the men who hated Lloyd Jones thought it was funny to hear the Russian psycho howling. If he wasn't bright enough to stand back when Lloyd approached, then he deserved everything that he got.

They reached the top landing and turned for the cells. Lloyd put his food tray into one hand and grabbed Jack by the scruff of the neck, yanking hard on it.

'I have to be seen to discipline the people who let me down, Jack,' Lloyd said.

Jack gurgled as he lifted him up and tossed him over the railings. He somersaulted in the air before he hit the safety nets fifteen feet below and bounced like an injured trampolinist. The nets held him and stopped him hitting the concrete below but he was hurt. PO's scurried along the landings.

'Jones!' Officer Clough shouted. 'In your cell right now. You're on report ...' he continued to rant but Lloyd couldn't hear him anymore. The laughing and cheering had reached epic levels. Everyone enjoyed seeing a nonce being thrown off the landing, even the screws enjoyed that. A kerfuffle began near the gates to the wing. The new daily intake had arrived. Lloyd looked down at the men behind the bars. Matt and Justin were being processed. They looked up and nodded a silent hello. There were four men on the wing that he could rely on. Now that Matt and Justin had arrived there were six plus himself, suddenly, the odds had evened up a little.

CHAPTER 29

Mr Ahmed was waiting patiently in reception for the detectives to come down. His wife looked very worried and stroked his arm constantly. When the door opened and DC Will Naylor walked out, they stood up and greeted him. They were both speaking at the same time and he couldn't understand a word that they were saying. Will was a young detective with a promising future. Alan had already earmarked him for the sergeant's exam next year. He was dressed immaculately in a grey Armani suit with a matching shirt and tie. He held up his hands to quieten them.

'Mr Ahmed.' he spoke clearly but calmly. 'I'm afraid that your wife will have to stay here while we do the line-up.'

'No, no, no,' Mrs Ahmed said, distressed. 'He can't do it. The man said he would blow his brains out!'

'What man?' he asked, looking at Mr Ahmed. 'Have you been threatened, sir?'

'Yes.' Mr Ahmed replied. 'He told me that I must identify someone else or he will have me killed. I'm afraid I cannot tell lies so I don't want to do it.'

'Okay, let's go in here,' Will said, guiding them into an interview room. The paint was peeling and the walls had graffiti on them. It smelled of disinfectant and vomit. 'Sit down.' The couple sat down and she began stroking her husband's arm again. 'Tell me what happened.'

'I was driving my cab,' Mr Ahmed began.

'He was in Bangor,' Mrs Ahmed added.

'A chap got in and asked me to take him to the White Eagle on the island.'

'The Rhoscolyn entrance he said, didn't he?' Mrs Ahmed filled in the details.

'Mrs Ahmed,' Will said, smiling. 'I really need you to shut up. It is very important that I hear what Mr Ahmed has to say, okay?' His smile covered over his abruptness but it had the desired effect. 'You took him to the White Eagle?'

'Yes. But when we got to the bridge, he pulled out a shotgun, a short one.'

'A sawn-off with two barrels?'

'Yes. Just like the one he shot the man outside the Paradise club with.'

'I see. And he threatened you?'

'Yes. He said that if I identify him then someone will come into my taxi and blow my head off.'

'Okay, Mr Ahmed. Listen to me very carefully.' Mr Ahmed nodded and held his wife's hand; she stroked his arm again with the other hand. 'You witnessed this man attempting to murder another man. Your witness testimony will put him in prison where he belongs and where he can't shoot you.' Will sat back and looked serious. He held up his index finger. 'If you don't identify him then he will be freed today. We don't have any other evidence that will stand up in court. The problem, Mr Ahmed, is that he will always be worried that you might change your mind at some point in the future. He will be free to make sure that you don't ever change your mind. Do you understand me, Mr Ahmed?' The couple looked at each other and nodded. 'Good. then let's go and put him behind bars, shall we?'

Fifteen minutes later, Mr Ahmed picked Derek Makin from a line-up. Alan was watching as he did so. He didn't flinch or falter. There was no doubt in his mind.

'Look at the expression on Makin's face,' Alan said, grinning. 'He didn't believe for one minute that he was going to be identified. That has spoiled his day no end! Take him back to the interview room and charge him.'

Will Naylor nodded and smiled. 'I'll enjoy that.'

'I bet you will.' Alan said, smiling.

Kim walked into the room. She had watched it from inside. 'That came as a surprise to him,' she said, chuckling dryly. 'They have recovered a nine-millimetre Beretta from a drain outside the Paradise club. Dr Martin called.'

'And,' Alan asked.

'An attempt was made to score the inside of the barrel with something metal, like a screwdriver, but Dr Martin reckons that he can ignore the score marks and lift the rifling pattern from underneath, especially from inside the suppressor. He's begun preliminaries and he said not to quote him yet but he's almost one hundred percent certain that it is the gun that was used to shoot Stuart Radcliffe and Walter Ricks.'

'Which puts Jones in the woods.'

'Almost,' Kim agreed. 'Let's hope that he can tie the gun to Jones with forensics.'

CHAPTER 30

Fifteen miles away, on the island, on the outskirts of Rhosneiger, a renovation was underway. The farmhouse and its outbuildings were being gutted and turned into luxury apartments, aimed at affluent kite surfers who wanted to see grass, trees, and cows from their kitchen windows. Bolek, a Polish joiner, had the job of stripping the main kitchen before the electricians and plasterers could come in. Once they were done, the painters would do a first fix and then he could do his real job, fitting the wood, the kitchen units, skirting boards, and doorframes. Until then, he was a labourer. Not that it mattered. As long as they paid him, he would brush the floors. He had a different attitude to a job than the local tradesmen. Their favourite saying was, 'That's not my job, ask the ... blah, blah, blah.' Painters would do nothing but paint, plumbers nothing but plumbing and fuck everybody else on site. Bolek didn't get it. They were lazy in this country, always looking for an excuse and someone else to blame.

He was using a claw hammer to dismantle a row of cabinets, although most of it was crumbling away in his hands. The bolts that had fixed them to the walls were rusty and stubborn. They would take some shifting. He hooked the head of one of them and pulled hard. The entire wall tilted and collapsed. He stumbled and fell backwards onto his back. The shelves and cupboards fell on top of him, pinning him to the floor. An entire section of kitchen had come down, with the wall behind still attached to it. He cried out and the other tradesmen came running to help him. They grabbed both ends of a stud wall and lifted it from him. The entire wall was one unit. Bolek was shocked but not hurt as he brushed dust and rotten wood from his clothes. As he looked up, he could see the other men staring at something that had been behind the wall. He couldn't tell what it was at first, then he realised that it was a video library of epic proportions. Hundreds of VHS tapes were lined up on shelves, which were fixed from floor to ceiling. At the centre of the wall was a door. They looked at each other as they studied the metal chain and the padlock that fastened it closed.

'We should call the police,' one of the men said. He was an Estonian bricklayer. 'That isn't good.'

'And tell them what?' Bolek asked. 'We have found a door in an old

farmhouse. Let's see what is behind it before we do anything. There could be something valuable in there.'

'Look at all those tapes, Bolek,' another man said, pointing. He walked closer and studied a shelf full of tapes. 'All the labels are girl's names, arranged in alphabetical order. This doesn't feel right to me.'

'Nor me,' another agreed.

'Can't hurt to look,' Bolek argued. 'Might be some mad old farmer's treasure-trove. It could be full of family jewellery and collectables.' He took his hammer and walked to the door. He looked around the anxious faces of the other workmen. 'Are we all agreed?' They nodded but looked unsure at best. He hooked the claw beneath the clasp that held the lock. The rusty chain was intertwined through the clasp. He pulled but the lock didn't budge. Pulling the claw harder, he tried again, leaning back using all his bodyweight to add pressure. The wood creaked and the doorframe splintered. He staggered backwards, one of his co-workers stopped him from falling again. The lock fell to the floor with a clunk. A spider scurried from under the door, it stopped to see what was going on before retreating to where it had come from. As small as it was, its arrival made some of the workers nervous.

'We should call the police,' one said.

'Definitely,' another agreed.

'I don't want to lose my job,' a third added.

'Why would you lose your job?' Bolek argued. He stepped towards the door.

'You are breaking into a locked door in a property that belongs to our employer. It is like burglary, stupid!'

Bolek stopped and looked at the man. He thought about it and stepped back. The man was right and he couldn't afford to lose his job. It was then that he got the first whiff of decay. He gagged and put his arm across his face.

'What is that smell?' he said, walking away from the door.

'Oh, my God,' another said, almost vomiting. 'Something has died in there.'

'Get the foreman in here,' one of the builders shouted.

Two of the men walked away to find the project manager. The others moved as far away from the door as they could but the stench followed them. A few minutes later, the foreman arrived, his hard hat in his hand, he looked flustered and angry.

'What the fuck is going on?' he whined. 'We're already two weeks behind on this job. Are you trying to get us all fired?'

'Look,' Bolek said, pointing at the door. 'The wall was false. It came down on me when I was pulling the cabinets out. The smell coming from behind it is rotten. Something is dead behind there. We should call the

police.'

'Not a chance!' the foreman snapped. 'If the police come in here, they will stop the job and we're all screwed. It's probably rats.'

'It must be a big rat to stink like that,' Bolek cautioned. 'But if you want to look then I'm with you. I can't afford to lose any money.'

'Open it and see what is there,' the foreman said.

'Okay,' Bolek said. He approached the door and kicked the chain out of the way. It grated along the floorboards. He reached for the handle tentatively, as if it might be hot. It wasn't. He turned the handle and pulled the door open. It creaked and groaned as it moved. The stench hit him like a sledgehammer. He put his arm over his nose and mouth. 'Oh my God, it is even worse in here. Pass me a torch.'

'Use your phone,' the foreman said.

Bolek shrugged and took out his Samsung, turning it to torch mode. The darkness retreated as he aimed it at the doorway. Flecks of dust floated around like stars against the backdrop of the universe. He swept the doorway left to right and back again. Bare floorboards formed a small landing, the walls were lined with VHS cassettes. There was another door to his left, the handle was covered in dust. A keyhole winked in the light. He stepped onto the landing and tried the handle but the door wouldn't budge.

'It is locked!' Bolek called. The stench of rotten flesh was more pronounced. 'Pass me a jemmy.'

One of the men picked up the metal bar from the floor, which they used to pull fitting from the walls. Bolek slid the narrow end between the door and the frame and pushed it against the lock. The wood cracked; age had weakened it. Another push and it sprung open with a bang to reveal wooden stairs which led down to a cellar. Dust and splinters filled the air and the stink that rushed up from below could have been sent from the pits of hell.

CHAPTER 31

Assistant Chief Constable Dafyd Thomas knocked on Alan's door and popped his head around it. Alan was on the phone to his son Dan, trying unsuccessfully to explain why he had not been home to feed the dogs. Saying that he had been home, briefly before a murder suspect had been picked up wasn't doing anything to lessen the onslaught. He waved to the ACC to come in and explained bluntly to Dan that he would have to call him back later, to which he had told him to stay there as long as he wanted and not to bother going home at all. He reminded him why Kath had left. It was true that his priority was work. He was only doing his job to the best of his ability, if only he had tried as hard to be a good husband, she might have been happy. He thought about that for a second and decided that she wouldn't be. Some things just couldn't be saved.

'Come in, sir,' Alan said, apologising. 'Sorry about that. The son is on the warpath again. It's time to circle the wagons and defend myself.'

'Oh dear,' Dafyd said, rolling his eyes. 'What have you done this time?'

'The same as usual, fuck all,' Alan sighed. 'What can I do for you?'

'I want to catch up on what's happened so far. Things seem to have rattled along at some speed.'

'They have indeed. It would seem that the Matrix informers were compromised somehow and it has snowballed from there. Lloyd Jones is at the centre of it all but we have had the forensics back on the weapon that he used and it is conclusive. It was used to shoot Stuart Radcliffe and Walter Ricks; the ballistics match; and Dr Martin managed to recover skin tissue from the trigger housing.'

'I thought it had been under water?'

'It was but the trigger housing on a Beretta is sealed so the trace was inside the gun and was preserved. Will Naylor is going to HMP Liverpool to charge him with both shootings. He's down for a long time.'

'Good work, Alan. How are the others linked? What's the score with that Selby chap?'

'Brian Selby seems to be a square peg in a round hole. He doesn't fit with that outfit for a second. I think he was bullied into smuggling drugs into Berwyn with a drone,' Alan paused. 'He builds them himself. Anyway, I think he was dragged into their plot and was unfortunate enough to be there when Jones decided to shoot Radcliffe. I think he was forced to help

to bury the body but Radcliffe wasn't dead. The forensics say Selby struck the blows which killed him. He doesn't seem to realise that killing someone who he thought was already dead is a crime. We've charged him this morning. He's on his way to remand.'

'Didn't he claim that Jones did it?'

'Yes. He wasn't very convincing though. The forensics will clear Jones and convict Selby all day long. He'll go down without a doubt. I just hope he gets a good barrister to plead collusion. He shouldn't have been there in the first place but he was forced to be there. It doesn't excuse what he did but I genuinely don't believe he would have hurt anyone intentionally. I think he was under duress and panicked.'

'It's not for us to worry about or explain, Alan. You've done your bit, let the courts deal with him now.' The ACC said, nodding. 'Very good work, Alan. Very good indeed.'

'You're right. On the flip side, Derek Makin knew exactly what he was doing when he emptied both barrels at Jones. Luckily our taxi driver didn't frighten when Makin threatened him. Jones will testify that Makin shot him and our witness nails him down. He's not as squeaky clean as he looks, that man. We've made some enquiries and it appears that he is a high-end dealer. I think he was a customer of Jones and there was some kind of fall out between them, whatever it was, they can rot.' Alan said with a sigh. 'The rest of Jones's outfit are either running or banged up. We'll get them all in the end, just a matter of time, sir.'

'Outstanding work, Alan. You and the team deserve a pat on the back.' Alan was thinking that if anyone tried to pat him on the back, he would punch them in the face, when Kim knocked on the door. 'Come in, Kim,' he said. Her perfume drifted to him.

'Sorry to interrupt but I thought you would want to see this,' she said, holding her laptop up. 'We focused on the surveillance tapes from February just like you said, Alan. Watch this.' She brought up a recording which had been filmed on a belt-camera. It showed a group of men walking through an industrial unit of some kind. 'That is Jones and look who that is!'

'Viktor Karpov,' the ACC answered. 'Well, bugger me.'

'Not right now, sir,' Alan said, dryly. The ACC blushed and cleared his throat. 'I don't like the look of this.' Alan watched as they approached a badly beaten man who was tied to a chair. Two Russian gorillas stood aside as they approached. There was a brief exchange of words and then Viktor pulled out a Glock-17 and put a bullet through the centre of the man's forehead. The back of his head exploded up the wall behind him. 'Jesus Christ!' Alan said, inhaling sharply. 'Who was that?'

'We don't know yet but we think he was probably one of their own. When they speak, here,' she said, pointing to a frame. 'He asks if he has said anything and he answers that he admitted taking the money and the drugs.

A translator at the university said that the word he used would be related to a consignment or a package. Like a delivery.'

'So, you think he was a courier,' the ACC asked.

'Maybe. We've passed it on to the Met. They are going to arrest Karpov this afternoon.' Kim grinned from ear to ear. Alan nodded slowly and thought about how he had come by the information. He was now convinced that Lloyd Jones had had a hand in delivering the message. Karpov had put a contract out on him and this was his way of hitting back without looking like a grass. Jones was a dangerously clever man.

'If they manage to lock that man up, there will be street parties from here to Siberia,' the ACC said, excitedly. 'Bloody well done, you two!'

'Don't get too carried away just yet, sir,' Alan said, cautiously. 'He's a slippery bastard and no one has managed to get a grip of him yet, not through the lack of trying either.'

'True, true, true,' the ACC said, looking out of the window. The Straits looked grey and choppy. A seagull was battling against the wind but the wind was winning. It soared and then dived out of view. 'You should be very pleased with your results. Outstanding work, both of you.' He patted Kim on the shoulder, awkwardly. Alan smiled to himself at the expression on her face. She threw daggers at him from narrowed eyes, knowing exactly what he was thinking.

'Thank you, sir,' Alan said. 'I think we'll take the team for a few beers after work.'

'So, you should!'

'Are you buying?' Kim asked, looking at the ACC. He blushed again and smiled.

'Keep up the good work,' he said, making a mock salute. He stepped out of the office and closed the door.

'He's not a bad old stick,' Alan said.

'What is an old stick?' Kim asked.

'It is just an old saying.'

'It must be very old because I've never heard it. I don't think you should use old sayings. They make you sound like a wrinkly.'

'I feel like a wrinkly,' Alan said, smiling.

CHAPTER 32

Bolek began to descend the steps slowly, the jemmy in one hand and his phone in the other. His foreman was right behind him, holding a torch that someone had retrieved from their van. He had a cloth to his nose but it wasn't helping to dampen the stench. The wooden stairs creaked and groaned beneath their weight. Gossamer webs hung from the walls and ceiling and a warped handrail was attached to the bare brick wall. Bolek used his phone to illuminate each stair, half expecting them to collapse at any moment. Halfway down was a small landing and the staircase bent to the right out of sight. They reached the landing and the foul smell intensified. Bolek thought he was going to vomit at one point. They paused on the landing and looked back. Worried faces peered around the doorframe at the top of the stairs.

They aimed the lights down the staircase. The cellar floor was concrete and covered in dust. They set off cautiously, testing each step as they descended. Bolek had to duck beneath a low wooden beam at the bottom. He pointed the phone at the walls, his foreman doing the same with the torch. They looked at each other as the lights revealed the contents. A filthy mattress lay on the floor in the centre of the room, the material was discoloured by age and there were dark stains all over it, like ink on blotting paper. Dull metal anchor rings were fixed into the floor at each corner of the mattress. Two tripod cameras were standing in the far corner of the room, both aimed at the mattress. A desk and solitary chair were positioned against the far wall, piled high with DVD'S. A row of shelves was packed with laptops, their screens covered in dust. Cardboard boxes, marked *memory sticks*, were piled three high in another corner.

'This is weird, Bolek,' the foreman whispered. 'I don't like this one little bit!'

'Why are you whispering?'

'Because I'm nervous.'

'Stop it. Whispering is making me nervous,' Bolek said, shaking his head. 'Over there, look,' Bolek pointed to a door to their right. The smell reached a new low. The foreman gagged. 'Do you still think it's a dead rat?'

'We don't know what it is yet. Could be anything,' the foreman said stubbornly but he didn't sound convinced. 'Rats, cats, dogs. It could be a freezer full of gone off food.' Bolek smiled nervously. He didn't think it was

any of those things. 'We've come this far, let's get the job done. I don't want the police in here unless it is necessary. Use that jemmy again. I'll shine the torch on it.'

Bolek approached the door and looked at it closely. There were three mortice locks fitted to the door.

'Don't you think that is overkill for a freezer?'

'Just open the door. This place is giving me the creeps!'

Placing the jemmy next to the highest lock, he pulled hard on the metal bar. The frame splintered and cracked, exposing the brass plate. He moved down to the middle lock and forced the bar between the frame and the door. A good hard tug cracked the doorframe and the lock popped free; the brass deadbolt glinted in the torchlight. The last lock took the most effort, both men leaning on the bar to crack the wood. Finally, it gave way and the door creaked open. They aimed their torches into a small room and both stepped back instinctively from the horror within. Three bodies were sitting on the floor, their arms chained to the wall above their heads. Their eyes were sunken black sockets, their teeth yellowed and bared into a permanent smile, their lips long since rotted. Long scraggy hair hung from paper thin scalps, two blonds and one brunette. They were clothed only in underwear, which had been discoloured by their bodily fluids. Their flesh was blackened and split in places; bony toes had popped through the skin. The smell was so bad that both men vomited simultaneously as they turned and ran for the stairs.

CHAPTER 33

Lloyd Jones was gutted. He felt like had had been stabbed in the stomach with a giant corkscrew and someone was twisting it. DC Naylor and a female DC, whose name he couldn't remember, had taken less than ten minutes to charge him with the murder of Walter Ricks and Stuart Radcliffe. The CPS had decided that he was equally as guilty as Brian Selby for the murder in the woods. Even the silky-smooth Jacob Graff couldn't throw him a lifeline. He said that his chances in court were zero and the best thing that he could do was to plead guilty and hope for a chance of parole in later life. It was a severe mental blow to realise that his liberty was probably gone forever. He would probably not leave prison alive. Somewhere in his subconscious, he had genuinely thought that he would wriggle out of it. The meeting with the MIT detectives had blown that assumption to smithereens in eight minutes. They hadn't even asked him any questions. It felt like being in an open coffin while someone closed it and then screwed the lid down with a drill. He felt crushed by the thought of being locked up for the remainder of his days. It was claustrophobic.

The PO's escorting him back to the wing were cautiously quiet. They knew what the detectives had done and they knew what it meant. Life behind bars. They were experienced enough to know what that kind of news could do to a man, even a hardened ex-con like Jones. Men reacted in different ways to news like that. Some would implode and end up on suicide watch while others would blame the world for their plight and lash out at the nearest target. Others would explode mentally and physically, endangering themselves and anyone in the firing line. They had seen it all, dirty protests, self-harm, hanging, slashed wrists and throats, and violent attacks on officers and fellow prisoners. Prison life was always volatile but when men were given the news that they would probably never get out, extra care and attention had to be applied.

They reached an intersection where the corridors split and ran to the other wings. A series of locked sterile areas separated them from C Wing. Lloyd was in a world of his own, his thoughts jumbled and dark. He looked up and saw two PO's escorting a prisoner onto the landings of C Wing. He recognised the bloated body, hunched shoulders and awkward gait. Brian looked like a frightened rabbit in the headlights of an oncoming truck. His eyes darted about nervously. Lloyd smiled.

'Hey, fat boy!' he shouted. Brian jumped and looked through the bars. His face reddened when he saw Lloyd. He seemed to sink in on himself as if he was deflating. 'You've been telling lies about me, Brian.' Lloyd pointed a finger at him. 'You're not just a grass, you're a liar!' Lloyd lunged at the bars. 'You cut Stuart's throat with a spade, Brian. You did it and told them it was me!' The PO's on both sides guided the men away from each other. Brian began to cry; the trepidation and fear had pushed him over the edge. He wanted to see his mum. 'You're nearly dead, Brian!' Lloyd shouted as they dragged him away. 'I'll get to you. Just you see if I don't. Watch your back, fat boy!'

'Alright,' Officer Clough said, through the bars on B Wing. 'That's enough, Jones!'

'Fuck you,' Lloyd snarled.

'Just calm down.'

Once Brian was out of sight, Lloyd calmed down from boiling to simmering but the anger in him was intense. His stomach knotted again as he thought things over in his mind. The PO's guided him through three sets of gates onto the landing at B Wing and walked him towards the stairs that climbed to the upper landing. The usual suspects shouted abuse but Lloyd didn't respond. He was in no mood for joisting. Their insults washed over him without consequence. There had been whispers on the landings earlier that the governor had drafted in more PO's and that they would be taken off lockdown within the next few days. That would sort out the men from the boys. His tormentors were brave while they were safe behind locked doors. It would be different when the doors were opened and everyone was free to roam the landings. He would see how brave they were then. Anyone who fancied their chances would be welcome to try. Lloyd didn't care who came for him or how many. He felt like he was about to detonate.

'We're going up the far stairs, Jones,' one of the PO's said. 'We don't want the barmy Russian winding you up today.'

'I'm just in the mood for that silly bastard,' Lloyd said, calmly. 'Ripping his throat out might make me feel better.'

'That's why we're going up the other stairwell.'

'Hey, Lloyd,' a familiar voice shouted from somewhere to the right. He looked up to see Matt in his cell.

'That's where they have put you, eh?' Lloyd called back. 'I wondered where you were.'

'Have you listened to the radio today?' Matt shouted.

'No. I've been busy,' Lloyd said, sarcastically.

'They arrested Viktor Karpov yesterday afternoon on a murder charge. They've sent him to Belmarsh.' Matt banged on the door with a metal cup. 'Did you hear that, you retard?' he shouted to all who could hear him. 'Viktor Karpov is in the slammer! No one is paying out on his bullshit

contracts!' The news was passed on from cell to cell in a murmur. 'Looks like you're off the hook, Lloyd!'

'You're a jammy bastard, Jones!' someone called from above. 'I was going to buy a new car with that money!'

'Lucky fucker,' another voice added.

'Fucking hell,' Lloyd said, under his breath shaking his head. His thought process changed. The contract had gone, no longer hanging over him. If he was going to be inside for good then he needed to take control to survive.

CHAPTER 34

Alan and Will Naylor navigated their way down a farm track, nearly running over a gaggle of enthusiastic reporters on the way. They avoided any questions and hardly slowed down at all. A uniformed officer kept them a safe distance from the crime scene. Alan pulled up at the farmhouse and turned off the engine. Tall trees encircled the building, their bare branches swayed in the wind. It was a secluded spot with an eerie atmosphere around it. Crime scene tape flapped in the breeze. The outbuildings were windowless, the tile roof half finished. Scaffold covered the visible brickwork of the gable end. CSI officers milled about in white over suits and uniformed officers guarded the scene. The farmyard was a quagmire of mud and building materials. Alan opened the door and climbed out. Will followed suit and closed the door a bit too hard. It was one of Alan's pet hates. Alan bit his lip, wanting to call him a clumsy twat but didn't want to dent his confidence. If he corrective-coached him on how hard to close his vehicle door at this stage, their relationship would be doomed from the start.

'It's an ideal spot to keep your activities secret,' Will said, looking around. 'No one would hear you screaming out here.'

'And the town is only a few miles away if you need another victim.' Alan agreed. 'Who is tracing the previous owners?'

'Johnson.'

'Google?'

'That's him. He's like a rat up a drainpipe.' Will grinned. 'Google is compiling a list. If there's anything to help us there, he'll find it.'

'I don't think our man will be on that list,' Alan said, thoughtfully.

'You don't?'

'No.' He didn't expand on his thoughts. He wanted to see what had happened inside. They walked towards the farmhouse and exchanged greetings with the officers on the scene. A local CID officer met them at the door. Alan knew him as DS Metcalfe. 'Afternoon, sergeant.'

'Afternoon, sir,' Metcalfe said. 'Hello Will,' he added, smiling. 'I heard you were with MIT now. Well done, mate.' They shook hands. Alan knew they had been on the force about the same length of time and figured they had been in uniform together. 'Will and I were in uniform together,' Metcalfe confirmed what he was thinking.

'Small world, eh,' Alan said, with a nod. 'Run us through what we have

we got so far.'

'Come this way.' Metcalfe turned and walked through the house to the kitchen. Plastic sheets covered the windows, and they flexed and flapped noisily in the wind. Metal supports held the wooden joists up where a supporting wall had been removed. The upper floors were exposed. Sawhorses and bags of cement were scattered about, making it like an assault course. They picked their way through the building site carefully. As they reached the kitchen, Metcalfe pointed to the wall of video cassettes. 'The builders were disassembling the kitchen when this false wall toppled over revealing this. They would not have been on the shelves at Blockbusters, that's for certain.'

'Have they been looked at?' Will asked.

'CSI have looked at about half a dozen randomly. They're all pornographic, bondage stuff. The victims are clearly being raped. There are a number of different men in them apparently but the victims are a mixture of girls and boys and all young, early teens and younger so far.'

'Get them over to the tech lab. Run the men on the tapes against facial recognition. They're old but you never know, we might get lucky,' Alan said, looking from left to right, studying the labels. He counted over fifty different names, with multiple copies of each, taking the number of tapes into the hundreds. 'This is a library,' he said. 'But a very dated one.'

'I was thinking the same thing,' Will said. 'DVD's came out in the late nineties, right?'

'I had a VHS player up until two thousand and five,' Metcalfe said. Alan looked at him surprised at the detailed memory. Metcalfe grinned. 'The European cup final, Istanbul. The missus taped it for me because I was on nights.'

'That makes these tapes obsolete ten to fifteen years ago,' Alan said, making a note of some of the names in his mind. 'It meant something to someone, that's why they're still here. They were proud of their collection.' He walked along the rows of tapes. 'Whoever set this up was selling these tapes commercially. They make the film, copy the ones which are selling well and label them up so it's easy to find them. It looks like a well organised rape-porn factory from the nineties.'

'My thoughts exactly. Have a look at this,' Metcalfe said, heading through the doorway onto the stairs. Temporary lights had been brought in to illuminate the gloomy farmhouse. 'The builders didn't want to bother us because they knew that we would stop the job so they came down here and had a look for themselves.' He gestured to the floor. 'The operation became digital at some point. There are laptops, memory sticks, SD cards, everything you would need to sell your smut online.'

'It would be simple to run once it was set up,' Will said. 'Especially if they transferred all the material on the tapes to disk.'

'It would be but what you need to ask yourself is why is it still here?' Alan said, looking at the mattress.

'The stains on the mattress are human blood, several different types apparently. CSI are confident that they can separate the types and crosscheck for anything in our database.' Metcalfe paused to explain. 'This room is where all the tapes that they have glanced at were filmed. The memory sticks too from what they have seen so far. All the victims were tethered to these anchor rings and assaulted on the mattress.' He noticed Will wrinkle his nose at the smell. 'It does hum a bit, doesn't it?'

'Just a touch,' Will agreed.

Metcalfe took them across the room and pushed the door open, standing aside to allow them to see inside. Will and Alan looked at the victims and then looked at each other. The three victims stared back at them from empty eye sockets, their skeletal smiles almost mocking them. 'CSI can't see any obvious trauma that would have caused death. They said that they were emaciated and that they probably starved to death. One of them bit her tongue off.' There was a long few seconds of silence. The girls would have suffered terribly while they were alive, their death an agonisingly long process.'

'The cold hard facts are that this may look like it was run by Ted Bundy but it is, in fact, a money-making operation run by some very smart people,' Alan said, looking around. 'And the kind of people who do this, don't just up and leave valuable assets like their products and equipment behind. They certainly wouldn't have left these poor girls to starve to death. They were way too hard to come by to allow them to die like that.' He looked at Will. Will looked confused. 'This place is frozen in time. We're looking for someone who left here in a hurry and never came back. We are looking for someone who either died suddenly or went to prison.'

'That should narrow it down,' Will said, impressed by Alan's logic. 'I'll pass it on to Google.'

'How long have they been dead?' Alan asked.

'Best guess at the moment is two to three years,' Metcalfe said. 'Obviously it could be more or less. The temperature down here would have kept them fresh longer.'

'Get the team to look for missing teenage girls from the local area. Let's say Merseyside, Cheshire, and North Wales. Go back the last four years to start with. Let's run tests on all the cases that we already have DNA samples for. I don't want to go asking parents for combs and brushes until we've exhausted the samples that we have already.'

'I'll call it in now.'

'And another thing,' Alan said, turning to Metcalfe. 'Looking at how many names are on those tapes and how far back they go, we need to be searching the surrounding land for bodies. There are two decades of films

there and that is a lot of victims. There's no way they let the victims go.'

'Do you want me to call in the dogs or the GPR unit.'

'Ground penetrating radar and the dogs,' Alan said. 'Get everything that we've got on this. I'll sign off the cost. There are a lot of tapes on that wall. There are only three bodies in there so where all the others?'

Will nodded and took a last look at the three girls. He couldn't imagine being chained up in there and brought out only to be raped and then returned. It might have been a blessing that their captor left them to starve to death in the darkness. One thing he was sure of, someone needed to pay for it.

CHAPTER 35

Jack Howarth was in agony. He had broken several bones in his leg when he hit the safety net. The pain killers that the prison doctor had administered hadn't touched the pain. His right leg felt like it was on fire inside and his foot was facing in the wrong direction. He was dizzy with the pain and complaining loudly. The doctor said that he would have to be sedated and taken by ambulance to Ysbyty Wrexham Maelor for a series of x-rays, explaining to the governor that he suspected a spiral fracture, which could lead to an amputation if it wasn't operated on immediately. The prison hospital just didn't have the specialist equipment to deal with severe injuries. The governor was annoyed but there was no alternative. Moving prisoners to and from hospital was expensive but Jack was inside for grooming so he was hardly a high security risk. He signed the transfer papers and an ambulance was called. Public sector guards from G4S would oversee the transfer, freeing up his PO's.

Jack drifted off to the dark place in his mind where he always went to when he was in pain and frightened. He had found the place during the years of abuse he had suffered at the hands of a catholic priest at the orphanage where he was brought up. It was a place where he could switch off what was happening to his body. He could hide there in his mind while the torment continued to his physical being. It was also the place that he went to when he was abusing others. A place of no emotion. The walls and floors were as cold as ice, as cold as his evil heart. He had no empathy for their pain and no sympathy for their cries. Their tears and pleading did nothing to stop him hurting them.

No one had listened to him when he was crying for help while the priest buggered him. Everyone at the orphanage knew what the priest did. He knew that they could hear him begging for it to stop. The other boys pretended not to hear because if someone else was screaming and getting the priest's special attention then he was leaving them alone. Others knew what he did too. The nuns, the social workers – they must have known. Those in charge were aware but they chose to brush it under the carpet. Nobody wanted the spotlight on the orphanage, the embarrassment would damage the church and stifle donations. There had been complaints for years but they were ignored. No one had helped Jack when he was suffering. That was just the way of the world. Bad people hurt vulnerable people and all the other people turned a blind eye because the reality is that

no one gives a fuck really. *I'm all right, Jack.* He always chuckled when he said that to himself. *I'm all right, Jack.*

He had said that when they charged him with grooming and sent him down. Had they looked deeper into his background; they would have found much darker deeds. He had plunged the depths of depravity, assaulting, raping and eventually, he had escalated to killing too. That seemed to be the ultimate thrill. Listening to them when they knew that they were going to die was like adrenalin being pumped through his veins. Watching the life leave their body and the sparkle in their eyes fading away was orgasmic, literally. The police had been so proud of themselves, setting him up in a sting for grooming, that they hadn't seen past that. They hadn't asked what else he had done. They told the judge and jury that Jack had planned to meet the teenager for sex in his campervan and that he travelled around the country in it trying to procure teenagers for sex.

They had it partly right but he had planned to do much worse than just have sex with her. He had planned to keep her for himself until he bored of her, then he would have either killed her or sold her on the black web as a sex slave to another pervert just like him or even worse. He took great comfort from the fact that there were worse than him out there. Much, much worse. His plans went far beyond what they had imagined. Sometimes he didn't know that they were going to die until it was too late. He never knew which way it would go. That was part of the buzz. He had no boundaries. Society could not tolerate sex that ended with the death of one of the participants, especially when they hadn't agreed to participate in the first place. Society would call him a monster. He didn't think that he was a monster, he just got carried away sometimes. Society would never accept his needs, in fact, they would punish him for his sexuality. It didn't seem fair to Jack. Some people are born heterosexual, some bisexual, others gay. They can't change what or who attracts them and neither could he.

They got the travelling part wrong too. He did travel in his campervan but not all the time. When he did, he often followed travelling communities. Their children were very vulnerable and easy to steal. The police didn't put half as much emphasis on missing travellers as they would for other members of society. They only did half the job when they arrested him. He thought that they would uncover his dirty, evil past and lock him up forever. If they had, they would have thrown away the key. They were too busy patting each other on the back to look beneath the surface. They hadn't seen the need to delve into previous addresses in detail. He said that he had lived in his van for years and they had believed him. When they sentenced him to five years for grooming, he was delighted. He felt that he had gotten off lightly. *I'm all right, Jack.*

Voices brought him back to reality. They were talking about him. His injuries were severe, the pain was unbearable. He felt another injection

being administered. A feeling of warmth spread through his veins. The pain faded and he drifted off like a helium filled balloon on the breeze. He felt the trolley being pushed, turned, reversed, and finally lifted. The wind touched his face for a few moments. He knew he was outside. Suddenly, the wind was gone and he heard doors being slammed. An engine started and sirens blared. The motion of the vehicle calmed him. He wasn't sure if it was because it was taking him away from prison. Maybe that was a psychological lift. Or maybe it was the drugs in his bloodstream.

He drifted away and only became aware when a doctor was moving his injured leg. Despite the drugs, he nearly jumped off the trolley. Voices told him to relax. He wanted to tell the voices to fuck off and stop twisting his leg but his motor functions were disabled. One voice stood out from the others. He wasn't sure why but it triggered some far away memory in his mind. It was a good memory but it wouldn't come into focus. His eyes flickered. There were glimpses of faces, nurses, doctors, a G4S guard. Someone was directing the process; his clothes were being removed. There was pain when he was moved, shooting pain that felt like it would make his brain explode. He felt his muscles spasm involuntarily. The cramps made his body twitch. He opened his eyes for a second and looked at the faces above him. A nurse saw him looking and smiled. Her lips moved but he didn't hear what she said. He was listening to the voice, trying to remember. He knew that voice but couldn't place it.

'I need these handcuffs removed.' The voice ordered. It wasn't a request.

'I'm not supposed to do that. I ...'

'Take them off or take him back to your prison hospital. This man needs surgery and I'm not operating on a man wearing handcuffs. Take the things off or get out of my hospital!'

The voice held authority in it. He wasn't messing about. There was a job to be done and it needed to be done urgently. *Take the things off or get out* ...

The memory was there again like a phantom in the corner of his eye, when he turned to look at it, it was gone. Jack felt the cuffs being removed. It felt nice to be free of them. His eyes flickered open again for a second and he looked into the doctor's eyes. Then he remembered where he knew that voice from. He felt an injection in the back of his hand and drifted away once more.

CHAPTER 36

Matt walked into the visiting room and looked across the lines of tables. Sandra was sitting alone waiting at one of them. She looked as gorgeous as ever. Her hair was down and her top was tight beneath a black leather jacket. There was no sign of the kids. She half smiled and waved her hand, nervously. He wasn't sure how he would feel when he saw her. She had sent several letters which were banal at best. There had been no apologies in them and that had pissed him off. He sort of understood why she had caved into the pressure from the police. The threat of losing their home had been too much for her to take. She had turned him and while he understood, he thought that he deserved an apology. He swallowed hard and walked across the room towards her. She didn't stand up when he leaned across the table to kiss her. The smell of her perfume filled his senses and he could feel himself growing hard. He had missed her touch at night. She turned her cheek away. It wasn't a warm reception, more like kissing a distant aunt. He was surprised and disappointed by her reaction. They had always been physically attracted to each other, no matter what but now she was cold to touch.

'How are you?' he asked.

'How do you think I am?'

'Sorry,' Matt said, begrudgingly. 'Silly question. How are the kids?'

'Fabulous,' Sandra said, sarcastically. 'Shelby wakes up crying every night and Lucas hasn't come out of his room for days, except to go to school. He hasn't spoken to me since you were arrested.' She paused; her eyes filled with tears. 'I think he blames me for you being in here.'

'I can't understand that, can you?' Matt said, dryly.

'Fuck you, Matt!' she hissed. She stood up and her chair scraped on the floor. The PO's looked on, concerned. 'Don't you blame me for being in here! You're in here because you were working for a drug dealer.' She jabbed at the air with her index finger. 'That's nothing to do with me. That is on you and Lloyd Jones. Lucas thinks the sun shines out of your arsehole and I'm the bitch who turned you in, well let me tell you, Matt, he'll find out one day exactly who you are and what you did. I won't be able to keep it from him, his mates at school are asking questions already. My mum and dad are asking questions and what am I supposed to tell them?'

'Tell them that you grassed me up and that's why I'm banged up.'

'How dare you blame this on me!' she shouted. All the heads in the

room were looking at them.

'Sit down and calm down, San,' Matt said, calmly. 'I'm sorry, okay. Let's start this all over again.' He tried to smile and took a deep breath. 'I'm not blaming you. It was my own fault. I knew the consequences if we got caught and I chose to take the gamble.' She sat down in a huff and folded her arms. He reached across to touch her hand but she pulled it away. That hurt. He needed a demonstration of emotion, no matter how small. Just something to make him feel human again.

'Did you really know the consequences, Matt?' she scowled. 'Did you really know the consequences?' she sniffled. He didn't answer, just looked her in the eyes and shrugged. 'Do you think that this is it? Do you think that this is all it is?'

'What do you mean, San?' he sighed.

'This,' she waved her arms. 'Prison. Did you think that this was the only consequence because this is fuck all to what I'm putting up with on the outside? It's me that must deal with our kids. It's me who must deal with our family. It's me who must deal with the sly looks at the school gate, listening to people gossiping about me. *There she is, the gangster's wife. No wonder she had such a nice car. I bet she has Botox, be nice to be able to afford it. I feel sorry for her kids. I've told mine not to talk to them. I don't want my kids near druggies!'* She exaggerated their accents. 'It goes on and on and never stops!'

'I'm sorry, San.'

'Jacob Graff thinks that they might freeze our bank accounts while they investigate you,' she lowered her voice and leaned forward. 'How the hell am I going to pay the mortgage if they do that?'

'I'm sorry, San.'

'You're sorry?'

'Yes, I'm sorry. What more can I say?'

'Try and think of something else to say except you're sorry.' She wiped tears from her cheeks. Mascara was smudged at the corners. 'I know you're sorry but it doesn't help me, does it?'

'It won't come to that.'

'Why won't it? What if it does?'

'Your mum and dad will look after you and the kids,' Matt tried to calm her. 'You'll be fine.'

'Mum and Dad are pensioners living in a terraced house that they have re-mortgaged twice to bail out my twat of a brother!' she hissed. 'How the hell are they going to be able to help me and the kids? There's enough money in the bank to pay the mortgage for the next nine months and then what am I going to do, Matt?'

'I'll sort something out, don't worry.'

'Erm, hello!' she said, sarcastically. 'Earth to Matt, Earth to Matt. Are you receiving me?' she frowned. 'You're in prison, Matt and from what that

useless wanker, Jacob Graff has told me, you will be for the next ten years.' She shrugged and looked into his eyes. 'The money will last nine months. Ten years minus nine months is a lot of mortgage payments.' She stifled a sob. 'What the fuck am I going to do?'

'I'll have a word with some friends,' Matt said, quietly.

'Friends?' Sandra repeated. 'What kind of friends will you have a word with?'

'Just friends.'

'Drug dealing friends?' she snapped. 'The kind of friends that could get me and the kids thrown out of the house for associating with them? Do you know that they think I'm complicit in all this? They will be watching me and if I make one wrong move, I'll be in here and our kids will be in care. I can't take a single penny from your friends, Matt.'

'Sorry,' he mumbled. 'I wasn't thinking.'

'That is the problem. You don't think. You didn't think about any of this shit while you were running around thinking you were El Chapo did you?' She paused for a breath and rubbed the corner of her eyes again. 'I'm not sure if I can do this, Matt.' She stood up and walked away quickly without looking back.

'San!' Matt called after her. All eyes in the room stared at him again. 'San!' She didn't stop. She reached the door and officer Clough let her out with a sly smile on his face. 'Sandra!' he shouted, but she was gone.

CHAPTER 37

The body dogs jumped out of the van and sat down, excitedly, their tails wagging. Their handlers were talking to Kim, who gestured with her hands where they should begin. Alan didn't think that it mattered where they started. He knew that there were bodies on the farm. There had to be. The video library went back decades. If the youngsters in the videos were alive, they would have grown up and complained to the police. At least some of them would. Moving a dead body is a risky business and no sensible criminal would take the chance unless there was no other option. Burying the victims on the farm would be the easy option. They were nearby and he knew it.

The handlers started their sweep of the area. Alan had ruled out the outbuildings for now. The smell of decomposition would make its way to the surface eventually. There was plenty of land to bury bodies where no one would ever smell decay. No human anyway, but the body dogs could. He watched them sniffing at the ground excitedly. Their handlers seemed to be enjoying themselves as much as their dogs. Kim was on her mobile chasing up any new information that had come in. Alan liked her style. She was always keen and eager to learn. She didn't know it all and she didn't pretend to. It was easy to mould a detective like that. He didn't want a team full of yes-men. That would stifle their development. He just wanted to make them the best that they could be.

Alan pushed his hands into his raincoat pockets and walked towards the outbuildings. From their shape, he assumed that there had been a barn, some stables and maybe a machine shed for storing tractors and the like. The fields beyond were a mixture of cattle grazing and rapeseed. In the far distance, Holyhead chimney stood against the backdrop of the mountain. He reckoned the land around the farm was about twenty-acres. It was being farmed and was populated with sheep. Only the land immediately around the farmhouse was untended. He made a note to find out who farmed the land in the close vicinity. They may have seen people coming and going. It narrowed the search area. A farmer would notice straightaway if the land he tended had been disturbed. The sudden appearance of broken earth would be spotted, whether it was in a cow field or amongst the crops. They had buried the bodies close to the farm; he was positive. He walked around the old stables and stopped at the edge of an untended field. The grasses were

knee high and he stopped to take in the scene. Four white vans were abandoned in a line, almost hidden by grass and bushes. They had been parked many years ago, stripped and left to rot. The wheels were gone, doors and seats salvaged. Vegetation had grown through the space where the windscreens had been. To his right an old plough was rusting away next to an equally decayed tractor. They had been there for decades, just like the bodies they were looking for. Alan guessed the farm equipment belonged to whoever had worked there before it became a paedophile nightmare. He envisaged an elderly couple who had worked the farm all their lives, grown old there, died there, and left it to their children who had no desire to be farmers; children who worked and lived in the city and had rented the farmhouse out to long term tenants, splitting up and selling the land to neighbouring farmers. It had happened all over the country. The last generation of farmers was literally that, the last generation. Rising at stupid-o'clock to milk cattle seven days a week for a few pennies on a pint was not what the younger generations wanted. It didn't have the appeal of high paid jobs in the cities. He thought that whoever had rented or bought the farmhouse had done so with the specific intent to use it as a porn factory. They had spent weeks and months if not years searching for the perfect venue, isolated yet well positioned for the road networks. The only piece of the puzzle that he hadn't worked out yet, was why they had left it in such a hurry. Prison or death were the most obvious.

He walked through the grass towards the vans and studied them. They were all Ford Transit models from the seventies onwards. The early model had round headlights, the later square. He moved closer to look at the number plates, only one remained. It was fixed to the latest model, probably from the late nineties, he thought. The engine was exposed but it was still in place. All the other vehicles had been stripped by scavengers. He walked towards the van and leaned over the engine bay and looked inside. Rust had eaten most of the hull and the gearbox was clearly visible. The others were in a similar state apart from the nineties model. He looked inside the engine bay and saw what he was looking for. Reaching in, he rubbed oil and dirt from a silver plate that was riveted to the hull. The VIN-number was still there.

Two ducks flapped overhead noisily and he looked to see where they had come from. A hundred yards away to his right, hidden from the farm by a slope, he noticed that a clump of trees occupied a dip between two fields. A stone wall ran north into the distance and a barbed wire fence ran south. He walked towards the trees and neared the rotting tractor, stopping to look at it. The huge rear tyres were flat and torn, holes the size of a fist had appeared. There was no cab and he wondered how cold and uncomfortable it would have been, driving it through the winter.

'Guv!' Alan heard Will calling him from the farmyard. Another brace

of ducks took to the air. He looked down at the coppice and saw water glimmering at the centre. There was a pond there. Alan decided that Will could wait and walked down the hill towards the trees. The lay of the land meant that the pond had been formed by surface water running from the gradients surrounding it. Long grass and shrubbery covered the slopes and barbed wire separated farmland from the coppice. Farmers didn't want their animals getting stuck in the trees and stumbling into the water. He walked further and reached the barbed wire fence. Touching it with his hand, he used a fencepost to support his weight as he climbed between the wire. A barb caught his trousers, ripped the material, and scratched the skin. He swore beneath his breath as he stood up on the other side. The ground beneath his feet became spongy, decomposing leaves and twigs had formed a layer above the soil. The undergrowth became thicker as he neared the water's edge. He pushed a sapling to the side to take a better look. Across the pond, Alan could see a scar on the land, an overgrown gulley that ran from the water through the trees. 'Guv!'

'On my way,' Alan muttered. He took another look around and then turned and walked back up the hill, glancing at the Transits briefly. His brain was churning like a washing machine as he made his way around the stables. When he turned the corner, Kim was on the phone. Alan's mobile began to ring. 'Are you calling me?' Alan said, looking at his screen. The screen said, Kim.

'I was shouting you,' she said, ending the call. 'I didn't know where you were.'

'What is it?' Alan asked.

'The dogs have swept the farmyard, nothing yet, guv.' Kim tiptoed through a muddy patch to reach Alan. 'And Google called.'

'What has he got?'

'The farm was owned by a family called Critchley as far back as he can go. The surviving relatives were Mary and Dennis Critchley, both are in their seventies. They're brother and sister and both are in nursing homes with advanced dementia. They sold off the workable land in the eighties but still own the farmhouse. The house was leased out to a local doctor, named Thomas from 1989 onwards until he died in July two years ago.' Alan nodded. It was never that simple but if the doctor had rented the farm for the best part of twenty-years, then he had something to do with it. 'The place had stood empty until a development company called Henderson's Homes bought it. If the doctor is our man, then it looks like a dead end.'

'He didn't do this alone.' Alan walked back towards the stables. He gestured for Kim to follow him. 'Whoever organised this operation was a clever man and clever men aren't easy to catch. They think of everything that can go wrong, plan for the worst but hope for the best.'

'I'm not following you,' she said, stumbling over a discarded brick.

'Has Google looked into Dr Thomas?'

'Yes. He was a consultant at Ysbyty Gwynedd for twenty years and then he set up his own practice as a GP in Llangefni. He ran it until he died.'

'What did he die of?'

'His death certificate says swine-flu apparently.'

'That's the downside of being GP. Contagious diseases. They can't avoid them.' Alan frowned.

'What's up, guv?'

'That doesn't fit the puzzle. Swine flu,' he said rubbing the dimple on his chin with his index finger. 'He would have been very ill but he had time to arrange for someone to clean up, get rid of the evidence, get rid of the girls.' He put his hands in his pockets and walked towards the rusting vans. 'Follow me and bring your phone.' Kim followed, picking her footing carefully. Alan made for the vehicle. 'See these vans, same make, different models, different years.'

'So?'

'That is a seventies model, that one is early eighties, that one is late eighties and that is nineties.'

'Okay,' she said, shrugging.

'They were used and then retired and then stripped of everything that could be used to identify them,' Alan said. He pointed to the youngest wreck. 'All except this one. They had started to strip it but not finished. There was no rush, you see?'

'Not really.'

'I should say that they thought there was no rush. Get this number plate and the VIN number called in. Tell Google to run anyone connected to that van in any way ASAP. I want to know who owned it, who insured it, who borrowed it, and even who washed it!' Alan paused and looked at the pond once more. A shiver ran down his spine. He looked at the dog handlers who were painstakingly searching a grid pattern around the farmhouse. One of them caught his eye and he waved them over.

'What are you thinking, guv?'

'I'm thinking where I would bury bodies on this land, especially if I had medical experience. I would know exactly what destroys DNA and trace evidence.'

'Water.' Kim followed his gaze to the pond.

CHAPTER 38

Lloyd Jones had spent the night planning for today. The PO's had told everyone that breakfast would be organised as normal with all three landings eating in the dining hall. B-Wing was off lockdown. It made doing time so much easier than being caged in an eight by four cage for twenty-three hours a day. Hours became days, days, weeks. Time dragged by so slowly in a cell. At least they could shower daily, get some fresh air, and socialise a little. Conversation could keep a man sane inside.

Lloyd knew that despite Viktor Karpov being arrested, he wasn't off the hook completely. The rest of the wing wouldn't bother to act on a contract from a man looking at a life sentence but Karpov's men would. Their families back at home would be looked after and their status in the organisation would be enhanced no end. He knew that they would try to get to him, especially Volkov. Volkov was a raving lunatic and he would come at him like a raging bull at a red flag. He wouldn't be motivated by the money totally; he had taken things personally. Lloyd didn't regret winding him up; if anything, it had been funny but with the doors opened, he had to be ready.

He checked his watch. Ten minutes. A murmuring was growing louder across the landings. The inmates were restless; ready to be freed and ready to be fed. Lockdown had been a hard slog this time around, longer than usual. He finished listening to a Kings of Leon track on the radio and then turned it off. Unfastening the back, he removed the batteries, all six of them and slipped them into a sock. Then he slipped the sock inside another sock, reinforcing the material. He pushed the heavy batteries tightly into the toe and then fastened a knot in the foot to keep them in place. He felt the weight in his right hand and nodded. It was enough to do substantial damage to a human skull. Lloyd picked up his three biros and held them tightly in his right hand, taping them together with his left. He double-checked that the point of each pen was out and then slipped them into his back pocket. He stood up and faced the cell door and waited for it to be opened.

CHAPTER 39

Javed Ahmed pulled up at the taxi rank and watched a scruffy man climb into his cab. He was wearing a baseball cap and a parka, like most of the men in the city his age. It was difficult to tell how old they were nowadays, drink and drugs made them look older but Botox and fillers made others look younger. The fact that middle-aged men now dressed like boys didn't help, long-shorts, trainers and sportswear were standard issue. Javed studied his passenger in the mirror. When he had opened the door and climbed in, his expression had showed disdain. Javed saw it a dozen times a day. They didn't have to say it; it was written on their faces. *Oh no, not another Paki taxi driver! I've watched documentaries on you lot grooming young white girls ... dirty bastards!*

The government and the press ranted and raved about racism and equality but it was mostly vote-winning bullshit. Javed was on the coalface. He saw racism every day of the week, every week of the year. It was there, entrenched in the British psyche. The multiple grooming and sexual abuse cases and the rise of radical Islam hadn't helped and he understood that. But it wasn't just racism against Muslims that he witnessed. He listened to customers ranting daily. *Brexit this and Brexit that. Europeans trying to hold us hostage they are! I'd send them all back and tell them to fuck off!*

Javed used to try and engage in balanced conversation in the early days but racism isn't balanced. Following the Manchester Arena bombing, one customer had reiterated the age-old adage, *we should send the lot of them back where they came from!* Javed tried to explain that many of the recent extremist attacks were perpetrated by British born Muslims, to which the customer replied, *if a pig is born in a kennel, it doesn't make it a dog, does it? Send them back to where their parents came from.*

Javed gave up at that point and tried hard not to have an opinion. It wasn't worth the hassle, especially after five o'clock when most customers were intoxicated.

'Where are you going?' Javed asked, as they pulled into the traffic.

'Caernarfon, Holiday Inn side,' the man said. He was local. The accent was unmistakable. It had taken Javed years to understand the lingo. The accent was harsh and guttural and they spoke too quickly. If they were pissed, then forget it. He had told them to enter their postcode into the Satnav themselves a hundred times. It was an impossible task to understand them. 'And don't go the long way around either,' the man added. The slur

in his voice indicated that he had been drinking. 'One of you lot tried to charge me a tenner last week. He was taking the piss!'

'One of you lot?' Javed repeated, quietly, wishing he didn't need the money sometimes. He pulled up next to a bus and nodded a silent greeting to the driver. The driver looked away as if he wasn't there. Javed looked at his passenger in the mirror. He was staring into his eyes, hatred or something similar burned in them. The thought of Del Makin paying someone to blow his head off sprung to mind like it did a dozen times an hour. Every customer was a potential assassin. He had his back to everyone permanently. It was such a vulnerable position. The police had reassured him that Makin wasn't a major player in the city. If he had been, he wouldn't have tried to kill Jones himself. He would have paid someone with more experience and skill to do it properly. Despite their assurances, he felt frightened but he knew that it would pass. The more time that went by without incident, the more likely the concern would fade.

Javed put his headlights on and navigated his way through the traffic, using bus lanes where he could. It was a three-mile journey that would take twenty-minutes. The meter was clicking over and he knew that it was going to approach the ten-pound level before they stopped. His colleague had been right and honest with the fare. He sensed there would be trouble at the other end. It came before he had anticipated.

CHAPTER 40

Lloyd stepped onto the landing and looked over the handrail. There were two guards on each tier as was the norm; hopelessly outnumbered. Matt caught his eye from the second tier and patted his pocket to let Lloyd know that he was tooled up. It was reassuring to know. There was no sign of Jack Howarth outside of his cell. Jack was a nonce but he was okay. He didn't pretend to be anything but who he was. Lloyd felt a bit guilty. Not much but a bit. He had heard that his leg was badly broken in the fall. That would probably result in a loss of privileges for a while but what else could they do to him? He would tell the governor to shove his privileges up his massive arse hole.

The prisoners were filing noisily towards the dining hall, descending the stairwells in some semblance of order. Only one man was walking against the flow. Volkov. There were shouts from below and two prisoners on the bottom tier began fighting. Lloyd didn't know who they were but he had a hunch that they were Karpov men creating a diversion and sure enough, the guards on every landing left their posts to attend to the trouble before someone was injured badly or the fight spread to involve others and became uncontrollable.

Volkov sensed that his time had come. He drew a shank that had been crafted from a radio handle. Tape covered one end, the other had been honed on the stone floors to a jagged edge. He held it up his sleeve and climbed the stairs to the top tier quickly, pushing smaller inmates out of the way as if they were children. As he reached the top tier, the other inmates had reached a frenzied pitch, cheering the fight below. Only a few had realised that it was only the prelim to the event that was about to take place on the top landing. Matt stopped walking and looked up to watch. He was one landing down on the opposite side of the wing. There wasn't much he could do from there.

Lloyd stopped and faced Volkov. He took out his makeshift club and waited. Volkov bared the blade and ran headlong at him. There wasn't much room to manoeuvre on the landing but Lloyd managed to turn sideways and deflect the onrushing Russian into the wall. He fell sprawling onto the metal walkway, cracking his nose. Lloyd remained calm and set himself. Volkov regained his feet, wiped the blood from his nose and rushed at him again. This time Lloyd aimed his weapon and gauged it well. The battery filled sock cracked the Russian on top of his skull with

sickening force. Blood sprayed up the walls. The blow was too powerful for the flimsy material and the sock ripped; batteries exploded from the rent clattering across the landing. The noise of metal on metal alerted the inmates to where the real action was and all eyes turned to the top tier. The volume increased to deafening levels. Volkov was stunned. He staggered forwards and Lloyd headbutted him with thunderous force. The Russian was stopped in his tracks and he fell to the floor, clutching his face. Blood poured between his fingers. He shook his head to clear his mind and tried to regain his feet. Lloyd was on him in a second, all the anger and frustration inside him exploded. He kicked the Russian in the face, landing on his jaw with incredible force. Volkov screeched in pain as his jaw was dislocated, the ligaments ripped from his skull. Fragments of teeth showered the landing, falling noisily onto the floors below. The Russian slashed at Lloyd with his blade, catching his cheek. A wicked gash opened and blood poured freely from it. Lloyd pulled out his biros and swung them in a lethal arc upwards at Volkov's throat.

'Jones! Don't do it!' Officer Clough shouted, rushing up the stairwell but it was too late. The improvised weapon penetrated the Russian's throat and went up through the flesh into his mouth. Lloyd pushed the weapon harder forcing it up into the nasal cavity and into his brain. Volkov began to twitch violently as Lloyd lifted him off his feet and tossed him over the railings onto the nets where no first aid could reach him. Lloyd looked down at Matt, his face splattered with the Russian's blood. He smiled and winked. Matt looked at him eyes widening, finger pointing. His mouth opened and he shouted a warning. Lloyd had begun to turn to look behind him when two razor blades cut through the side of his neck into the carotid artery. Arterial spray gushed from the wound like a crimson fountain, splattering the landing with blood. Lloyd collapsed against the wall, clutching at the gaping wound. His attacker, another of Karpov's men, pulled his head back and slashed at his throat again and again, slicing the jugular veins. By the time the PO's reached them, Lloyd Jones's head was practically severed.

CHAPTER 41

Javed indicated off the dock road into Beaumaris. The Beaumaris Eye was turning slowly, majestically spinning against the darkening sky. The north star was glinting above the Straits, soon to be joined by a trillion others. It would be dark within the hour.

'Is that meter on double time, Taliban?'

'What did you call me?' Javed asked, enraged. He slammed on the brakes. Crowds were gathering outside the castle five-hundred yards to his left. This part of the town was quiet and he could stop on the cobbled road without causing an accident. He turned to face the man. 'You are a racist!'

'There's no need to freak out,' the man said, laughing. 'You want to be careful. You're trying to rip me off in my own town. I was born and bred here. I know how much it is from town to the docks and it isn't a tenner!'

'I am not trying to rip you off,' Javed said, trying to remain calm. 'You can see that everything is done by the meter. I do not set the meter. The council sets the meter.'

'Whatever,' the man said. The heavens opened and rain began to bounce from the pavements. 'My car is over there.' He pointed to a small car park next to the canal lock. 'Take me over there and you can stick the tenner. Robbers usually wear a mask. Cheeky bastard,' he muttered.

Javed turned the cab around and pulled into the car park. It was dark and unlit and he didn't feel comfortable. He parked as close to the road as he could. Across the canal, crowds were drifting beneath the huge Ferris Wheel, queuing at food stalls and bars. The meter read just over ten pounds. He turned around and took the ten-pound note from the man and then released the lock to allow him to open the door. He just wanted him out of the cab. Fifty-pence wasn't worth arguing about.

'Keep the change, knobhead,' the man said, slamming the door.

Javed took a deep breath and turned the taxi around. He waited for the man to get into his car and drive off before he moved. He thought about reporting him to the police for drink driving but decided that he couldn't be bothered. Karma would bite him on the arse one day. Every action has a reaction. He relaxed as the man turned onto the coast road and mingled with the traffic. A knock on the window startled him. A woman with a baby in a pram was huddled against the pouring rain. She smiled and mouthed 'are you free?'

He nodded and opened his door to help her to get the buggy into the

vehicle. She opened the rear door and stood back. Javed lifted the buggy up the step and fastened it into place with a safety belt. He glanced at the child and realised too late that it was a doll. Before he could register the thought, Lucy Makin blew his brains all over the back of his cab.

CHAPTER 42
ONE WEEK LATER

Alan was standing in front of a bank of digital screens. He was leaning against a desk. His legs felt weary. Over sixty detectives had been summoned to the briefing. The discovery of bodies at the farm had attracted national and international press coverage. The senior brass and the Home Secretary were pestering constantly for news of progress. Their interest was hampering, not helping, the situation. Images from the farmhouse flashed before them as he spoke.

'Nineteen bodies have been recovered so far. All of them were buried in a ditch next to this pond. We think they used a JCB or similar to excavate the trench deep enough to be below water level. They dug the trench long enough that it could be used multiple times. The bodies were dumped into it, covered in quicklime and buried. Because they were below the waterline, eventually they became immersed in water too. Between the quicklime and the water, there isn't much left to examine. There certainly won't be DNA trace, although we should be able to identify most of them if we can get a match against what we have.'

He turned to look at the gathering. They were focused on his every word, their expressions grim.

'We know that the farm was used to manufacture kiddie-porn on an industrial scale. We also know that the doctor who rented the place died suddenly, leaving those girls trapped in the cellar.'

'I thought you had ruled him out?' someone asked. They had been drafted in that day.

'I need you all to get up to speed as quickly as possible,' Alan said, standing up. 'The death certificate was entered onto the system as swine flu by an admin clerk. When we traced the original notes, he was killed by a heart attack brought on by swine flu. Dr Ian Thomas is our prime suspect but we know from the tapes that he didn't work alone. We have a team working through every tape crosschecking the offenders with our database. Some of the men wore masks so we're trying to match tattoos, scars, moles, freckles, and the like. You all appreciate how long this will take.' The gathering nodded. 'In the meantime, the laptops have given up over a hundred email addresses. The UK clients are being traced and rounded up as we speak. Everything else has been passed on to Europol and the NCA.'

He paused. 'We have teams trawling through the victims' backgrounds trying to find a link between them. Why them?' Alan asked, pointing to the screens. 'How did they target their victims?'

'We have checked the families that we have identified and none of them were on the doctor's lists, either at the hospital or at the surgery,' Kim added.

'Guv,' Google interrupted excitedly. He had entered the MIT office in a fluster, wearing an anorak and a beanie hat. 'I've got something on the Transit.' He looked around the room and realised that the entire gathering was looking at him. He blushed and took off his coat. Alan waited for him to compose himself.

'Take your time,' he said, calmly. 'What is it?'

'You were right about it being stripped to mask its history.'

'Go on.'

'The number plates were stolen from another van which was reported stolen in ninety-five but the VIN number was kosha. I went back through the previous owners and one name jumped out.'

'Don't keep us in suspense,' Alan joked, a flutter of hope in his guts.

'The van was owned by Lloyd Jones from ninety-six to ninety-nine. After that it was never taxed or insured.'

'Lloyd Jones?' Alan repeated, incredulously. He looked at Kim. Kim shrugged and shook her head. 'For those of you who aren't familiar with him, we locked him up last month for two gang related murders. He was attacked and killed in HMP Berwyn a week ago.' Alan sighed and looked at the ceiling. Another dead end beckoned, literally. 'I don't believe Jones was involved in that. It just doesn't fit.'

'Maybe not,' Google interrupted. 'But there's more.'

'What do you mean?' Alan asked, confused.

'He had three named drivers on the insurance, one of them has form for sex offences.' Google paused and pulled out his information from a folder. 'A nonce that we locked up two years ago for grooming.'

'Jack Howarth,' Alan and Google said at the same time.

'Where is he now?' Alan asked, excitedly.

'According to his records, he is still in HMP Berwyn.'

'Kim,' Alan said, turning to her. 'Get over there and speak to him. Take Will with you. Nail the bastard to the floor. He was the doctor's accomplice.'

'How can you be sure?' Will asked, frowning.

'The doctor had a heart attack and Howarth was lifted and jailed for grooming two years ago when the doctor died.' He pointed to the screen. 'You see? That is why nobody went back to clean up. I bet Howarth didn't even know that he was dead. He wouldn't have expected any contact from him in jail in case we had stumbled across this. I bet Howarth thinks the

doctor is still alive and that he just cleaned up the operation and retired to Marbella.'

'Makes sense,' Will said, picking up his jacket. 'I'll get over there now.'

'What about the others?' Google asked. 'The men on the tapes.'

'We stay on it until we have nailed every one of the bastards. If we get one name from facial recognition, we can lean on them for the others involved. Jack Howarth is our key into the operation. I guarantee it.'

CHAPTER 43

Alan was sitting in his office, allowing himself to be a little bit excited. He'd had a feeling about those vans the first time he had laid eyes on them. They had been parked, side by side in a line by an organised mind and stripped of their identification. In hindsight, he knew that the doctor had been a cautious man. He had probably used the vans for kidnapping several times and then retired them from use. Scrapping them wasn't an option. There would be records created. So, he left them nearby yet invisible to the world and systematically stripped them to nothing but lumps of rusting metal. It would have worked too if he hadn't died and Jack hadn't been arrested at roughly the same time. A knock on the door disturbed his thoughts.

'Alan,' ACC Thomas poked his head around the door. 'Have you got a minute?'

'Of course, sir,' Alan said, standing.

'Sit down,' the ACC said. He had a worried expression on his face. 'I'm the bearer of bad news, I'm afraid.'

'Oh?'

'How is the Javed Ahmed murder going?'

'We are working on it, sir. Amongst other things. I can see the spot where he was killed on CCTV footage,' Alan said.

'Of course, you can,' the ACC said. He coughed and cleared his throat nervously. 'I'm afraid the CPS are dropping the charges against Derek Makin.'

'What?'

'Ahmed was the only witness. Jones is dead and Makin's wife is giving him an alibi for the time he arrived home. There's no way that he could have hung around the Paradise club until Jones came out and made it home in that time.'

'She's lying,' Alan said, angrily.

'Of course, she's lying!' the ACC snapped. 'Everyone is always lying. They lie, we lie, it is just a case of who the CPS thinks the jury will believe. We have no witnesses left to testify.'

'They can't let him out. He shot Lloyd Jones and he threatened Mr Ahmed at gunpoint.'

'They can and they have, I'm afraid.'

'For fuck's sake!' Alan slapped the desk. 'I sometimes wonder why we

bother. It's a joke!'

'You're not going to like this either,' the ACC mumbled. Alan looked at him and sat back in his chair. 'The CPS has deemed the video evidence against Viktor Karpov is inadmissible. It was gathered by criminals during criminal activities. If it had been filmed by undercover officers, it would have been okay but this way. The criminals were coerced and they were allowed to continue with their involvement in criminal behaviour.' He paused. 'I can see their point. They released him this morning.'

'And Jones's men?'

'Their lawyers are all over it. It's the same evidence gathered the same way. DI West didn't do her due diligence. They'll be out by the morning.'

'So, the only man left in jail is Brian Selby. The most unlikely criminal that I've ever met. I'm beginning to think that justice is as rare as a hen's tooth.'

'We can only do what we can do, Alan. You're a good detective but we have rules to follow and a system to abide by. Well done. You have done your best.' Alan looked at him and nodded. He just wanted to go home and attack the whisky. Sleep would be hard to come by without it. The ACC turned and walked out of the door without another word. There was nothing else to say.

CHAPTER 44

Jack was sitting in a wheelchair, a blanket over his legs. The doctor pushing him was sweating nervously. He checked that the corridor at the back of the X-ray room was empty. It was. The G4S guard was outside the main entrance, reading the paper and texting his wife's sister on his phone. He had been trying to get into her pants for months and she was finally coming around to the idea of an affair. Her husband had left her a year ago and the idea of no strings attached sex appealed to her. She had never got on with her sister anyway, so banging her husband a few times a week would be a thrill.

The doctor pointed down the corridor. He gave Jack a baseball cap and a coat and a thousand pounds.

'The taxi rank is at the end of that corridor,' he said. 'We're even. Now fuck off out of this hospital and don't ever come back. If I ever see you again, I'll kill you.'

'There's no need for that, doctor,' Jack said, grinning. 'We had some good times, didn't we?'

'Fuck off! Go before I change my mind.' He watched Jack wheeling himself towards the exit and hoped that he would never see or hear from him again.

He turned around and pushed open the door of the X-ray waiting room. Stepping inside, he closed the door and held his breath. Memories of the cellar at the farm came flooding back to him. They were memories that sickened him and excited him too. It was more than sex. He couldn't explain what it was. In his day job, he stopped people hurting; he stopped their pain. In the cellar, along with others, he had inflicted it on the weak and vulnerable. He used the words underage where society would call them children. When he looked at his own teenage daughters, he felt sick and twisted about what he had done but there were dark times when his mind wanted to return to the tears and the sobbing. He had supressed his evil desires as best he could for years. In the beginning, it was supposed to be sex but they started hurting the victims more and more and he loved it. The first time he saw one of them murdered, he never went back. That was a step too far. He began to question how he had become involved in such evil. Ian Thomas, the consultant who rented the farm had befriended him and one drunken night they confessed to having similar taste in underage sex. That was the beginning. They were friends for years but they fell out

when he stopped going to the farm. The consultant was worried that he would talk. He warned him that if he ever spoke of the farm to anyone, he would have someone visit his family. He had also told him that everything he had done had been filmed and if they were caught, he would take him down with him.

He pushed the memories from his mind and looked around and then gritted his teeth before slamming the back of his head against the wall. The impact split his scalp and left blood trickling down the magnolia paintwork. He lay face down on the floor and waited for someone to discover that Jack Howarth had pushed him against the wall, knocking him out and escaped via the back door.

CHAPTER 45

Matt arrived home from prison in a taxi, paid the driver and climbed out. The place was in darkness. A *for sale* sign flapped in the wind. He walked up the drive and looked into the living room window. The lights were out but he could see that the furniture had gone and the floorboards were bare. His heart sank. He took out his mobile and dialled San for the fifteenth time. The answering service said that the number was no longer in service for the fifteenth time, just in case he hadn't believed it the first time. He walked to the front door and tried his key. It didn't fit. She had changed the locks too. He thought about going to her mother's house but he knew that she wouldn't be there. Wherever she was, she would make sure that he couldn't find her. He called Justin's number. Justin answered; the background noise told him that he was in a pub somewhere.

'Hey.'

'Where are you?' Matt asked.

'In Holyhead. Where are you?'

'At home.'

'How's that going?'

'Sandra has fucked off with the kids. It's a long story.' 'What are you going to do?'

'I'm going to come to town and get smashed. We've got a busy day tomorrow.'

'What the fuck are you talking about?'

'I know where Lloyd kept his emergency stash.'

'What?'

'There's usually ten grand and two kilos there.'

'You're bullshitting me?'

'Nope. Tomorrow morning we're back in business.'

'I'm in the Welsh Fusilier,' Justin said, excitedly. 'I've been shitting my pants about what to do when I got out!'

'We'll do what we're good at. Without Lloyd around, we've got a good chance of making it too. He was a crazy bastard. I'll see you in half an hour. Wait there for me.'

'I'll see you in a bit.'

Matt cut the call and glanced back at the house. This was it. He had a choice, find Sandra over the next few weeks, go straight and get a job

working nine to five and bring up his kids like any normal dad or start up in business again tomorrow, make a shit load of money, drive nice cars and lay pretty women. He put his phone into his pocket and walked away. Starting again was exciting and this time, he was the boss.

CHAPTER 46

Brian Selby was numb with pain. It felt crippling. The prison councillor had summoned him to an interview on D-Wing. He'd been escorted there by Officer Clough who was working on C-Wing that day. He insisted on calling him 'Lard Arse'. The news that his mum had suffered a stroke in the night and was found dead by a carer the next morning was devastating. He was sent to the pharmacy and given two sleeping tablets that were to be taken at lights-out. That was it.

'Your mother has died, here are some tablets to help you sleep. The funeral? No, you won't be able to attend. You are in prison on a murder charge, remember?'

Not being allowed to bury her was a hammer blow. He couldn't fathom how they could not allow him an hour to say his goodbyes. She had been the only constant in his life apart from being bullied; that would always be there. The sense of guilt was like nothing he had ever experienced before. If he had been at home where he should have been, he may have been able to save her. The fact that she had died alone was impossible to come to terms with. She had been there for him all his life and when she had reached her final moments, she had to face them helpless and alone. He simply couldn't deal with it.

The journey back to C-Wing was a blur. He was tripped up from behind by other prisoners three times. Three times in fifteen minutes. Officer Clough thought it was hilarious.

When he reached his cell, his personal belongings had been stolen. His soap, his deodorant, even his toothbrush. They had taken his new razor and left the old one on the floor. To top it all, his chocolates and crisps were gone too. He complained to officer Clough immediately but he said that prison was full of crooks and where did he want him to start looking? Wasn't he supposed to be protecting him? Obviously not. It was like being back at school only ten times worse and now there was no going home to his mum, not ever. It would be like that every day until he was old. Bullied and pushed around and the target of cruel taunts, fatty this and fatty that and fatty the other. He was sick of it. He was sick of living. When lights-out came, he lay in the half darkness and listened to the sound of prison. Laughter, abuse, crying, anger and frustration saturated the very fabric of the building.

Brian took his sleeping pills and washed them down with water. Water that had a metallic after-taste. Even the water was bad. How could they get

water wrong? He reached down for his razor and picked it up. The thin metal blade glinted dully in the nightlights. He pressed the edge against the metal bedframe until the plastic cracked, exposing the blade. *It was time to leave and be with Mum.* He had no idea where but he knew that she would be waiting for him when he arrived. The tablets were making him sluggish. He put his head on the pillow and turned onto his back. Placing the blade against his wrists, he paused to think about the pain. It would hurt. Dying that way wouldn't be pleasant but then living was agony. The alternative was the easy way out. A few painful slices through the flesh and darkness would come. The pain would be gone, so would the name calling, and so would being fat. He could start again. Taking a deep breath, he made the first cut vertically from the wrist to the elbow, long and deep. Tears trickled from his eyes and he had to bite his lip to stop himself from crying out as he made the second cut. The blood flowed, the warm sensation on his skin not unpleasant. He changed hands and sliced the opposite wrist and then dropped the razor onto the floor and closed his eyes. The pain became a dull ache. His mind became fuzzy, his muscles weak. Darkness became darker still. He was drifting away, dying, leaving this earthly plane. Everything was peaceful.

The observation hatch opened and officer Clough looked in. Brian was on fifteen-minute observation checks. It was standard operations following the death of a parent or child on the outside. The alarm blared and the door burst open and his peace was shattered. He came rushing back into the chaos that was life. Brian felt them tugging at his limbs. He felt his arms being wrapped in material. Voices called out; orders were given. He felt warm breath on his ear.

'Oh no you don't, Lard-Arse!' Officer Clough whispered. 'Not on my nightshift, you're not worth the paperwork.'

Brian felt sick to the pit of his stomach. They wouldn't even let him die in peace.

EPILOGUE
ONE YEAR LATER

Jack Howarth was standing next to Lloyd Jones's grave. He hadn't brought flowers. That wasn't necessary. Lloyd wouldn't have wanted flowers. He wasn't a flower type of guy. Jack spat on his grave and unzipped his jeans. He took out his penis and pissed on the gravestone. Lloyd would have appreciated that. Whatever level of hell he was suffering in, it would bring a smile to his lips. Jack finished urinating and zipped himself up. He patted the headstone and walked away. His limp wasn't as bad now and the aching pains had subsided. It was nearly time to go back to work. The urges were becoming irresistible. He was set up on the internet again and the demand had not diminished, in fact it had intensified. It was a shame that the doctor and Lloyd were dead. Jack was a master of acquiring victims. Some sites online were calling disappearances as the work of the Child Taker. Lloyd and Dr Thomas had had a knack for disposing of bodies. Lloyd had been secretive about what he did with them but chatter on the landings had mentioned that Lloyd had put brothers from a rival outfit through an industrial mincing machine. When he had heard that, Jack realised what he had done. The doctor had become concerned that the trench was full and that as the bodies decomposed, the surface would subside, leaving a visible scar on the land. He said that he would have to keep levelling it off to hide it and that any activity with a digger was too visible. Lloyd had said that he would dispose of the bodies, no problem. When asked how, he used to tap his index finger against his nose.

'Best you don't know,' he would say, with a wry smile.

Jack smiled at the memories. He always knew that there were sicker people than him out there. Lloyd Jones had been one of them and it had been an absolute pleasure to have known him.

THE END

Nearly Dead is part of The Anglesey Murders and the prequel to the bestselling Detective Alec Ramsay Series, which is seven novels long. Conrad has written 24 crime thrillers. To read the entire series for less than £6, click here; https://www.amazon.co.uk/gp/product/B01MQGCR6S

If you enjoyed *Nearly Dead*, then please leave a review. They help the author with visibility which is the only way they can keep writing the books you enjoy. The 3rd Anglesey book will be published in September. Many thanks for your time.

CONRAD JONES

PROLOGUE

The machine whirred into life. Metal hooks slotted onto the meat hopper and an automated hoist kicked into motion. A metal chain rattled. It lifted the rear of the hopper and tipped the bloody contents into the huge, stainless steel funnel that fed the meat grinder. Half a ton of pig bits slid noisily towards the spinning cogs. Ears, noses, tails, skin, offal, and bone were crushed and ground into mincemeat in minutes. The pale pink mince was forced through a sieve the size of a bin lid and collected in another meat hopper beneath it. The smell of dead flesh hung heavily in the air.

'Half a ton of flesh and bone processed in under four minutes,' Lloyd said, without turning around. He rubbed his tattooed hand over his shaven head, feeling the stubble. A vein throbbed at his temple and the muscles in his jaw twitched. He looked angry but then, he always did. Three men were standing behind him. Two were holding the third between them; blood dripped from his nose onto his Armani shirt. He looked confused, frightened and exhausted. 'It is an amazing machine. It allows us to use almost every bit of the animals that come in. Nothing is wasted. Impressive, isn't it?'

'Why am I here?'

Lloyd watched another hopper full of pigs being minced. He ignored the question.

'Who are you and what do you want from me?' the man asked, again. Lloyd continued to stare at the machine and ignored him once more, fascinated by the grinder.

'Please! What am I doing here?' the frightened man asked. His voice was quiet and reedy. Lloyd glanced at him and put his index finger to his lips to shush him. The man looked around the abattoir, the smell making him gag. He could hear pigs squealing in a different part of the building. They could sense death was close too. The atmosphere was oppressive, tainted with fear. The odour of blood and animal excrement made him want to vomit. The machine finished its business and fell silent. Lloyd grinned and nodded. He looked over his shoulder at the man.

'Okay. Let's get straight to the point. You are a regular customer of the Wicks brothers,' Lloyd said, turning to look at the man. The man looked at his feet, not wanting to make eye contact too long. Lloyd waited for a reply but none came. 'I'll say it again; you are a regular customer of the Wicks brothers.'

'I don't know what you're talking about.' The injured man said, shaking his head.

'You don't?'

'No. I don't.'

'The Wicks brothers?'

'I don't know them.'

'You don't?'

'No.'

Lloyd punched him on the nose. The nasal bones shattered with an audible crack. The blood flowed faster now.

'Lie to me and I'll hurt you. Okay?' Lloyd said. The man nodded. 'I asked you a question.'

'Okay.'

'Good, let's be clear about things. You are a regular buyer from the Wicks brothers.' The man shook his head to the negative. 'That wasn't a question, by the way. You are a customer of theirs. That is a fact.'

'I don't know them.'

'You don't know them at all?' Lloyd tilted his head as if he was talking to a child. The man continued to shake his head. 'You are telling me that you have never heard of them?'

'I've never heard of them.'

'You're lying to me.' Lloyd headbutted him. The thud was sickening. His knees went weak and he had to be held upright. A gurgling sound came from his throat as he swallowed his own blood. His eyes rolled back into his head.

'I swear that I don't know them.' The man began to cry. His lips quivered and saliva mixed with blood dripped from his chin like a sticky red stalactite. His breath was coming in gasps. 'Please, don't hurt me anymore. I don't know them.'

'You do.' Lloyd grinned. 'Do you know how I know?'

'No,' the man replied, his voice a whisper.

'They told me that you are a customer, so there is no point in lying to me.'

'What?'

'The Wicks brothers themselves told me that you buy from them regularly.'

'I don't know ...' Lloyd lifted his finger to silence him.

'They told me that you buy a kilo of coke from them every Thursday. You have been buying a kilo of coke from them every Thursday for five years.' Lloyd paused and smiled although there was no warmth in it. 'They like you. You're a good customer. You're never late and you never ask for credit. You pay them sixty-five grand a kilo, right?'

'Look. I don't know who you are,' the man moaned, shaking his head.

His eyes were full of fear and suspicion. 'I can't talk about stuff like that. They're nutters. They would kill me.'

'I understand. You are afraid of the Wicks brothers?'

'Yes, I'm afraid of them and so should you be.'

'I'm afraid of no one and you don't need to be afraid of them either.'

'Look,' the man spoke, calmly. The fear in his eyes couldn't be concealed. His voice was shaky, tinged with fear. 'With all due respect, I don't know who you are but you clearly have no concept of who the Wicks brothers are or what they're capable of. They are dangerous.' He nodded and looked at the men one at a time to reinforce his point. 'If I talk to you, I'm as good as dead.'

'Sorry, I'm not making myself clear, Del,' Lloyd said. 'Do you mind if I call you, Del?' Del shook his head, almost imperceptibly. 'Let's clear this up right here, right now. I want you to call Dave Wicks on your phone so that we can straighten this out.' Del shook his head. His eyes widened in fear. 'Go on, call him right now,' Lloyd said with a shrug.

'What do you want me to say?' Del looked confused.

'Whatever you normally say. Do it. Take out your phone and call him before I lose my temper with you.' Del took his mobile from his pocket and scrolled through the contacts. He found the number for Dave Wicks and called him. A mobile began to ring nearby. Lloyd took the mobile from his pocket and grinned. There was blood on the screen. He held the screen towards Del so that he could see it. 'Can you see that?'

'Yes.'

'This is Dave's phone.'

'I know it is,' Del said, quietly.

'He has you stored in his phone as "Big Nose".' The men holding Del laughed. 'Why do you think that is, Stuart?' Lloyd asked one of his men, who was standing behind him.

'I think it is because Del has a big nose, boss.'

The men laughed louder. 'He does, doesn't he?' Lloyd giggled for a few moments. He stopped suddenly and looked at Del with piercing blue eyes. His face was like thunder. 'You have got a big nose, Del,' Lloyd said, seriously. 'You know that, don't you?' Del nodded. 'You do know. You must know. I bet you got bullied at school, didn't you, Del?' Del nodded again. 'There was no need for him to set it as your caller ID was there?'

'No. There wasn't,' Del agreed, finding his voice.

'Dave Wicks was a cheeky bastard, eh, Del?' Lloyd smiled and walked towards a line of meat hoppers beneath the grinder. He looked into each one as he went by.

'Why have you got Dave's phone?' Del asked, concern in his voice. He noticed a smirk on one of the men. A shiver ran down his spine. There was something very scary about his captors. They had menace coming from every pore. 'Where is he?'

'Come and see this.' Lloyd ignored the question. He gestured towards the hoppers. Del was helped along on unsteady legs by the men that held him. His eyes darted left and right nervously. 'Notice how the colour of the meat varies slightly from skip to skip. No two are the same. This place is not a completely legitimate slaughterhouse. Some of the animals that come here never existed.' Lloyd tapped his nose with his forefinger. 'Black market meat is big business. There are none of the usual restrictions involved.' He tapped his nose with his forefinger again. 'Of course, some of it goes back into the industry. You could say it goes missing. I know a pig farmer who buys this stuff, boils it up in huge vats with cereal and oats and turns it into pig swill. They love the stuff. Have you ever heard the noise pigs make before feeding time?' Lloyd looked Del in the eyes and waited for an answer. Del looked confused. 'Are you listening to me?'

'Yes.'

'I asked you a question.'

'Sorry.'

'Don't be sorry just answer the question!'

'No. I haven't heard the noise pigs make before they eat,' Del mumbled.

'It is deafening, Del. They go bananas. When they smell that swill being cooked, you can't hear yourself think. They go into a frenzy, bumping and charging each other away from the troughs. The strongest eat first and the weak get the leftovers.'

'This is all very interesting but could you please tell me what the fuck I am doing here?' Del said, finding some courage. Lloyd nodded to the men holding him. One of them grabbed his testicles hard in a vice like grip and twisted. Del's mouth opened but no sound came out, the air was trapped in his lungs. It was five torturous seconds before the grip was released. 'I'm sorry,' Del gasped. 'No more, please. I'm listening!'

'Good. It is rude of me not to explain myself properly. Come here,' Lloyd gestured for the men to bring him to the line of meat hoppers. 'You see how they're all pretty much a uniform colour, except this one.' Lloyd pointed. Del looked inside. The meat in that hopper was much darker. 'All the other hoppers are full of pig. This is a different colour. Do you know why?'

'No,' Del whispered.

'Can you guess?' Lloyd grinned. Del shook his head. 'This meat is much darker in colour because that is what remains of the Wicks brothers.' Lloyd grinned widely. 'They don't look scary now, do they, Del?' Del looked like he had been punched in the guts. The colour drained from his face. His mouth opened to speak but he couldn't find words. 'You should have heard them squealing, Del. They made so much noise, cried like babies. Some people can't die with dignity, Del.' Lloyd let the gruesome news sink in. Del looked like he was going to be sick. He couldn't take his eyes from the dark, human mince. 'Anyway, as you can see, they won't be trading anymore. I'm taking over their business and their customers. Everything will stay the same for you, almost.' Del was stunned. 'Did you hear what I said?'

'Yes. You said, almost?'

'You will buy a kilo a week from me just as you did with the Wicks except the price is now seventy-five grand.'

'That's ten grand a kilo more …'

'You can add up,' Lloyd said, sarcastically. 'This is not a negotiation. Let me explain.' He leaned closer to Del's face. His breath smelt worse than the abattoir. 'You are Del Makin. You live in a three-bedroom detached in Rhoscolyn. You drive a new Lexus and your wife drives a Mercedes. She works in a dental practice in Valley next to the Valley Hotel. She's very pretty by the way,' Lloyd patted him on the shoulder and winked. 'You're punching well above your weight there, Del.' Del started to tremble. 'Your daughters go to a private school on the mainland. Jessica is nine and Emily is twelve. They leave home at eight thirty every morning and get the bus home at four o'clock every day.' Del was about to speak but Lloyd put his index finger to his lips. 'You have a nice family and I'm sure you want to keep them safe, don't you?'

'Of course, I do!'

'Good. Then listen to me carefully. If you try and buy from someone else, they're dead. If you try and shaft me, they're dead. If you moan about the price, I'll go straight to your dealers and cut you out permanently. You and your family will be pig swill just like your friends here, understand?' Del nodded that he understood. He was pale and shaken. The skin beneath his eyes was swelling and turning black. Blood still pumped from his shattered nose. 'I asked you a question.'

'Yes. I understand.'

'Good. Then we're done here,' Lloyd said, an evil grin on his face. 'It's been nice doing business with you, Del. Your first delivery will be Thursday. Make sure you're there on time with the money, you hear me?'

'I hear you.' Del wiped blood and snot from his chin with the back of his hand.

'Good man. I can see we'll get on. Not a word to anyone mind, got it?' Lloyd gestured to the remains of the Wicks brothers. He pulled up a video on the mobile phone that he had taken from Dave Wicks and clicked play. The images of the Wicks brothers being tossed into the grinder played. As their limbs were sucked into the grinder's spinning cogs, their screams were desperate and bloodcurdling. The sound of bones splintering filled the air. Their bodies were pouring through the sieve as mince long before they stopped screaming. Del couldn't take his eyes from the screen. He turned white and then vomited onto his shoes.

****

Across the island, Jack Howarth was sitting in his camper van, waiting for his newest project to arrive. He had spent three months talking to her in online chatrooms. At first, he had posed as a teenage boy to break the ice. He sat patiently waiting for her icon to come online night after night and then he would chat to her. Not too heavy at first, just talking about school and stuff. She started talking to him regularly and eventually gave him her real name. Then he really got his hooks into her. She wanted to add him on Facebook but he lied and said his parents had deactivated his profile as a punishment but he spent hours on her Facebook page researching his target. He knew her location, where she went to school, who her best-friends-forever were, what football team she supported, and what her favourite music was. Everything that he needed to know about her to get inside her head was there and he had used his new-found information to groom the unsuspecting child.

As their friendship developed, he set up a PayPal account for her and began to send her money so that she could buy music, clothes, jewellery, and whatever she wanted. Not much at first, ten pounds here and there. He told her to be careful what she spent it on so that her family didn't begin to ask where things were coming from. She told him that her parents were cannabis smoking alcoholics who wouldn't know what her name was if they hadn't tattooed it on their arms. This information gave him more ammunition, pandering to her problems and feeding her desires. He became her knight in shining armour. Once she was hooked, he admitted that he wasn't thirteen and that he was in fact an adult. He also told her that he had fallen in love with her. That was always the vital link in the grooming chain. He always covered his tracks by using VPN software to hide his IP address just in case.

At this point, she would either flip and tell her parents, who would in turn notify the police or she would continue the virtual relationship. Her relationship with her family was tenuous at best so she did the latter after a brief period of sulking, which ended when he sent her a hundred pounds to apologise. Pretty soon she was talking about running away, about hating school and her dysfunctional parents. A few months later, she had agreed to meet him. He had told her that he was an adult with adult needs and that if she loved him as she said that she did, and then she would want the same thing. She agreed to have sex.

He checked his watch and looked around the park. There were a handful of dog walkers and joggers but the rain was deterring most people.

It suited him. The camper was the ideal vehicle for illicit sex with a minor. A movement to his right caught his eye. He saw her beneath an oak tree, a hundred yards away, huddled beneath an umbrella. At least, he thought it was her but couldn't be sure. She waved and summoned him over. He waved back and gestured to her to get into the camper. She shook her head and called him over. He didn't want to get out of the van but she was obviously nervous. It was understandable. He checked his appearance in the mirror and pulled a beanie hat on to hide his receding hair. She would not be attracted to him in anyway. None of them ever were but the three crisp twenty-pound notes in his pocket would sway her. It was a fortune to a girl of that age. He opened the door and climbed down, closing it behind him. The wind tugged at his dark coat. He buried his hands deep into his pockets and jogged towards her. She looked nervous but managed a half smile. He kept his head down so that she couldn't see his face clearly. A dog walker and a jogger crossed his path and blocked his view of her. He tried to look around them but they were in the way. They moved by and he caught a glimpse of her. She looked sexy in jeans and trainers. Her blond hair was shorter than in her pictures. It was a different shade too. As he neared, he noticed the lines at the corners of her eyes. Her teeth weren't as pearly-white as they were in the pictures on her Facebook. He walked closer but alarm bells were ringing in his head. Despite wearing foundation to smooth her complexion, she looked older than thirteen. Much older.

'Jack Howarth?' a voice said from behind him. Jack turned to see two plain clothed detectives and two uniformed officers surrounding him. One of them reminded him of someone. The jogger and the dog walker had turned to block his escape. The German shepherd reared up on two legs and bared its teeth, barking angrily. He realised that they were police officers too and that he had been tricked – hook, line, and sinker. 'You're under arrest, sunshine. I hope you brought a toothbrush in your camper van because you'll be going away for a while,' Alan Williams said, squeezing the cuffs on a little too tightly. 'I hope that hurts, you horrible little man. Let's get you locked up where you belong.'

CHAPTER 1
TWO YEARS LATER

Brian looked over his shoulder again. He stared into the gloom and tried to make sense of the shifting shadows. The sound of footsteps in the distance drifted to him but he couldn't see who they belonged to. Every time he turned around, the footsteps slowed and the sound faded in the darkness. When he stopped, they stopped. The wind whistled through the trees that lined the road, their naked branches reached towards him like bony fingers, pointing, warning him of the evil that followed, as if they knew who was there. Rain dripped from their boughs, soaking his clothes and absorbing his body heat. He pushed his hands deep into his pockets and shivered against the cold, listening intently to the whispering breeze. The footsteps appeared to have ceased completely. He began to question if he had heard them at all. Fear and angst made his stomach knot. He felt sick with nerves and something else. Fear. It was pure unadulterated fear. His head was spinning. He wanted to turn back and go home. This was not his world. He didn't belong in it. It scared him. He wanted to go home to his warm house and his mother.

The sausage dinner followed by ice cream that she had fed him earlier, threatened to come back up. His breathing was laboured and his knees were creaking beneath the substantial weight that they carried. He wanted to stop now before it was too late. The sound of a throaty cough floated to him on the icy breeze. He listened intently, frozen to the spot. Was it a cough that he had heard or was it an evil chuckle or was it neither, just a trick of the wind? He swallowed hard and caught his breath and scanned the horizon again, then he turned and walked into the biting cold. Rainwater ran down his nose and dripped from his chin. His exposed skin was cold and numb. The joints in his podgy fingers ached and his feet were sore. Every step was a chore. Only fear drove him on.

A security light came on to his left, triggered by his movement. It made him jump but he was grateful for its luminance. The darkness was pushed back a few yards if only for a short while as he travelled through its field of operation. He could see a mechanic's garage. Its signs advertised MOT and cheap tyres. The security light illuminated the forecourt where half a dozen vehicles were parked. On top of a pole, a CCTV camera overlooked the scene. He suddenly felt exposed and vulnerable in the circle of light. The feeling that he was being watched was overwhelming. Brian looked behind again nervously. He studied the shadows. Nothing. There was no sign of anyone there. He turned up his collar in a vain attempt to keep the rain out and jogged away from the light into the darkness once again. As the night enveloped him, he took small comfort that it offered him camouflage. He jogged awkwardly for a minute. The fat wobbled from side to side. He struggled on until the sweat was running down his back. His nerves were jangling and he felt the muscles in his chest tightening as his lungs gasped for air. He promised himself that he would make a serious effort to lose weight but he knew that was a pipe dream. Being obese was something he had lived with all his life. He was the fat kid at school, college, and university. His fellow students had been cruel. The insults had cut him deep emotionally. It was something that he blocked out. He would go home from school crying most days. His mother would comfort him with sweets and chocolate and she would repeat the old saying.

'*Sticks and stones can break my bones but names will never hurt me*'.

What a load of bollocks that was. It had been made up by someone who wasn't fat. They had never had to endure a barrage of abuse all their life. The name calling had hurt him. It still did but it wasn't life threatening. He had reached his late twenties safely despite the bullying but his life was in danger now. Real danger. It swung in the balance and there was no way out. He steeled himself against the storm and cursed himself for getting into this situation in the first place.

He wished that he had never agreed to it. Not that he had been given any choice. His life had been turned upside down since Lloyd Jones had entered it. The man was deranged. In fact, deranged didn't cover half of it. One minute he was everyone's brother from another mother, the next he was a violent lunatic. He had no sympathy for those he hurt; in fact, the pain and the terror he inflicted on them amused him. Brian had seen it first-hand. He had encountered many bullies through his life but Lloyd was on a different scale. He was a cocaine fuelled psychopath. Lloyd Jones frightened the life out him. He frightened the life out of most people and that was why it was better to do what he was told to do, no matter what the consequences. If Lloyd Jones said jump off a bridge, you asked him which one, Britannia or Menai. Jumping would be easier than pissing him off. He wasn't right in the head. He picked on Brian constantly, much to the amusement of his thugs. Lloyd and his men bullied him relentlessly. Brian was used to being bullied but this was a different level of abuse. They kicked him, punched him, stabbed him with their steroid needles, and burnt him with cigarettes. He was constantly nursing one wound or another. They never hurt him enough to warrant going to a hospital but his mother was beginning to ask questions about the first aid supplies being depleted. If she had known, she would have made a fuss and called the police and that would have been even worse. He had never grassed on the kids at school and he wasn't going to start now. Being the fat kid at school had made him accustomed to violence and abuse and things hadn't changed when he became an adult. That had disappointed him. He had expected it to stop the moment that he walked out of the school gate for the last time but fatism was everywhere he turned. It always had been and always would be.

Brian stopped in his tracks as a car appeared over the hill and he turned his face away so that the driver couldn't see him. It went by without slowing. He watched the rear lights grow smaller and then disappear around a bend. The road was silent again. Behind him, the security light at the garage switched off, plunging the street into darkness once more. Brian kept jogging at an unsteady pace, trying to place his feet carefully. The last thing he needed now was to trip. His hands were in his pockets and if he lost his footing, he would fall on his face. Things were bad enough without any more facial injuries. The scar on his cheek was still red and angry. Fourteen stitches had held the flesh together until it knitted but the scar would be there to remind him what happened if you questioned Lloyd Jones. Lloyd had smiled as he sliced Brian's face, slowly and calmly with a serrated steak knife. Brian had nightmares about the twinkle in Lloyd's eye as he cut through skin and muscle and scraped bone; the blade had nicked his cheekbone. The doctors weren't sure if he would recover the use of the left side of his face beneath the scar. It had left him with a crooked smile. He hadn't looked in the mirror for days. His reflection had always made him cry but now it was worse. He wished Lloyd Jones would succumb to a long and painful disease and die screaming. Until then, he had to do whatever Lloyd asked.

A hundred yards on, he saw the barrier that blocked vehicle access to a lane. It ran through a copse of trees towards the rear of Berwyn prison on the outskirts of Wrexham. He checked both ways before crossing the road. At the barrier, he paused and studied the pavements on both sides of the road. He looked left, right and behind him. There was no sign of life. He hoped that the mysterious footsteps he had heard were a figment of his own tortured imagination. There were no monsters or demons stalking him; his tormentor was human. His waking nightmares revolved around one man. Lloyd Jones. He was far more frightening than any imaginary being. Brian took one last look in each direction and then turned and waddled into the trees.

The darkness took on another shade, darker and deeper than before. It seemed to shift, expanding and contracting around him. Dark shadows shifted position, drifting, floating, reaching for him. He slowed his pace and stuck to the middle of the lane. It was familiar to him. He had walked the route a dozen times before Lloyd had made him fly a drone over the wall into the prison. Lloyd didn't know that Brian knew where he was to fly the drone. He thought that his security was tight but Brian had used his eyes and his ears to learn things that others missed. Picking bits and pieces from whispered conversations, Brian had worked out what Lloyd wanted him to do and where. It was one of his few talents.

It was all Brian's idea from the start. He hadn't thought for one minute that having an idea would take him to the edge of a precipice. He had simply been thinking aloud at the time. It was just an idea to begin with but when he had shared it with a work colleague called Luke, he hadn't expected him to discuss the idea with his cousin, Lloyd Jones. Lloyd had listened to it, liked it and embraced it with fervour. He had waited outside Brian's workplace the next day, approached him with a charming smile and a firm handshake, introducing himself as Luke's cousin. Before Brian knew what was happening, he was persuaded to get into a Jaguar with three of Lloyd's henchmen. They took him to a very swanky gin bar, in Trearddur Bay, called the Black Seal, told him jokes and made him feel like one of them. Brian didn't have many friends. He had always been shunned because of his weight. Lloyd and his colleagues had made him feel like they were friends at first and he enjoyed himself for the first time in years. They were big men, heavily muscled and tattooed. Lloyd was shaven headed and tall with a back like a grand piano. The sinews in his forearms looked like they were made from wire. He wore an expensive grey suit with an open neck shirt and snorted coke from a silver business card holder every ten minutes or so. The rest of his friends wore jeans and designer polo shirts underneath dark leather jackets. The evening had gone by in a blur. As soon as their glasses were empty, another round appeared. Once Lloyd was convinced that Brian was drunk and relaxed, the real reason that he wanted him there surfaced and the atmosphere changed very quickly. By that time, it was too late. They took him across the road to the Trearddur Bay Hotel, where it was a little quieter. When they'd ordered drinks and shots, Lloyd turned serious.

'Tell me about your drones, Brian,' Lloyd had said, as he snorted a thick line of white powder. The question came out of the blue. His smile had vanished and his eyes seemed to look into Brian's head, searching for lies. Brian was suddenly frightened by Lloyd. It changed that quickly.

'My drones?' Brian was confused by the sudden change of subject. He looked around the faces at the table. 'How do you know that I have drones?'

'My cousin, Luke told me. You work with him.'

'Oh, I see,' Brian said, shrugging. 'What can I tell you about them that won't bore you to death?' Lloyd had stared at him, no expression on his face. The silence was threatening. Nervously, Brian stumbled through a summary. 'Erm, I am a bit of a drone geek, so I don't want to drone on about it,' he said, trying to make a joke but no one smiled. He could sense the menace coming from each of them. 'Well, where do I begin? I have four drones, two small ones and two big ones. I mess about with them and put cameras on them and make videos of flyovers for my website.'

'Videos of what?' Stu had asked. His voice was thick and gravely.

'All kinds of things,' Brian had explained. 'I fly them over the island, the mountain, Holyhead harbour, the breakwater, Trearddur Bay. I've been all over the mountains in Snowdonia too. You know, that kind of thing?'

'How many videos have you uploaded?' Lloyd asked, pretending to be interested in his hobby.

'I'm not sure. Over a hundred.'

'These drones can carry things?'

'Yes,' Brian said, nodding. His fat jowls wobbled. He felt like he had been tricked but he didn't know why. 'Obviously, the bigger the drone, the more weight it can carry.'

'Obviously,' Stu said sarcastically. The big men grinned at each other.

'Tell me about your idea of using a football to smuggle drugs into a prison,' Lloyd's tone changed. All eyes seemed to bore into Brian. Two men on another table had overheard Lloyd and turned around to look at them. 'What the fuck are you pair of nosey bastards looking at?' Lloyd snarled at them. They stood up and put their coats on, leaving their drinks unfinished. He watched them leave and then turned back to Brian. 'Tell me about the football idea.'

'The football idea?' Brian said, almost in a whisper. The colour had drained from his face. 'I was just thinking aloud when I came up with that. How do you know about that?'

'My cousin told me.'

'Of course, he did,' Brian muttered. His mind was spinning. What did this man want? 'He told you what I said did he?'

'Yes. Explain it to me properly.'

'It was nothing really. We were just talking about an article online.' Brian laughed dryly but no one else laughed with him. They stared, their faces deadpan. 'It was an article about dealers flying drones into prison grounds delivering contraband.'

'Tell me and the boys about the story,' Lloyd said, emptying his gin and tonic. He waved a tattooed hand at the barmaid and indicated that they wanted another round and then snorted another line. 'From the beginning.'

'Okay.' Brian shrugged as if he couldn't see the point. He had wanted to leave but knew that he couldn't. Droplets of sweat formed on his top lip and it began to tremble just like it had at school when the bullies had surrounded him in the playground. The familiar desire to run crept into his mind. He had run once at secondary school but his tormentors caught him and beat him. Running wasn't an option then and it wasn't now. He had to tell Lloyd what he wanted to know. 'It was a story online about a dealer inside, who had someone fly a drone over the wall of the prison, using a camera to steer it once it was out of sight. The pilot flew it to a first storey window, packed with a drug called spice and a mobile phone,' he explained. 'It was a legal high before the government outlawed all of them.'

'We know what spice is,' Stu growled.

'Of course, you do,' Brian mumbled nervously. 'Apparently, that stuff is like gold dust inside. Anyway, to cut a long story short, the drone he used was too small for the weight and the weather conditions and he couldn't pilot it properly. The drone veered off track and went to the wrong window and the drugs fell into the wrong hands. According to the article, a fight broke out in the prison. Two men died, all because they used the wrong drone. It wasn't big enough, a schoolboy error really. They overloaded it.'

'Tell me about the football.'

'It was just an idea,' Brian said, blushing. 'It was nothing.'

'Don't be shy. Tell the boys your idea.'

'Well, prison officers are on the lookout for drones nowadays. My idea was to use a drone with a camera to see what kind of footballs they use during exercise time. You know, in the yards?'

'What do you mean?' Stu asked, frowning. Deep wrinkles creased his protruding forehead. Brian thought he could model as a Neanderthal man.

'My idea was to fly over and film the exercise yard. Then source the exact same type of ball, fill it with drugs or whatever you like and then fly it over the wall, drop the ball in the exercise yard and then fly the drone out. You could mark the ball so that the recipients inside can identify it without touching it. Once the coast is clear, they could empty the contraband out of the ball. If anything goes wrong and they are caught going near the ball, they can deny all knowledge of what is inside. They play with that very same type of ball every day, after all. The guards would have no way of pinning the drugs on anyone until they emptied the ball, obviously.' Brian sat back and sipped his gin. He smiled, impressed with himself. His new friends looked equally impressed. That was his first mistake. They were not his friends. It had been a violent rollercoaster ride ever since.

Brian felt the ground beneath his feet becoming muddy. The condition of the lane deteriorated the deeper he ventured into the trees. He heard shouting coming from beyond the walls. He couldn't understand the words but he could tell that one of the inmates wasn't very happy. A searchlight switched on to his right. The guard in the tower aimed it at something inside the walls. The powerful beam swept left to right and back again. Brian crouched and ran off the lane and into the trees. He ducked beneath the branches of an ancient oak and watched as more lights came on. More men began to shout and a siren started to wail. The volume went up as the lights crisscrossed the interior of the prison. It was obvious to Brian that something had kicked off inside. He checked his watch. It was nearly midnight. Brian reached into his pocket and took out his mobile phone. He ran back to the lane and headed deeper into the trees until he reached a rusty gate, where he recovered an entrenching tool that he had hidden in the long grass. Brian looked at his phone and scrolled through his contact list until he had the right number and then he hit dial. Beneath the ground, a Nokia 105 began to ring. He picked that mobile because its battery life was thirty-five days. The ringtone was muffled but he could hear it well enough. He followed the sound until he was directly above it and then he started digging. Within minutes, he had uncovered the rucksack that had the drone and the remote inside it. He had buried them the week before, after flying the drone into the prison and before making his escape on foot. Burying them had seemed like the sensible thing to do but Lloyd Jones didn't think so. When Brian had told him that he had buried the drone near the prison, Lloyd went ballistic. Apparently, leaving evidence behind was a big no-no, even if it was underground. He accused Brian of trying to get him nicked and gave him a good hiding for his troubles. The next morning, Lloyd got the news that the drugs and mobile phones that were inside the football had been intercepted. Apparently, the guards were waiting to pounce. They had been tipped off that the drop was coming. Lloyd had a sneak in his operation and he flipped, accusing every man and his dog of being the grass. His paranoia deepened. He questioned everyone. Brian's interrogation involved the steak knife. Lloyd's men on the inside had been rounded up and transferred to different prisons the next day, where they were rearrested and charged with several offenses, all of which would add several years to their sentences. Lloyd had been pulled in and questioned but following a 'no comment' interview, he was released quickly. He was rattled and he ordered Brian to recover the drone and dispose of it somewhere it could not be found and used as evidence. He had accused Brian of burying it so that he could use its location as a bargaining chip should he be arrested for his part in the operation. Brian didn't think like a criminal but he could see Lloyd's point and he promised to recover the drone as soon as it was safe to do so. Lloyd said that wasn't good enough. Brian had to recover it that night or lose his fingers and toes. He had no option but to do as he was told.

With the rucksack recovered, Brian wiped the sweat from his brow, bent low and headed down the lane towards the road. He counted each pace from the gate. When he had reached one hundred steps, he turned and walked off the lane into the trees. Ten paces in, he dug another hole and reburied the drone. He patted the soil and stamped it down with his feet and then hid the entrenching tool at the base of a sycamore tree. He had told Lloyd exactly where he had buried the drone the first time, now if he went to check if he had disposed of it, it was gone. There was no way Brian was going to destroy his best drone. He had hand built that machine and it flew like nothing else he had tried. It was mint. Lloyd Jones could go and fuck himself.

Brian stomped the mud from his boots and headed back to the road. He reached the barrier, grateful that the rain had eased a little. Checking that the road was clear, he turned left and crossed. As he stepped onto the pavement, headlights appeared over the rise ahead of him. He put his head down and walked as fast as he could without running. His heart was pounding in his chest. He could hear the engine and the tyres cutting through the surface water. The headlights dazzled him, turning raindrops into diamonds falling from the darkness above. As the vehicle approached, he glanced up. It was a dark van. His imagination filled it full of Lloyd's men, armed to the teeth with hammers; knives; axes; baseball bats with barbed wire wrapped around them. He imagined Lloyd at the wheel, sneering at him through the windscreen. He felt his heart rate quicken and his hands turned into fists in his pockets. The van seemed to slow. He stole a momentary look at the driver, a face he didn't recognise. It wasn't Lloyd Jones and the driver was alone. It roared by him into the night.

Brian sighed with relief and broke into a lumbering jog; his midriff wobbled from side to side. His car was a half a mile away, parked on an empty industrial unit. The quicker he got to it, the quicker he could go home, eat a curry, have a hot shower and warm his weary bones. He would ring Lloyd and tell him that the drone was in the river and if he went to check that he had moved it, which he would, it wasn't where he had buried it anymore. The man was a paranoid wreck but a very dangerous one. Brian had already decided that he wasn't going to do anything else illegal. He had heard Lloyd and his cronies chatting about using drones to case robberies, lookout for police cars, even to deliver drugs across the city. None of them had the expertise to pilot a drone carrying thousands of pounds worth of merchandise so he had to assume that they meant to use him to fly them. He wasn't going to do it. No way. Lloyd could fuck off. Brian had thought about his options, which were limited indeed and the only viable option was to move away without telling anyone where he was going. The problem was that he didn't have any money to live on while he looked for a job and then there was his mum. She was getting old and Brian was her only carer. He had played out the different scenarios over and over in his mind but he hadn't come up with any answers. The security light at the garage flicked on and he jumped as the light illuminated the forecourt.

'Hello, Brian,' a familiar voice growled. He knew it was Stu immediately. His bulky figure was silhouetted in the bright light. 'Now then, where have you been?'

'Me?' Brian looked around nervously. He wanted the ground to swallow him up. 'What are you doing here?' he waffled. He looked up and down the road, praying for help to appear on the horizon. 'I was sorting out the drone. You know, like I promised Lloyd.'

'That's good to hear. Where is it, Brian?' Lloyd asked from behind him. His voice made him jump. Brian turned quickly. His mouth was open in surprise. Lloyd's huge frame was bathed in light, making him look even bigger. Brian couldn't answer. His top lip began to quiver again, just like at school. 'The drone, Brian, where is it?'

'I moved it.' Brian blurted without thinking. He couldn't lie to save his own life. 'I was going to take it to the sea but when I was digging, the sirens went off at the prison.' He looked from Stu to Lloyd. Their eyes bored into him. 'You heard the sirens going off, didn't you?'

'I didn't hear any sirens, did you, Stu?'

'Nope. I didn't hear any sirens.'

'They did go off, honestly. I was digging and then all the lights came on and then the sirens went off. It sounded like chaos in there. Anyway, I panicked. I didn't want to get caught in the open on the way back to my car so I thought I would just move it. I panicked.' He tried to smile but his lips wouldn't do as they were instructed. His knees were trembling and he could feel his fingers shaking. He tried to swallow but his throat had dried up. He coughed. 'It is safe for now, Lloyd. No one can find it but me. It's safe as houses. Honestly it is.'

'Honestly?'

'Yes.'

'I don't think that you even know the meaning of the word, Brian,' Lloyd said, shaking his head.

'What do you mean?'

'I mean that you're telling me lies, Brian and then you're using the word 'honestly'. You moved the drone and then you were going to go back when you thought that I had forgotten about it, weren't you?'

'I just thought it would be okay there for now, that's all.' Brian shrugged. The nerves at the corner of his lips twitched. 'I mean, it's a perfectly good drone.' He looked at Lloyd like a child caught stealing from a shop. 'I built that with my own hands. It's my best drone, Lloyd. I just thought it would be okay there for a while and then I could recover it later.'

'And then what?'

'I was going to dismantle it and use the parts to build another one.'

'There we are,' Lloyd said, smiling. 'The truth. You see, that didn't hurt, did it?'

'No,' Brian said, shaking his head. He was confused and frightened. 'I'll go back and get it if you want me to and I'll toss it in the bay.'

'Good man. That's what I asked you to do in the first place,' Lloyd said. 'We'll come with you this time, just to make sure that you do what I asked you to do.'

'You don't need to go to all that trouble.' Brian looked from one man to the other. He felt like he was going to lose control of his bowels. 'I'll be fine on my own, Lloyd, honestly.'

'There goes that word again, Brian. It just doesn't sound right when you say it.' Lloyd shook his head and grinned coldly. 'You shouldn't use that word if you don't mean it.'

'I do mean it, Lloyd,' Brian said as calmly as he could. 'I will go and get the drone and throw it in the Straits.'

'What do you think, Stu?' Lloyd asked, without taking his eyes from Brian. 'Do you think that we can trust Brian anymore?'

'Not a chance,' Stu replied gruffly. 'Look at the size of the fat bastard. He has no will power and no self-respect. You can't trust a man who has no self-respect. If he doesn't respect himself, how do you expect him to respect you?'

'There you have it, Brian,' Lloyd said with a shrug. He took a pack of Lamberts from his pocket and lit one, inhaling deeply. He exhaled as he spoke. 'You can't be trusted.'

'You can trust me,' Brian said, feebly.

'I am cold and I am wet and I am very fucked off that we can't trust you to do a simple job.' Lloyd looked up the road towards the trees. 'You had better take us to the drone before I lose my temper and it had better be where you say it is or mark my words, you will be sorry.'

'I'm already sorry,' Brian muttered. He turned and crossed the road, the big men followed him, one on each shoulder. 'I didn't mean to cause any problems. I panicked when the sirens went off.'

'Shut up. We should take him to the abattoir and have done with the useless lump,' Stu growled. 'He would feed the pigs for a week.' He shoved him hard in the back and Brian stumbled, almost falling. Images of school flashed by in his mind. Being tripped in the corridors, morning breaks, dinnertime breaks, and afternoon breaks was part of his day. Walking more than twenty paces without someone kicking at his ankles from behind was an anomaly. Learning to keep his balance had been essential to remaining upright.

They reached the barrier and Brian paced out his steps. He took out his mobile and dialled the Nokia again. Lloyd and Stu looked at each other as the mobile's muffled ringtone came from beneath the earth. Brian went to the base of the sycamore tree and picked up the entrenching tool. He knelt and began to dig. Lloyd stubbed out his cigarette as he watched Brian digging. The earth was still soft and loose and he reached the rucksack in minutes. He picked it up and held it up to show Lloyd. Lloyd reached into his coat and took out a silenced Beretta.

'Keep digging, fat boy,' Lloyd said, gesturing with the gun. Brian looked shocked for a moment; his mouth open. 'I said, keep digging!'

'Lloyd, please don't do this,' Brian muttered. His hands began to shake as he plunged the spade into the soft earth. 'I am more use to you alive than dead. I didn't mean to cause any trouble for you. I only did what I thought was right. I didn't mean any harm.'

'Shut up and dig,' Stu snarled. 'Dig the hole longer!'

'Lloyd,' Brian said, his voice almost a whisper. 'I look after my mum, Lloyd. There's only me left. I'm all she's got. Give me one more chance, please.'

'If you speak again, I'll shoot you in the face,' Lloyd said calmly. 'Dig it longer. A few more feet this way and another six inches or so down.' Brian dug with shaking hands for fifteen minutes. 'That ought to do it, eh, Stu?'

'It should do it.' Stu grinned in the darkness.

Brian felt his heart racing. Sweat poured from every pore. His mind searched its darkest recesses for a solution but he couldn't think of anything to say that would save him. This was the end of the road. Shot dead and buried in a shallow grave. He had always hoped that things would improve as he got older but they hadn't. Things were always just a different shade of shit but they were always shit. Being buried in a muddy hole was probably all he should have aspired to. It was probably more than he deserved. Tears ran from his eyes, mingling with the rainwater as they crossed his chubby cheeks. He tried to slow down as the hole reached the perfect length for hiding a body. Even a body the size of his. His chest heaved as he tried to control the sobbing. Despite the shitty life he had, he wasn't ready to die. Not yet. Not like this.

'Please, Lloyd!' Brian whined.

'Shut your mouth!'

'I'm sorry. Really, I am. I didn't think.'

'How much did they pay you I wonder?' Lloyd asked thoughtfully.

'Who?' Brian asked, confused. 'How much did who pay me?'

'I told you to shut up, Brian.'

'Sorry.'

'It was a big score for them,' Lloyd said, tilting his head. 'There was fifty-grand in coke in that football. That was worth ten times as much on the inside. I bet the Drug Squad thought all their Christmases had come at once when they got that tip but what was it worth to you?'

'I don't know what you're talking about,' Brian sobbed. He wiped snot from his nose with his sleeve leaving a snail trail. Images of school flashed in his mind once more. His school blazer was always striped with snot on the sleeves. 'I don't know anything about any Drug Squad.'

'I told you to shut up and I won't say it again,' Lloyd said flatly. 'I guess that I'll never know how much a grass gets paid for that kind of information,' Lloyd sighed. 'How much was it, Stu?'

'What?' Stu looked confused.

'How much did they pay you to rat me out?' He raised the Beretta and fired twice into Stu's chest. One bullet shattered his breastbone before veering upwards and leaving through the shoulder. The second went through his left lung. Stu collapsed to his knees, a surprised look on his face, before toppling forward onto his front. The muzzle flash blinded Brian and he squeezed his eyes closed tightly and waited to die.

'Help me get him into the hole,' Lloyd said. Brian opened his eyes and looked at Stuart's dead body.

'What just happened?' Brian whispered to himself.

'Grab his legs and pull him into the hole!' Lloyd snapped. 'Hurry up.'

'But what just happened?' Brian seemed dazed as he grabbed Stu's feet and dragged his body into the grave. Lloyd kicked the limp arms into the hole. 'What happened, what happened, what happened?' Brian muttered.

'Bury him properly. Make sure he is well covered and hurry up about it.'

'I don't understand what just happened,' Brian sniffled. He shovelled earth onto the dead body. The rain threatened to wash it away as quickly as he put it on. He muttered to himself as he toiled. 'One minute I thought they were going to kill me, the next I'm burying a body. What just happened?'

'Will you stop wittering for fuck's sake!' Lloyd snapped.

'I'm sorry but I'm a bit shocked. You just shot Stuart,' Brian said in a panic. 'Twice!'

'Get a grip, Brian. Stuart was a grass,' Lloyd said, as if it was obvious.

'A grass?'

'A dirty grass. He was feeding information to the police. He made the mistake of thinking that he was smarter than me and that was where he fucked up.'

'Bloody hell,' Brian muttered. 'Stuart was a grass. I never expected that.'

'He was very convincing but he wasn't as smart as he thought he was,' Lloyd said. He tapped the side of his head with his forefinger. 'That was a huge mistake. You don't think you're smarter than me do you, Brian?'

'No,' Brian said nervously. He shook his head and shovelled dirt as fast as his body would allow. There was no doubt in his mind that he was smarter than Lloyd. Lloyd was average intelligence at best but telling him that right now was not the best plan. 'I don't think that I'm smarter than you. Not at all. I made a mistake but at no point did I think that I was smarter than you, Lloyd. Not for one minute did I think that. Never in a million years would I think that. Not me. No way.'

'Good because we don't want you and your old mum ending up in an accident, do we?'

'My mum?'

'Yes. Your mum. If you fuck up, I'll feed her to the pigs, understand?' Brian nodded that he did. 'Is that what you want?'

'No, Lloyd,' Brian said quietly.

'No, Lloyd is the right answer. Now hurry up and bury that turd and then throw that drone into the river, understand?'

'Yes, Lloyd.' Brian gulped.

'We'll send the boys back tomorrow night to dispose of him properly. I have someone else that I need to go and see. Call me when it is done.' Lloyd checked his watch and walked away into the night.

Brian knew then that running away from the island was a fantasy. He was burying a dead body. A murdered body. He had colluded in the disposal of a murder victim. There was no way back now. Lloyd Jones had his hooks into him and there was nothing that he could do about it. He was working out his options when a hand gripped his ankle tightly, the nails piercing his skin. Brian tried to turn around but the grip on his leg was too tight. He stumbled onto his knees and cried out.

'Get off me!'

The ground beneath him began to undulate. Another hand broke through the soil and clawed at his face. Brian grabbed it and pushed it away from him but the blood-stained fingers clawed at him. He stared at the hand, holding it as far away as he could, panic rising. The other hand shifted and gripped his throat. He could hear muffled cursing coming from below him. Fingernails dug deep into his neck; blood trickled from the indents. Brian couldn't pull away. He gripped the wrist as hard as he could and tried to pull it from his throat. The ground began to rise. He looked to his left and spotted the shovel. It was within his reach. Brian let go of the wrist and scrabbled for it. His fingers touched the handle and he fumbled to pick it up. He wrapped his hand around it, lifted it high above his head and plunged it hard into the loose soil. The grip on his throat loosened. He raised it again and thrust it into the ground. The hand seemed to stiffen and then went limp. Brian lifted the shovel one more time and brought all his weight down on it. Stuart's attempt to escape his grave ended as the blade crushed his larynx. Brian collapsed in a sweaty heap, his breathing deep and laboured. He closed his eyes and tried to fathom what he had done.

CHAPTER 2

Peter Clough picked up his fish and chips from the counter and walked towards the door. The Globe chip shop was on his way home from his local, the Holland. He checked the time. It was just before one o'clock in the morning.

'You're the last customer tonight. Goodnight, Peter,' the owner called after him. 'Will we see you tomorrow?'

'I'm on nights until Wednesday,' Peter said, grimacing. 'I'll see you Thursday.'

'Take care until then.'

'Will do, night mate.'

The smell of vinegar was making his mouth water and he plunged the plastic fork into the tray and came out with a chip that was smothered in mushy peas. He blew on it twice and then put it into his mouth. It burned as he chewed it but it was worth the brief pain. He was starving hungry. An eight-hour shift and four pints of lager had given him an appetite that he hadn't had for weeks. The death of his father the month before had hit him hard and he was struggling to deal with it. Eating had been the last thing on his mind. Work had been very kind to him. They insisted that he took leave and didn't return until he was ready. And they had continued to give him full pay all the time he was off. The press and the public were quick to bash the prison service at every opportunity but they didn't see past the headlines. The service was like a family. There were some bent officers, bad apples but they were in every workplace. Most of the time, everyone had each other's back. They looked out for their colleagues. They had to; it was a dangerous environment to work in. He couldn't thank them enough for the support they had shown to him while his father was dying and following his death. The three weeks leave had given him time to grieve and put things into perspective. Things were slowly returning to normal, his appetite included.

Peter stopped in the doorway for a second to shovel another forkful into his mouth. They tasted divine. He ate there most nights of the week when he wasn't working. It was possibly the best fish and chip shop that he had used since that trip to Betws-y-Coed. The chippy on the bridge in the middle of the village was his favourite. The memory made him smile. His dad had been sharp and agile back then. That was before the cancer came. The disease had devoured him internally until the pain was unbearable. That was the worst bit. Watching him suffer had been soul destroying to the point where he wanted the hospital to ring him in the middle of the night to say that he had passed. It had made him feel so guilty but he had wanted him to die so that it would be over. When the call did come, it was almost a relief. At least he was free from the pain now. Life had to carry on regardless. The world didn't stop revolving for anyone, grieving or not.

Peter stepped out of the doorway and turned left, tucking into his chips as he started the short journey home. His flat was a hundred yards from the pub and two hundred from the chip shop. That was a key factor in where he wanted to live following his separation from his wife. His marriage equated to fifteen years down the toilet. Fifteen years of walking on eggshells to keep her happy. The miserable bitch wouldn't know happiness if it crept up behind her and bit her on the arse. If it wasn't one thing then it was another. At first, his job as a sales rep wasn't good enough. It was commission only and his wages were too unreliable. Then he joined the prison service but she didn't like the night shifts and he didn't get promoted quickly enough. She could emasculate him with her tongue. Nothing he did was good enough. The crux of the problem was that she had wanted children but it didn't happen. They went through three rounds of fertility treatment before the NHS pulled their funding and another one paid for by themselves before their money ran out. Her moods became worse and more unpredictable as time went by and then one day she turned around and asked for a divorce. 'I'm not happy,' she had said. No shit Sherlock. She had never been happy. She wouldn't know happy if it punched her in the face.

A week later, Peter was moving into his flat. It was a massive relief at first. He went out wherever he wanted, whenever he wanted. The divorce went through a year or so later and everything was done amicably. No one had lied or cheated after all. They had simply grown apart. Things trundled on for a while and then a year later he bumped into her on Market Street, in the centre of Holyhead. She was obviously flustered and embarrassed but she managed to introduce her new husband, Rupert. That hurt more than he thought it would but not as much as spotting the huge bump in her stomach had. He didn't ask how far gone she was, the words just wouldn't come. She had pulled her coat closed so he couldn't see it but it was too late. He had seen it. She was pregnant. As he walked away, tears had trickled down his face. She had been impregnated by a man called Rupert. He felt emasculated yet again. Rupert had refreshed the parts that Peter hadn't reached. Frustration and anger bubbled beneath the surface, forcing more tears from his eyes. He felt jealous. That was an emotion that he never expected to feel about her. Jealous. He was jealous and angry that she was having a child with another man. Another husband. Another life. A family. That was his dream when they had married and it had been shattered. Now another man was living his dream with his wife and it didn't seem fair. All that time and heartache that they had invested trying to conceive and he had nothing to show for their pain. He had nothing and now she had everything. It wasn't fair. It was at that moment that he realised how desperately lonely he was. He gravitated to his only remaining parent, his father. They regularly went for a pint and played golf once a week. It filled a void in his life. Eighteen months later, his father was diagnosed with pancreatic cancer and his world was shattered once again.

Peter mulled things over as he walked and chomped on his takeaway. He had taken some emotional knocks but he had weathered the storm. There was only one way from the bottom and that was up. He would take each day at a time and he would grow stronger. It wasn't too late to be happy. One day, he would meet his soul mate and he would have a family. Maybe he would meet a woman who already had children. That would be ideal. He would make a good dad even if the children weren't biologically his. He genuinely believed that it would happen, it was just a matter of time.

A car pulled up alongside the kerb, disturbing his thoughts. The passenger lowered the window. His face was vaguely familiar and a shiver ran down his spine. He couldn't put a name to the face but he knew that it wasn't a face that he wanted to see. There were two more men in the back seat. Peter sensed danger immediately.

'Good evening, officer Clough,' the passenger said, making a mock salute. He had a twisted smile on his face. 'It's been a long time. You're out and about late, aren't you?'

'Do I know you?' Peter said, glancing at him. He looked up and down the street, hoping to see someone that he knew but it was deserted.

'You don't remember me?'

'No., Should I?'

'I'm Lloyd,' the man said, grinning. 'Lloyd Jones.' The name echoed around Peter's brain. 'Don't tell me that you don't remember me?'

'I can't say that I do.' Peter lied.

'That hurts my feelings,' Lloyd said sarcastically. He opened the door and climbed out. Peter kept on walking. He picked up the pace, trying to put distance between them. 'Don't walk away, officer Clough. I just want a quick chat.'

'I've got nothing to say to you,' Peter mumbled. He pushed chips into his mouth and looked over his shoulder. Now he could see him properly, the memories rushed back. Lloyd Jones was a big man, an unforgettable man. Peter remembered him alright and he remembered that he was trouble. Big trouble. He was a bully inside, a nasty piece of work but he was also wary of the big fish back then. Lloyd Jones wasn't on the top tier of the underworld but he wanted to be. Peter didn't doubt that he would get there in the end.

The car pulled ahead of him and the men inside opened the doors and climbed out, blocking his path. They formed a wall of muscle and ink. There was nowhere to go. Peter had no choice but to stop and turn to face Lloyd.

'Alright, I remember you vaguely. What do you want?'

'Just a little chat. You could call it a business opportunity.' Lloyd stepped closer.

'I have no interest in your business.'

'You haven't heard what I have to say yet,' Lloyd said calmly. He reached into Peter's tray of chips and grabbed a handful, stuffing them into his mouth greedily. 'They're nice aren't they.' Bits of fish and potato sprayed from his lips as he spoke. 'Grab a chip, lads,' he said, gesturing to his men. 'Officer Clough won't mind sharing.' The men crowded in on him and grabbed handfuls of his dinner. Peter snatched the tray away from them and glowered at them. 'What's up, officer Clough?' Lloyd sneered. 'Are we not good enough to share your chips?'

'What the fuck do you want, Jones?'

'Like I said, I have a business opportunity for you.'

'And I told you that I have no interest in your business.'

'That's a shame,' Lloyd said, shaking his head. 'You could be missing a golden opportunity.'

'I doubt that very much.'

'I've heard that you have had a rough time lately.'

'You've heard wrong.'

'I heard that you might need to earn a few extra quid.'

'I don't know where you get your information from but I'm fine.'

'Funerals and divorces are expensive,' Lloyd said. 'You have had both haven't you?'

'That's none of your business.'

'I heard your old man snuffed it?' Lloyd feigned sadness. Peter was stunned. 'My sincere condolences. I lost my father a few years back. I mean it, sincere condolences.'

'Thanks,' Peter muttered uncomfortably.

'It's never easy losing a parent.'

'No.'

'How did the funeral go?'

'As well as can be expected,' Peter answered, frowning. 'Look, I don't have the time or the inclination for this conversation.'

'Sorry to bring up the funeral.' Lloyd raised his hands in apology. 'I couldn't go to my old man's funeral.' Peter shrugged. 'Because you bastards wouldn't give me a pass out for the day. I spent the day in my cell, crawling up the walls.'

'That's nothing to do with me. Decisions like that come from the governor. You know that.'

'Oh, I'm not blaming you,' Lloyd said, looking around. 'I know what a tough time it is, that's all I'm saying. An expensive time too. Funerals cost a small fortune nowadays.' Peter remained quiet. 'I heard that you were struggling and could use a bit of extra cash.'

'You've heard wrong. I don't need extra cash and I certainly don't need any cash from you.' Peter held Lloyd's gaze. 'So, if we have that straightened out and that's all, you can take your gorillas and fuck off and leave me in peace to eat my chips.'

'There you go again, being rude,' Lloyd said, wagging his forefinger in Peter's face. 'You could at least hear me out.' Lloyd winked at one of his men. The man sniffed and cleared his throat and then spat a thick green ball of phlegm onto Peter's food. Peter glared at the man but kept his temper under control. Reacting to these men was unwise. He had worked with criminals long enough to know that they would attack at the first opportunity. Despite his rising anger, he held his tongue. 'Ah, look at that. Your chips are ruined now.'

'I'd had enough anyway to be honest,' Peter said, tossing the tray onto the floor. His calmness rattled the men. He could see them getting angry. 'Okay, you have sixty seconds of my time. What do you want, Jones?'

'Jones?' Lloyd frowned. 'We're not on the landings now, officer Clough. There're no uniforms out here, no locks, no bars, no keys, no truncheons or pepper spray. You're on your own out here. This is the jungle and we're the predators. We eat people like you for breakfast. You're fuck all on the outside.' Lloyd paused to allow his words to sink in. Peter remained calm on the surface although Lloyd had seen a flicker behind the eyes. It was fear. 'I am a reasonable man, Peter. Can I call you, Peter?' Peter nodded. He didn't see the point in riling them. 'We do a lot of business on the inside. You know what I'm talking about.' Peter nodded again.

'You sell drugs.'

'We do sell drugs, you're right. They keep the inmates quiet and the violence down. We are doing you prison officers a favour really,' Lloyd grinned.

'Well, I'm sure we're all very grateful. Get to the point.'

'The prisons would explode without drugs. You must turn a blind eye to it every day. We have a lot of officers on the payroll but we don't have anyone working on your wing. There's a vacancy there that I need to fill. I'm offering you the position because we have history. We go back a long way.' Lloyd paused to gauge his reaction.

'Have you finished?' Peter asked, checking his watch. He looked from one man to another. Lloyd shrugged. 'I have given you my chips and I've given you my time and listened to what you had to say.'

'And?'

'The answer is no. Thanks for the offer but no. Now, if you don't mind, I'll be on my way.' A young couple walked by hand in hand. Neither looked at the men. They were too intimidating to make eye contact with. Peter grasped the opportunity. He sidestepped Lloyd and tried to pass. Lloyd stuck out his arm and blocked his path. 'Let me pass or I'll call the police.'

'Try and call them,' Lloyd said, in a whisper. 'You'll be dead before you dial the number.' One of the men opened his coat to expose a machete hung from his hip. 'I'll gut you and leave you to bleed out in the gutter.' Reluctantly, Peter stepped back. 'That's better. Let me explain a few things to you, officer Clough. We have officers working for us, some get paid for what they do and some don't. You really don't want to be in the 'not paid' category. They are my bitches. You might as well get paid for what you do for us.'

'I have no intention of doing anything for you, paid or unpaid. When I get home, I'll be calling the police and reporting you. I bet you're still on licence, aren't you?' Lloyd snorted and laughed. 'I bet you're in breach of your probation. I'm not frightened of you or the muscle-bound retards that you employ in your gang.'

'Is that right?'

'Yes. It is. Do you know why?'

'Enlighten me. Because I'm associated with a gang that is bigger than your gang. It's called the police force. Now, get out of my way!' Peter sidestepped him and tried to push his way through the men. Lloyd aimed a punch at the base of his skull and it landed heavily with an audible thud. Peter's knees folded underneath him as he crumpled to the ground. Lloyd grabbed him by the hair and put his face close to his.

'I don't see any of your gang around now, officer Clough.' He sneered. 'Put him in the boot of the car. We'll do this the hard way.'

CHAPTER 3

Brian Selby spent over an hour reburying the body. His head was in a spin. He had buried Stuart alive. Lloyd Jones hadn't killed him, Brian had. This fact was bouncing around in his brain like a marble in a jam-jar. There was no excuse. When Stuart reached out through the soil, Brian could have phoned an ambulance but he didn't. He had used an entrenching tool to murder him. He was a murderer. Try explaining that to mum.

Brian used the topsoil from the surrounding area so as not to leave any holes or divots that might alert a passer-by that someone had been digging. Then he gathered twigs and fallen leaves to cover the topsoil so that no one could tell it had been disturbed. He was nearly finished when he noticed the crushed cigarette butt.

Brian remembered seeing an empty mineral water bottle when he was foraging for leaves. He returned to the spot where he had seen it and picked it up. The top was missing but that was okay. He walked back to the grave and knelt over the cigarette stump, using the mouth of the bottle to lift it from the soaking dirt. He tipped the bottle and allowed the stump to fall inside before placing it in the rucksack. He muttered to himself as he cleaned the blood from the entrenching tool, sliding it into the rucksack with the drone. The bag slipped from his hands and clattered onto the floor. He stooped to pick it up, still muttering. *'Do everything that he said, Brian or he will shoot you just like he did to Stuart and then he'll kill Mum and put her through the meat grinder and feed her to the pigs.'*

It would pain him to throw them into the sea but he had no choice. He couldn't risk angering Lloyd. Watching him shoot Stuart was enough to convince him that he was capable of anything. He would have to bite the bullet and toss the drone into the drink. There would be other drones, he only had one mum. Lloyd Jones was a murdering psychopath. He had threatened his mother. Evil bastard. Who could think about putting a senile old lady into an industrial mincing machine? Lloyd Jones, that's who.

Brian wiped the sweat from his brow, put the rucksack on his shoulder and headed down the lane to the road. He tried to calm his breathing as he looked both ways and then clambered under the barrier onto the pavement. As he stood up, headlights bathed him in white light. He turned and looked into them, dazzled by their luminance. The vehicle was parked on the garage forecourt. He heard the engine start and its tyres squealed as it lurched over the pavement towards him. It screeched to halt next to him and his heart stopped when he saw the markings on the vehicle. The driver and the passenger doors opened at the same time and two, young-faced police officers climbed out, placing their hats on as they approached him.

'Stay where you are please,' one of the officers ordered. Brian froze.

'What is your name, sir?'

'Erm, Brian.' Sweat trickled down his temples, mixing with the rainwater. He wanted to vanish. His mouth went dry and it was difficult to swallow. He felt dizzy. His heart was threatening to jump out of his chest.

'Brian what?'

'Brian Selby.'

'Where are you from?'

'Anglesey.'

'You're a long way from home.' Brian didn't reply. 'Well, Brian Selby,' one of the officers stepped in front of him. 'Do you want to tell us what you're doing out here at this time of night?'

'Walking.' His top lip quivered as he spoke.

'Walking where exactly?'

'Nowhere in particular. I was just walking.'

'Just walking?'

'There's no law against that is there?' Brian tried a smile but it didn't work. It made him look more nervous, guiltier.

'What are you up to, Brian? You look nervous to me.'

'I am a bit.'

'Why would that be?'

'I don't know.'

'What's in the bag?'

'Nothing.'

'Nothing?'

'Your shoes are very muddy,' one of the officers said, pointing at his shoes. Brian looked down. They were very muddy.

'I stepped in some mud.'

'Did you step in it with your hands too?'

Brian looked at his hands. They were caked with dirt. He blushed red with guilt.

'I tripped.'

'You tripped.'

'Yes. It's very muddy on the path.'

'What happened to your neck, Brian?' Brian instinctively touched his throat. 'It is scratched. They look like finger marks to me.'

'Finger marks?' Brian scoffed but it came out a high-pitched squeak. 'Don't be ridiculous!'

'I'm not being ridiculous, Brian. You look you've been in a struggle and I need to know who with,' an officer challenged him.

'I must have got tangled in some branches, that's all. It was dark.'

'It tends to be dark at this time of night.' One officer commented.

'Where is your torch?' the other asked.

'What torch?' Brian stammered.

'Exactly. What torch. Why are you stumbling about in the woods in the dark?'

'Next to the prison,' the other officer added.

'You wouldn't be sending things over the wall, would you?'

'What wall?'

'The prison walls.'

'No. I didn't know that there was a prison there.'

'You didn't know there was a prison there?'

'No.'

'The big building with high walls and lots of barbed wire?'

'I hadn't noticed.' Brian's voice sounded childlike.

'What is in the bag, sir?'

'Just stuff.'

'We need to see what's in it.'

'Don't you need a warrant?'

'Not if we think you're in the process of committing a crime, we don't.'

'I see,' Brian mumbled. His mind raced for answers. He was useless at lying.

'Put the bag down, sir and step back from it.'

'It's a drone,' Brian blurted out. 'And an entrenching tool.'

'A drone and an entrenching tool,' one of the officers said, taking the bag from his shoulder. Brian could feel his bowels loosening. He felt like he was going to defecate in his trousers. His life was disintegrating in front of his eyes.

'An entrenching tool?' the other officer asked.

'It's a folding spade,' Brian explained.

The officer opened it and looked inside. 'It is a drone and an entrenching tool. Just like he said.' He took out the folded tool. The blade was thick with soil and something sticky. 'I'm not a detective, Brian but looking at this and your shoes and your hands, I would have to deduce that you have been digging.' Brian began to shake. 'And looking at your neck, I think you've been involved in an altercation.'

'I think there's blood on this blade,' the other officer said, shining his torch on the shovel.

'Blood,' Brian echoed. 'That's ridiculous …'

'Where were you digging, Brian?'

'Digging?'

'Yes, digging.'

'You think I was digging?'

'Yes. Why were you digging in the woods in the dark?'

'No comment,' Brian blurted. There was nowhere to escape from their questions. They had caught him red handed. He decided to shut up shop and say nothing. It was better than incriminating himself. If he said the wrong thing, Lloyd would hurt him. It was better to say nothing at all.

'You're not under caution yet, Mr Selby but if you don't come up with some sensible answers, you soon will be.'

'I don't want to be under caution.'

'Good, then tell me what you were doing in the woods?'

'No comment.'

'We're wasting our time. We'll have to seal off the woods. Read him his rights. I'll call this in. They won't believe this at the station.'

CHAPTER 4

Peter Clough came around in his armchair. His flat had been trashed. The settee looked like it had exploded, foam and springs protruded from it at right angles. His fifty-inch flat screen had a hammer through it and the kitchen cupboards didn't have a single door attached. The contents had been launched all over the flat, across the ceiling, the floor, and the walls. His dining table and chairs had been smashed into pieces, all bar one, which Lloyd Jones was sitting on.

'How's the head?' Lloyd asked as if nothing had happened. He snorted a line of coke from his silver holder.

'Fuck you,' Peter mumbled. His mouth was parched. He wiped his lips and realised that there was a rope noose around his neck. 'What is going on?' he said as he grabbed at the rope but someone tightened it from behind. Peter was lifted from the cushion and he began to choke.

'Relax and he'll take the pressure off.' Lloyd said, standing up. Peter relaxed and the rope became looser. He settled back in the chair and looked around, his eyes wide with fear. 'Stay calm and listen carefully.'

'What do you want?'

'I want you to work for me.'

'And I told you no.'

'Look at what is going on around you. Haven't you got it yet?'

'Obviously not.'

'We could string you up right now. When they find you hanging, they will think you lost it. You couldn't cope anymore. You smashed up your home and strung yourself up. No one will investigate it. You are recently divorced, you lost your old man, you got suspended from work, you hanged yourself. No one will give a fuck.'

'What are you talking about, suspended from work? I am not suspended from work.'

'You will be once we make a few anonymous phone calls to the governor. "Peter Clough has been smuggling drugs and phones into the nick."'

'No one would believe that. My record is spotless.'

'Wouldn't they? Are you absolutely sure about that?'

'Yes, so get lost!'

'Would they investigate the allegation?'

'Of course, they would.'

'Exactly. You're not thinking straight. You see, we have plenty of men on the inside who will back us up. They might be cons but there's no smoke without fire. They'll suspend you straightaway while they investigate, then they'll interview the cons who come forward with information. They will say that they have bought drugs and mobiles from you for months and you'll get screwed. You'll be suspended and then sacked. You might even do time. Then you will top yourself. I'll make sure that it looks like you did. And that will be the end of poor old Peter Clough and no one will give a toss about it.'

'Bastard!' Peter tried to shout but his voice broke with emotion. 'Do you think that you can get away with this?'

'Yes. I do.'

'Why are you doing this to me?'

'We need an officer on your wing, Peter and you're the most obvious choice. Take it as a compliment.'

'I didn't treat you badly when you were inside.'

'No, you didn't but some of the other bastards in uniform did and, where were you?' Lloyd scoffed. 'You were in the canteen turning a blind eye as usual. Now you can turn a blind eye for me. It is easy money and the risks are minimal. Or you can take your chances with the disciplinary but I don't fancy your chances.'

'I will not work for you. I'll take my chances. You can say what you want. They'll investigate and it will be my word against some cons. They'll take my word over your scumbag mates.'

'There's a little bit more than just the word of a few cons, officer Clough,' Lloyd grinned.

'What are you talking about?'

'Do you remember having a chat last week with a con who had been studying Roman history. He's a nonce in for grooming.'

Peter frowned. He didn't see the relevance. 'Vaguely.'

'You looked at some coins with him on C Wing?'

'Coins?' Peter was confused but he remembered something. One of the prisoners had shown him some copies of Roman coins that he had been given as part of a history class. They were in little plastic re-sealable packets. 'I remember. Why are you bringing that up?'

'The coins were in plastic packets,' Lloyd said, smiling. 'My man reckons that you handled at least six of the plastic packets.'

'And what?'

'Those packets have since been used to hold cocaine in them.' Lloyd shrugged. Peter felt his chest tighten. 'Do you see where this is going yet? We have your fingerprints on plastic packets that will test positive for cocaine. We have cons on the inside, who will testify that you have sold them drugs and phones and bingo, you will get shafted.'

'Bastard,' Peter said beneath his breath. He felt like he had been punched in the stomach. 'You dirty, underhanded scum.'

'Don't push it, Peter. You need to realise that you are screwed here. You will do as I say or you're finished.'

'I don't believe this.' Peter closed his eyes and tried to make sense of it all. 'You picked me because of what exactly?'

'I picked you because you're vulnerable. We could stitch you up in a few hours whereas some other prison officers would be much harder to bring onboard.' He gestured to the man behind Peter. He tossed the rope and it landed in Peter's lap. 'I appreciate that you're going to be angry at first. You'll be frustrated because there is nothing you can do about it but that feeling will pass. Once you get into the routine of taking stuff in for us, you'll realise that it's a doddle and the money is good.'

'I don't believe that this is happening to me.'

'It is. Get used to it. Worse things could happen.'

'Worse?' Peter snapped. 'How could this be any worse?'

'I could make you do it for nothing. Some do. The ones who piss me off. They do whatever I tell them for nothing because the situation is the same. I have a hold on them and they can't wriggle free. Doing it for nothing would be much worse, believe me. You are still in the paid category, don't piss me off and you can stay there. When do you retire?'

'What?'

'It is not a difficult question. When do you retire?'

'Four years.'

'Okay, let's work it out. Four years at a grand a month. That's forty-eight thousand pounds tax free to put into your retirement fund. I'll throw in a couple of grand as a sweetener to get a new telly and fix up your kitchen. Fifty-grand, Peter and you get to keep your job and your pension or I'll pay you fuck all and you will lose everything. You would probably string yourself up before I could get to you. The choice is clear. Make your decision wisely.'

Peter squeezed his eyes closed and put pressure on the bridge of his nose with his forefinger and thumb. 'I don't seem to have many options.'

'You have several but only one works out well and has a happy ending.' Lloyd shrugged. 'Are you in or are you out?'

'I'm in. I don't have a choice.'

'Good.' Lloyd said, nodding. 'I'll be in touch when your first shipment is ready. Let's go boys.'

The men filed out of the living room and closed the door behind them, leaving Peter with the shattered remains of his life. He couldn't believe that he had been so stupid as to be framed by touching those packets. No matter how he replayed things in his mind, the outcome would have been the same. He felt sick. The urge to phone the police was overwhelming but he couldn't help but think how it would look at work. Accusations of being bent happened to officers every week but even if an officer was cleared, suspicion lingered. And if they didn't believe him and he was found guilty of smuggling cocaine, he would be on the other side of the bars, which was not a good place to be as an ex-officer. Not if he wanted to remain anally retentive. He would lose his job and his pension and do time. Lloyd Jones had him over a barrel and he could only see one way to go. He looked out of the window as the men walked down Holborn Road towards the bridge. He couldn't see Jones. They would probably go into the Dublin Packet and the Holland Arms for a few drinks. He thought about phoning the police but what could he prove? Lloyd Jones would be smiling and laughing and celebrating his new recruitment. Peter felt sick inside; like a worm on hook and there was nothing he could do.

CHAPTER 5

Chris Cornell climbed into the driver's seat and started the engine. The dark X5 roared into life. He waited nervously for the others to return. Market Street was deserted, its inhabitants sound asleep, comfortable in their homes behind the curtains and blinds. It had been a long day and an even longer night. Things were beginning to unravel. He could sense that his boss was feeling the pressure and it was making him more unstable than usual. That had a knock-on effect on the rest of the outfit. He was casting aspersions in all directions; everyone was potentially a rat until proven otherwise. Everyone was on edge. The back doors opened and Matt and Justin climbed in. They both looked around to see if they were being watched.

'Where's the boss?' Chris asked, peering into the wing mirror. 'We can't hang around here too long at this time of night.'

'He's decided that he is going to take a shit in Clough's hallway, just to make sure that he gets the message loud and clear,' Matt said with a shake of the head. He rubbed his eyes. 'I swear he's losing his grip.'

'You need to keep opinions like that to yourself,' Justin said, looking over his shoulder through the back window. 'He's in a dark place right now. I have never seen him so agitated. Take my advice, keep your head down and your mouth shut, got it?'

'Got it, calm down,' Matt mumbled. They saw Lloyd approaching the vehicle and waited for him in silence. He opened the door and climbed in, taking out his silver box, he carefully tapped a line of coke onto it and snorted it loudly. Nobody spoke for long seconds.

'Did you do it?' Matt broke the silence as Lloyd squeezed his nose, shook his head and let the drug do its magic.

'Did I do what?' Lloyd asked, a sly grin on his face.

'Did you shit in his hallway?'

'Of course, I did,' he chuckled evilly. 'It was a 'welcome to the company gift'.' He chuckled again and lit a cigarette. 'I left him a big steaming welcome gift in his hallway.' He took a deep drag on the cigarette and then blew the smoke out of the window. 'Not all companies give new employees a welcome gift, you know,' Lloyd said sincerely. He looked at each man in turn, a serious expression on his face. 'He's a very lucky man to be given a welcome gift on his first day with the company. A personalised gift created by the employer himself.'

'He could let it dry out and put it on the mantelpiece'

'He might put it on his shelf next to the window,' Matt added sarcastically. 'It would look nice there.'

'He might have it engraved,' Justin giggled.

'I didn't get one when I joined,' Chris joked. 'You haven't always offered a steaming welcome gift, boss.'

'Not always,' Lloyd answered seriously. 'It's a recent benefit. It hasn't been available for long.' He turned to face Chris. 'If you feel like you have been overlooked, I'm sure that I can muster you one up?'

'No, no, no. It wouldn't mean the same now, Lloyd. Thanks for the thought though. Very considerate of you,' Chris said, nodding his head in appreciation. 'Very considerate indeed but I'll give it a miss.'

'What about you two?' Lloyd turned to face the men in the back seat. 'Would you like one to take home?'

They raised their hands in surrender. 'No need, boss. We feel appreciated,' Matt said. 'Don't we, Justin?'

'Very appreciated. No need for gifts.'

'Not steaming ones, anyway,' Matt added. The four men laughed as they watched the streetlights whizz by.

'Where are we heading,' Chris asked. He glanced at Lloyd. His boss was looking out of the passenger window, staring into space. Tendrils of smoke curled from his nostrils. 'Boss?'

'What?'

'Where to?'

'Where is your car parked?' Lloyd asked.

'At the unit in Morawelon. Matt couldn't pick me up this morning,' Chris replied, frowning. 'Why?'

'Where is your car, Matt?'

'On Penrhos industrial estate, around the corner from the lockup.'

'We'll go there.' Lloyd said, looking back out of the window. 'It's late. You can all go home once we're done and I'll drive this back to my gaff.'

'Nice one,' Chris said. 'I'm knackered. It's been a long day. My bed is calling me. I'll sleep tonight.'

'Are you sleeping alright?' Lloyd asked. The men looked at each other. No one replied. The atmosphere was tense. He snorted another line. Chris glanced at his boss, a concerned look on his face. 'I asked are you sleeping alright?' he said, turning to face Chris.

'Me?' The driver glanced at him and shook his head.

'Yes, you. It's not a difficult question. Are you sleeping alright?'

'I sleep okay but it depends how much brandy I have before I go to bed. The more I have, the better my kip is. Sometimes I'm too wired to sleep sober,' Chris said, shrugging. 'I toss and turn all night if I don't have a drink. You know how it is, boss.'

'I always said you were a tosser,' Matt joked.

'Fuck you very much,' Chris replied, looking in the mirror.

'You're welcome.'

'Maybe I should try brandy,' Lloyd sighed.

'Are you struggling to sleep, Lloyd?' Chris felt obliged to ask. Lloyd was acting weirdly. Weirder than usual and that was difficult.

'I haven't slept a wink since that drone got busted last week,' Lloyd sighed. He looked out of the window again and flicked the cigarette into the night. Sparks flew into the air as it hit the pavement. He gazed blankly into the darkness as they faded. 'Thinking about it keeps me awake all night long.'

'That was a tough one,' Chris said, glancing at him. 'Someone must have blabbed.'

'Oh, there is no doubt about that. Someone did.' Lloyd stared at Chris with a confused expression. 'That is what keeps me awake, you idiot! Knowing that one of my men is a grass keeps me awake at night.'

'Sorry, boss,' Chris said without making eye contact. 'Have you got any idea who?'

'Yes.'

'You do?'

'Yes.'

'Bloody hell, Lloyd!' Chris said, excited. 'You think that you know who it was?'

'Yes.'

'Who?'

'I can't say yet. I need more proof.' The men fell into an uneasy silence. Suspicion seeped through the confined space, no one knew who they could trust. The quiet was deafening. Lloyd let the silence reign for a while before speaking again. 'Do you know how much gear was in that football?'

'No,' Chris answered. He shook his head and stared forward through the windscreen, avoiding eye contact again. 'I have no idea what was in it but I'm sure it wasn't peanuts.'

'There was fifty-grand's worth of coke.'

'Fifty-grand?' Chris whistled.

'Yup. Fifty-grand,' Lloyd said, turning to the men in the back. 'We would have made ten times that on the inside.'

'Ten times?' Chris asked.

'Yes. That's what it's worth on the inside. Then there's the phones. They're worth five hundred each.'

'That's another three grand,' Chris said, shaking his head. 'That is a lot of money to lose. No wonder it has done your head in.'

'What do you mean by that?' Lloyd snapped.

'By what?'

'Saying that my head is done in.'

'Well, you know.'

'No. I don't know. Explain it to me.'

'I didn't mean anything by it,' Chris backtracked. 'I just meant that it would do my head in if I lost that kind of money. That's all.'

'He didn't mean anything by it, boss,' Matt intervened.

'How the fuck do you know what he meant or didn't mean?' Lloyd turned in his seat. His jaw was set, anger flashed in his eyes. 'What are you, a mind reader now or something?'

'No,' Matt shrugged and looked away. 'I was just trying to calm things down.'

'Why, who isn't calm?'

Matt didn't reply. Whatever he said would be wrong. Chris stared forward through the windscreen. The silence was oppressive. Lloyd snorted another line and leaned his head on the headrest. He closed his eyes and waited for the soothing rush. It seemed to calm him down a little.

'I lost over five hundred thousand pounds to be exact,' Lloyd spoke calmly as if nothing had happened. 'Half a million-quid burned because of some little rat.' He looked at each man in turn. 'And do you know what the worst thing is?' No one answered. He waited a minute for an answer but they dare not speak. 'I went in halves on the deal with Jaz.' He made eye contact with each of them. They looked shocked. 'You all know who Jaz is, don't you?' The men nodded but remained silent. Jaz was from Bangor. Everyone in the city knew who Jaz was, wrong side of the law or not. They also knew that he was a puppet for the most dangerous outfit around. A Russian mob known as the Karpovs. 'I was inside with him a few years back. We became friendly and he said he would help me get up the ladder. Jaz gave me the coke and I said that we would do the rest and split the proceeds.' He shook his head and shrugged. 'When the drone got busted, I offered to pay him the fifty-grand for the gear that we lost but that was when he stopped being my friend and business took over. His supplier, Viktor Karpov, stepped in,' Lloyd explained. 'Karpov doesn't want the money for the gear because it was my fuck up. He wants his share of what we would have made. He wants two hundred and fifty-grand plus interest. Grass or no grass, it is on my head to deliver.'

'Jesus,' Chris whistled through his teeth. 'No wonder you can't sleep.'

'Do you know what the interest on the debt is?'

'No,' Chris said, his voice almost a whisper.

'A grand a day,' Lloyd sighed. 'I've got until the end of the month to pay up.'

'Fucking hell. A grand a day? The thieving bastard.'

'That is more than generous, to be fair to him. If he didn't think that I could raise it, I would be dead already and so would you lot. We would all be toast.'

'Is that why you're recruiting and leaning on Clough and the others?' Matt asked.

'That is exactly why,' Lloyd turned to face him. 'We need to generate cash rapidly. We can do it but it will be tight.'

'All because of a grass. What can we do to help, boss?' Justin asked.

'Simple. You can make sure that everyone who owes us money, pays up this week. No ifs no buts, they pay up or bones get broken.'

'How much is outstanding?' Justin asked.

'About a hundred and fifty big ones.'

'We'll split up the debt list in the morning,' Matt said. The others nodded their agreement. 'We'll have what is owed by teatime.'

'Good. The next thing is we make sure that it doesn't happen again,' Lloyd said with a shrug. He snorted another line and then took out his mobile and sent a series of text messages. The men were silent while he used his phone. After twenty minutes or so, Lloyd spoke. 'Someone is a snake and he's right under our noses. We need to weed him out and hand his head to Jaz in a bag. If I can show him that we've plugged the leak, it might keep him off my back for a while. It might buy me some time.'

'How do we find the rat, Lloyd?' Matt asked. 'Point me in their direction and I'll make them talk. If there is one thing that I hate, it's a rat. Tell us what you're thinking, Lloyd.'

'I don't want to speculate just yet.'

'There's nothing wrong with sharing what you think with us, boss.'

Lloyd looked thoughtful. He nodded. 'Okay, here's is what I think. I've narrowed it down,' Lloyd said, lowering his voice. The men in the back leaned forward to listen. 'See if you can work it out too.' He snorted a line and then passed the gear around. They all took a line. 'Think about it clearly. Who knew about the drone going over the wall into Berwyn?'

Chris looked into the rear-view mirror. The men in the back looked at each other and frowned as they thought about it.

'Alright, let me think,' Matt said, using his fingers to count. 'Us four knew about it. Then fat boy Brian, Stu, and Robby all knew.' He shrugged. 'The rest of the lads knew something was happening but they didn't know the details. We kept it quiet for obvious reasons.'

'Hold on a minute,' Justin said, shaking his head. 'I knew about fat boy flying a drone but I didn't know when it was going over the wall or what was in it. I didn't know all the details.'

'Nor me,' Chris added quickly. He glanced at Lloyd, nervously. 'I didn't know all the details either. That's me and Justin out of it, eh Justin?'

'Is right. We knew fuck all.'

'That's very true,' Lloyd said, thoughtfully. 'You didn't know all the details and neither did Robby.'

'Okay,' Matt said nervously. 'That leaves fat boy, Stu, and me and you Lloyd who knew where and when. Obviously, Lloyd didn't grass on himself.'

'Neither did fat Brian,' Lloyd added. 'He didn't know where or when the drop would be until I picked him up with his drone. So that leaves Stuart and you, Matt.' He stared into Matt's eyes as he snorted another line. 'We've narrowed it down to two possible suspects.'

'I'm not a grass,' Matt snapped. 'You know that I'm not a grass.' He looked at the other men nervously, fear in his eyes. 'I don't believe Stuart is either. Where is Stu anyway?'

'He's out of the equation for now. Don't worry about him.'

'What do you mean, out of the equation?' Chris asked.

'Like I said before,' Lloyd shrugged. 'I narrowed it down. My contacts on the force made a few enquiries and guess what came back?'

'A name?'

'No.'

'What then?'

'They said that the information came from inside Berwyn itself.'

'No way,' Matt said, shocked by the news. 'Someone on the inside grassed?'

'Yes.'

'I still don't get it,' Chris said. 'One of the cons talked?'

'Yes.'

'Why the fuck would they do that?'

'They could be a plant or they made a deal for a reduced sentence.'

'Whatever their reasons were, the leak was on the inside.'

'I still don't get it,' Chris said, glancing at Lloyd.

'Think about it. Who was the go between for us with the boys in the nick?'

'Stuart.'

'Stuart?' Matt said, disbelief in his voice. Lloyd nodded. 'I don't believe it. He had me fooled. What a snake!'

'Bastard,' Chris hissed.

'I can't believe Stuart is a grass,' Justin said, astonished. 'Never in a million years.'

'He's out of the equation now. Forget about him.'

'Where is he, boss?' Matt asked.

'Which bit of what I just said do you not understand?' Lloyd turned to face him. 'I said forget about him.'

No one pushed the issue any further. If Lloyd had whacked Stuart, it was better that they didn't know. They travelled the remainder of the journey in silence. Chris indicated and pulled off the main road onto the industrial estate where Lloyd had a lockup unit. He put the headlights onto full beam to navigate through the maze of dilapidated units, some derelict, the rest almost there. The lights picked out Matt's Mercedes and Chris pulled the X5 to a halt nearby.

'Keep going. Drive around to the lockup,' Lloyd said, pointing. 'I want to show you something before we finish.'

'No problem,' Chris said, nodding. He steered the vehicle around the corner and pulled up outside the unit. The doors were open and two of Lloyd's men were standing on either side. 'What are they doing here at this time of night?'

'Take it inside,' Lloyd said, ignoring his question.

'Here we are,' Chris said, yawning. 'I don't know about you lot but I'm fucked.' He turned off the engine and stretched his arms out.

'You are fucked.' Lloyd grabbed his left arm and clicked a handcuff around his wrist.

'What the fuck are you doing?' Chris was stunned. He didn't struggle as Lloyd snapped the other cuff to the steering wheel. 'What the fuck is going on, Lloyd?'

'You tell me, Chris.'

'I don't know.'

'You don't know?'

'Whatever you're thinking, you're wrong. Very wrong.' He turned to the men in the back. 'Have a word with him will you, Matt! This is bollocks.'

'What is going on, boss?' Matt asked, concern in his voice.

'I'll tell you what is going on.' Lloyd snarled. 'A little birdie told me that the leak wasn't working alone,' Lloyd said, smiling thinly. His eyes had darkened. 'I didn't know who was working with Stuart until tonight. It is you, Chris.'

'I don't know what you're talking about, Lloyd. I'm not working with Stuart or anyone else!'

'You dropped yourself right in the shit, Chris.'

'Fuck this, Lloyd!' Chris struggled with the cuffs. He yanked at the wheel. 'I'm not working with Stu or anyone else. I'm not a grass. This is bang out of order!'

'Is it?' Lloyd grinned and shook his head.

'Yes, it is! Get these things off me.'

'How did you know about the mobiles, Chris?'

'I don't know what you're talking about,' Chris said, continuing to struggle with the restraints. 'You've lost the plot. Get these off me and I'm finished with this shit! I'm out. You can shove your paranoid bullshit up your ring. I'll go and work somewhere else!' Lloyd turned and punched Chris in the side of the head, just below the temple. His body crumpled, stunned by the force of the blow. 'Lloyd!' Chris mumbled, panic setting in. 'I work for you. I'm with you! You've got this wrong.'

'Have I?'

'Yes!'

'Tell me how you knew about the mobiles?'

'What mobiles?' Chris moaned, his voice childlike and frightened. 'I don't know what you're going on about.'

'You knew how many phones there were in the football.'

'I don't know what you're talking about!' Lloyd punched him again. Chris jerked violently in his seat. 'Fucking hell, Lloyd! I haven't done anything. I don't know what you're talking about!'

'Are you sure about this, boss,' Matt said, finding the courage to intervene. 'What makes you think that Chris is in on it?'

'I wasn't sure who it was until tonight.' Lloyd turned to look at him in the eye. 'I'll be honest with you, Matt, I thought it was you until earlier but then he gave himself away.'

'What are you talking about, Lloyd?' Chris asked in a panic. He pulled at the steering wheel. The cuffs rattled but didn't budge. 'How did I give myself away? I haven't done anything. This is all wrong!'

'You said the mobiles were worth three grand,' Lloyd said. He punched him in the face again, splitting his lips on his teeth. 'I didn't say how many there were. I said they were worth five hundred each on the inside.' Chris looked terrified. He shook his head and searched for an excuse but none came to him. 'You said that they were worth three grand. There were six mobiles in the package. I put them in myself. I was the only one who knew how many were in there apart from Stuart.' He punched him again. Chris howled like a wounded dog. 'I didn't tell you so how did you know that, eh Chris?'

'I don't know, honestly. You must believe me, Lloyd. Maybe I read it in the news or something.'

'The news didn't report the details. They said *a large quantity of class A drugs and a number of mobile phones had been intercepted*.' He punched him in the side of the head again. Chris cried out and reached for the door handle but Matt grabbed him from behind, pulling him back into the seat. 'Where are you going, Chris?' Lloyd asked, punching him in the face once more. 'We're just getting started here.'

'You grass!' Matt snarled in his ear.

'I didn't grass!' Chris sobbed. 'You have to believe me, Matt! I didn't grass.'

'Then explain to me, how did you know about the mobiles?' Lloyd asked, calmly. 'This is your last chance.'

'Okay, okay. Give me a minute. I can't breathe. Let me explain,' Chris said. His breath was coming in short gasps. He was shaking. 'I remember now. It was Stuart that let it slip. We had been drinking and having a toot. He told me about the phones in conversation but I didn't know he was a grass. It didn't cross my mind for one minute that he was a snake. I didn't think anything of it until now. I didn't know he was a grass, Lloyd. Honestly, I didn't.'

Lloyd smiled and then shook his head and punched him in the face again. His head rocked back violently and clattered against the driver's window.

'Why didn't you say that straight away?' Chris didn't answer. He cowered in his seat and spat blood into the foot well. 'The answer is because you're a liar, that's why.' He rained a series of heavy punches onto Chris's head and neck. 'Get this piece of shit out of my beamer. Looking at him is making me want to puke.'

Matt and Justin climbed out of the X5 and opened the driver's door. Lloyd unlocked the cuffs from the steering wheel and fastened both his hands together. Chris sobbed as they dragged him out, blood and saliva dripped from his chin.

'I'm not a grass, lads,' he muttered. 'I'm not a grass. Help me. Lloyd has got this all wrong. I would never rat on anyone. Please help me. Don't let him hurt me, lads, please. I'm not a grass!'

'Shut your mouth,' Matt snapped. He kicked him in the face. 'After everything I have done for you and you're a grass. You make me sick.'

'I'm not a grass, Matt,' Chris whined. 'You have known me for years. I've watched your kids growing up. You know that I'm not a grass.'

'Don't you talk about my kids, you snake. I thought I knew you. Turns out that I knew fuck all about you.'

'Matt,' Chris gasped. 'Please, mate. Listen to me. I am not a grass. Lloyd has got this all wrong!'

'Lloyd has got this all right,' Lloyd said, aiming a kick at his testicles. Chris screamed and doubled up in pain. He vomited onto the moss covered concrete. 'You had better start talking, Chris, because I need to know what has been going on and I need to know now.'

'Nothing has been going on, Lloyd!' Chris sobbed; his voice almost inaudible. 'Please believe me.'

'That is the crux of the problem, Chris,' Lloyd said, kneeling next to him. 'I don't believe you.' He stroked the back of his head. 'Don't take this personally. This is just business. I realise that there will be a reason why you have ratted me out. There is always a reason. However, I need to know who you have been talking to and what you have told them.' Chris tried to talk but Lloyd raised his finger to his lips and shook his head. 'Shush! This is the bit where you stop lying to me and you listen very carefully to what I am going to say. Are you listening to me, Chris?' Chris nodded, tears streaming from his eyes. 'You remember what happened to the Wicks brothers, don't you?' Chris screwed his eyes tightly closed as if the memory was too horrible to recall. 'And you will remember Kenny Jenkins too, won't you?' Chris nodded; his body began to shiver uncontrollably. 'You were there at the abattoir for all those men, weren't you?' Chris nodded again. He shook his head. His eyes pleaded for pity. Lloyd grinned. 'Do you remember Jenks was still screaming when his arms went into the grinder. Most people stop screaming at the thighs. You remember that, don't you?' Chris nodded almost imperceptibly. His lips quivered as if he was very cold. 'You were sick all over the floor, if I remember rightly. I should have known then that you had no spine.' Lloyd paused to find the right words. He leaned closer to Chris's ear. 'This is the important bit. Listen very carefully. If you don't tell me what you have been doing, I'm going to send the boys to your house and they're going to take your wife and kid to the abattoir.'

'No, no, no, no!' Chris became hysterical. 'Don't touch my family, Lloyd! Don't you touch them, you're sick! Don't let him do this, Matt. Don't you touch them,' Chris blubbered, saliva dribbled from his chin. Lloyd slapped him hard across the face, silencing him instantly.

'Shut up and listen! I'm going to let you watch your wife and kid go through the grinder, Chris and then we can feed them to the pigs together. Unless you talk to me, right now.' Lloyd stood up and walked to the X5, leaning his back against it. He snorted a line and shook his head. 'Five seconds, Chris. Four, three, two, one, too late. Go and get his wife and kid,' Lloyd ordered the two men who had opened the doors earlier. They moved towards a Land Rover without a question. 'Take them to the abattoir. We'll meet you there.'

'No, Lloyd!' Chris cried in a high-pitched tone. 'Don't bring them into this, please. Please, Lloyd, don't hurt them.'

'Talk now or they're mincemeat.'

'Okay, okay. I'll tell you what happened. Promise me you will not touch them!'

'You have my word.'

'Promise me, Matt,' Chris turned to look at his colleague. 'Promise me that you won't let him touch my family!'

'He gives his word too,' Lloyd said, impatiently. 'Get on with it before I change my mind.'

'Promise me, Lloyd!'

'You have had all the promises that you're going to get.' Chris closed his eyes. 'Get on with it.'

'We never set out to do it, Lloyd. I would never have turned against you if I'd had the choice. You must believe that. We had no choice.'

'Everyone has a choice. Tell me what happened.'

'We did a bit of business for ourselves last year,' Chris began. His voice was reedy and broken. 'The deal went to shit. We were set up by the Drug Squad and they lifted us with a kilo, a gun, and thirty grand in a holdall.'

'This is you and Stuart?'

'Yes.'

'When was this?'

'November last year.'

'Fourteen months ago?' Lloyd asked, surprised.

'Something like that.'

'And?'

'We were screwed, Lloyd. We were nabbed red handed with a kilo and a firearm. They said we were looking at a ten stretch at least. We've both got kids, Lloyd,' Chris sobbed. 'We couldn't do a ten stretch. They said we could walk if we fed them information.'

'So, you are a grass? You scumbag,' Matt hissed. 'You've given them information about us for fourteen months? There will be enough evidence to bang us all up for years!'

'Wanker!' Justin shouted and kicked Chris in the face. Matt joined in kicking the prone man until his cries became a whimper. He stopped struggling.

'Stop!' Lloyd shouted. The men backed off reluctantly. Lloyd walked to an old sink and filled an empty water bottle from the cold tap. He returned to the injured man and poured the water onto his face. Chris began to cough and splutter. He opened his eyes. 'Do the police know about this place?' Lloyd asked. Chris nodded that they did but couldn't speak. Lloyd looked around. They were surrounded by hundreds of brand-new stolen plasma TV'S and container loads of fake designer goods from China, all stolen from Holyhead port. 'Why haven't they swooped in and arrested us yet?' Lloyd frowned. He prodded Chris with the toe of his boot. 'Why haven't they lifted us yet, Chris?'

'Jaz and the Karpovs,' Chris moaned, hoarsely.

'What the fuck has Jaz got to do with this?'

'They knew that you were working with him more and more. They want to nab you and Jaz at the same time in the hope it might lead to Viktor Karpov.'

'They're going to use me to get to Viktor Karpov and Jaz?'

'I think that was their plan.'

'And then what did you think would happen, Chris? You and Stuart would have stepped in and took over while we were all rotting in the slammer?'

'I'm sorry, Lloyd. I couldn't go to jail, Lloyd. My missus would have left me and I would never have seen my kid again. I had no choice!'

47

'If Jaz and the Karpovs think that we've been leaking information from our outfit, they'll go ballistic,' Lloyd said, thoughtfully. 'They'll bury all of us.'

'Then we're double fucked,' Matt moaned. 'We'll have the police and Jaz all over us.'

'Not necessarily. Think about this rationally,' Lloyd said, scratching his chin. 'We have the upper hand now.'

'How do you work that one out?'

'We know that they know.'

'But they don't know that we know,' Justin added. 'We could sneak the gear away from here a little a time and they won't know we're relocating. Then we carry on as normal.'

'You have it in one,' Lloyd said, smiling. 'Tell me Chris, was it Matrix who set you up?'

'I think so. I was never sure.'

'How often did you communicate with them?'

'Once a week. The same place every time.'

'Where?'

'There's a litterbin outside of a pub called The Sportsman on Denbigh Moors,' Chris groaned. Talking was becoming difficult. 'We dropped the stuff there at seven o'clock in the morning every Wednesday.'

'What stuff?' Lloyd snapped. 'What stuff did you drop?'

'Mostly memory sticks, sometimes paperwork.'

'Memory sticks? What the fuck was on the memory sticks?'

'Pictures mostly.'

'Mostly?'

'Recordings sometimes,' Chris whispered.

'You were wired up and carrying surveillance cameras around us for fourteen months?'

'Not all the time.'

'How often?'

'A lot of the time. I'm sorry. They made us do it, Lloyd. It was that or do a ten stretch.'

'You wore a wire and a camera for over a year while you were around us?' Matt asked, astounded. 'You bastard! How much stuff have they got on us? I don't believe this. We'll go down for years. We won't get out until we're nearly dead!'

'That changes things dramatically,' Lloyd said, looking at his watch. 'I'm very, very fucked off with you, Chris.' He frowned, his face as dark as thunder. 'You never met your handler, everything was done remotely at this pub?'

'Twice we had a meeting with a big shot DI from the Drug Squad and a woman from the CPS. That was in the early days after we got lifted. After that it was just dropping shit at the pub.'

'How far away is this pub, about sixty miles?'

'About that. It takes about an hour and twenty minutes, roughly. I'm so sorry, Lloyd!' Chris began to sob again.

'Sorry doesn't change anything.'

'I know it doesn't. I wish I could take it all back!'

'You can't undo it. The damage is done.'

'I'll tell them that it was all bollocks,' Chris said, clutching at straws. 'I'll say we made it all up.'

'It's too late for that. Do you have any idea what you have done, Chris?' Lloyd asked, calmly. 'Jail would have been a doddle for you. You would have done it standing on your head and been out in five. Instead, you turned on your friends. You are a grass! What you have done is unforgiveable.'

Chris nodded. 'Yes, I know. I'm sorry, Lloyd. We had no choice. Really we didn't.'

'There's always a choice. You just picked the wrong one.' Lloyd climbed into the X5 and closed the door, lowering the window as he did so. 'Pick up his wife and kid and take them all to the abattoir.' Chris began to scream hysterically. 'Make him watch before you do him.'

'His kid, Lloyd?' Matt said, shaking his head. 'I've known that girl since she was born. That is too far for me, Lloyd. I can't do that!'

'Justin. What about you and you two?' Lloyd asked the other men. They shrugged that it wasn't too far for them.

'The bastard has been filming us for over a year. He didn't give a toss about me being with my family when he was doing that, did you, you rat?' Justin kicked Chris hard in the groin, doubling him up in agony. 'I'll do them, no problem and then I'll do him.'

'Good. You need to open your eyes, Matt.' Lloyd said, pointing a finger at Chris. 'That piece of shit has been stitching up you and your family for fourteen months. If we get nicked, you could be away from your kids for a very long time because of him.'

'I know he has it coming but not his kid, Lloyd, and not like that,' Matt said, shaking his head. 'I can't watch that.'

'Don't go soft on me, Matt. We need to send a message loud and clear that if you grass, you lose everything and everyone you love. Boom!' Lloyd clapped his hands together loudly. 'All your life gone because you talked to the police. If we don't respond to this, the Karpovs will crucify us.' He looked his men in the eyes, one by one. 'You know what we have to do. Call me when it's done.' He closed the window and started the engine.

'Lloyd, this is madness!' Matt shouted after him, trying to persuade him to change his orders. His boss ignored him. 'Lloyd! Come on, this is too far, man!' The X5 roared away into the night. Chris's incoherent pleas for mercy went unheeded.

CHAPTER 6

Brian Selby was sitting in an interview room wearing a blue forensic suit. He was biting his nails, muttering to himself and staring at his feet. His brief appeared to be taking notes although, apart from a few lines, the page was blank. The detectives across the table glanced at each other, checked their watches and stood up to leave. Detective Inspector Alan Williams watched through the glass. He was totally underwhelmed by the sight of Brian Selby. Master criminal he was not. There was something almost childlike about him. Alan rubbed his chin and his forehead wrinkled; deep creases appeared at the corners of his eyes. The door of the interview room opened and the detectives stepped out. DI Joanne West from the Drug Squad smiled as she greeted him.

'What are you doing all the way down here, guv?' she said, sarcastically. She flicked her raven hair from her shoulders and straightened her trousers and jacket. The smell of Chanel Chance drifted with her. 'Are you lost?'

'Cheeky bugger,' he chuckled. 'It has been a while since I've been down in the dungeons. I had to ask for directions but I found it.' He grinned. 'Seriously, I wanted to let you know that the DS from the search team at the prison called me,' Alan said, smiling. No matter how shit the day was, Kim made him smile. She just had an aura around her that made people feel comfortable. 'The dogs found a body. It's only been there a few hours.'

'Bloody hell!' Kim said, looking at Brian through the glass. He was still muttering to himself and staring at his feet. 'I don't know what I was expecting them to find but it wasn't a body.'

'He doesn't look like a killer to me,' Alan agreed.

'What have they got so far?' Kim asked.

'The victim is male, thirties, two gunshot wounds to the chest buried in a shallow grave. Estimated time of death is around midnight last night. They haven't got an ID yet.'

'Shot?' Kim was amazed. 'Any sign of a gun?'

'Not yet.'

'Dr Martin doesn't think the bullets killed him,' Alan said, staring at Brian. Kim frowned. 'There are three very deep lacerations to the face and throat of the victim. He thinks the blow to the throat killed him. Apparently, it smashed the larynx. There's evidence of internal bleeding, so he was alive when it was caused but the wounds are full of dirt.'

'Meaning?' Kim was confused.

'He's not certain but he thinks the body may have been buried when the lacerations were inflicted. The blade went through the soil before it pierced the skin.'

'Was the body in the woods?' Kim asked.

'Yes.'

'He was lifted coming out of the woods.' She looked at Brian again. 'It isn't looking good for him.'

'It isn't. What time was he picked up?'

'Just before one. They had him on suspicion of flying drugs over the wall but the custody sergeant noticed blood spatter on his face and clothes when he was booking him in and the scratches on his throat prove he was in some kind of altercation,' Kim said, staring through the glass. 'I think we should charge him now but this guy seems to be away with the fairies. He won't even confirm his name. I've sent uniform around to his home. The neighbours say that he lives with his elderly mother. She's infirm apparently.'

'Any other forensics in yet?' Alan asked, rubbing the stubble on his chin. There were more white bristles than black.

'Only the drug swabs. Selby and the drone both tested positive for being in proximity of cocaine recently. It's too early for GSR results.'

'I think he's playing the game,' Alan said.

'What do you mean?'

'He's playing dumb because he knows that we'll find the body and he doesn't want to say the wrong thing until he knows what we have. If he has gunshot residue on him, it's a slam dunk but somehow, I don't think it is going to be that easy.'

'Don't hold your breath on the results. I've never had a slam dunk yet, have you?'

'There's more chance of spotting a unicorn in the garden.' Alan said, patting her shoulder. 'I think you should give him the bad news about the body and see how he reacts.'

'Will do, Guv.'

'Keep me in the loop on this one.'

'I will do. Any special reason why?' she smiled, confused.

'I have a funny feeling there's much more to this than meets the eye.'

'So, do I,' she said, looking back into the interview room. Alan walked away towards the lifts. He waved a hand. 'I'll call you when we get anything.'

CHAPTER 7

Rachel Cornell stroked her daughter's hair. Claire had always been a difficult sleeper. She would wake most nights, about the same time, suffering with nightmares. Rachel put it down to her being too hot as the nightmares were usually accompanied by sweats. Tonight, was different and she had gone off halfway through her bedtime story and slept soundly. Rachel smiled as she watched Claire sleeping peacefully. She resembled her husband, Chris, so much that it was like looking at a tiny female version of him. Chris was working late again. The late nights were part of the job but recently, they seemed to be becoming more frequent. Their relationship was spiralling out of control. They were like ships that passed in the night, he slept when she was awake and he barely spent any time with their daughter. He wasn't happy at work but he was trying to hide it but she could read him like a book. Every line on his face told her a story, every expression betrayed what was going on in his mind. The year before, she had sensed that something had changed dramatically but he wouldn't talk about it. He had always been shady about his work but things were worse now. Worse than they had ever been before. It was getting to the point where she had thought about leaving. She didn't even know exactly what was wrong but it was something to do with his job. She didn't even know exactly what he did but she had a gut feeling that he was up to no good. The money that he brought home was enough to keep her from digging too deep. They lived in a detached house that was the envy of both their families, she drove a new car, and wanted for nothing. Whenever she mentioned the late hours, he said it was only for a few years until they were stable enough for him to change employer and get out. He mentioned his boss, Lloyd, sometimes but when she asked what he was like, he would clam up. She had overheard phone calls a few times and she had heard Lloyd shouting and being abusive towards Chris. When she asked him what he wanted and why he was being so nasty, Chris had said that he was just like that. He was adamant that he wouldn't be working for him forever. She wasn't sure what he would do if he did change careers because he wasn't the sharpest knife in the drawer so she didn't push too hard. He loved her and Claire and when he was with them, he treated them like princesses and that was all that mattered.

Headlights lit up the bedroom, sweeping left to right through the curtains, illuminating Claire's books and dolls. Their eyes seemed to twinkle and they looked so alive in the half-light. The sound of a diesel engine drifted to her. The nerves on her scalp tingled, sending shivers down her spine. She instantly knew that something was wrong. Danger was approaching. She didn't know how she knew but she did. The urge to look through the curtains was overwhelming but her survival instinct warned her not to. A twitch of the curtains would give away her position in the house. The vehicle wasn't Chris'. She knew how his engine sounded. She tucked the quilt around Claire and tiptoed out of the room, closing the door quietly. She heard the vehicle slow and come to a stop. The tyres crunched to a halt on the gravel driveway. She heard the doors opening and whispered voices then the sound of footsteps approaching the house. Her heart was pounding in her chest. She touched her pocket where her mobile lived and listened intently, her senses on overdrive. She felt ice-cold when she realised that the pocket was empty. Her phone wasn't there.

Rachel went to the spare bedroom and peered out of the window. There was a white van parked at the front of the house. The lights were on and the engine was ticking over, exhaust fumes climbed skyward from the exhaust. She saw movement directly below her and as she looked down, her heart nearly stopped. Her breath stuck in her chest. She put her hands to her mouth to stifle any noise she might make involuntarily. The instinct to scream gripped her but she knew that no one would hear her. Their nearest neighbours were half a mile away. She put her face nearer to the glass. Two men in balaclavas were looking up at the windows. They spoke briefly and then parted. One of them headed for the front door, the second headed towards the rear of the house. She could hear their footsteps on the gravel. Panic set in and she bolted. She ran to her bedroom and scrambled across the bed, looking frantically for her mobile phone. Her fingers reached for the bedside lamp, fumbled at the switch and clicked the light on. The charger was plugged into the wall, where it always was but the Samsung was not attached to it. She jumped up and tried to think.

'No, no, no!' she whispered under her breath. The blood was racing through her brain. She remembered that she had been texting her friend while she watched her soaps on catch-up earlier. It was on the coffee table downstairs next to a bottle of wine. She ran to the landing and looked over the banister. A dark shadow appeared at the front door. The doorbell rang. The noise made her jump. She bolted down the stairs and made it halfway down when the sound of the handle being twisted came to her from the kitchen. She could hear the door being rattled in its frame. The noise of breaking glass stopped her dead in her tracks. The back door had a glass panel. Chris always moaned at her for leaving the key in the lock. *'If a burglar breaks the glass, they can reach the key, Rachel. You might as well leave the thing open,'* she heard his voice in her mind. She heard glass shattering on the floor and the key turning in the lock. The front doorbell rang again and again followed by a loud persistent knocking. The letterbox rattled and then opened and she saw eyes looking at her. She thought they were familiar.

'Open the door, Rachel,' the man at the front door cagouled. 'We need to talk to you about Chris.'

Talk about Chris? Why would you come here in the middle of the night wearing balaclavas? Fuck that! You haven't come here to talk.

It spurred her into action. Rachel sprinted down the stairs, taking them two at a time. She had to reach her phone.

'Open the door, Rachel!' the man at the front door ordered. His voice had become stern. 'We're not here to hurt you. Chris sent us. Open the door quickly!'

'Fuck you!' Rachel ran past the door and stumbled down the hallway. She heard the back door rattling. The key was in the lock but she had remembered to fasten the bolts at the top and bottom. She didn't slow as she opened the living room door and sprinted to the coffee table. She reached for her phone and picked it up. Her fingers were shaking so much that she fumbled it. The phone fell and clattered onto the laminate floor, sliding towards the settee. She cried out as it disappeared underneath.

'No, no, no,' she said in a panic. She dropped to her knees and peered into the darkness. There was no sign of the phone. The sound of a heavy blow to the front door echoed through the house. It reverberated down the hallway.

'Open the door, Rachel!'

She heard the bolts being slid open and the back door fly open, the frame slammed against the fridge. Heavy footsteps stomped across the kitchen tiles. Rachel grabbed the settee and yanked it away from the wall. She scrambled on all fours and picked up her mobile, running as fast as she could for the hallway. The front door rattled in its frame as she reached the stairs and bolted up them, scrambling on all fours. She heard the kitchen door open and footsteps running along the hallway. They stopped at the front door and she heard the locks being unopened.

'Where is she?'

'She ran upstairs.'

'Get her quickly before she calls the police!'

Rachel heard them. Her mind was buzzing with questions. What did they want? Who were they? How the hell could she get Claire, phone the police, and escape?

There was no time. They were about to mount the stairs. She looked around for inspiration. A glass vase stood on an occasional table. The flowers in it were wilting. She grabbed it and launched it down the stairs. The thick glass exploded against the wall, spraying the men with a thousand tiny shards and water. They jumped back away from the stairs. Rachel ran back to the table and picked it up with both hands. She heaved it up and over the edge of the landing. It toppled end over end and crashed into the banister at the bottom. The legs wedged between the spindles. One of the men tried to clamber over it but couldn't cock his leg over it. They grabbed at the table trying to pull it free. Rachel looked around. They had been decorating. The spare bedroom door was open. She ran to the door and grabbed a set of wooden stepladders. Chris had used them to decorate a month ago and never put them back in the garage. Rachel picked them up and ran onto the landing. She hoisted them above her head and hurled them down the stairs. The ladders hit the first man in the face and he was knocked backwards by the force, sending him crashing into the second. They tumbled backwards in a whirlwind of arms and legs. The ladders opened and wedged behind the table between the balustrade and the wall. Rachel felt inspired. She ran back into the little bedroom and put her hands through the bars of Claire's old cot. They hadn't parted with it in case they had more children. She half lifted it and half dragged it to the top of the stairs and then launched it as hard as she could. It tumbled end over end before becoming lodged behind the ladders. The men were getting to their feet. A tirade of abuse drifted from the hallway.

'Bitch!'

Rachel wasn't waiting to see what happened. She ran back into the bedroom and dragged a single bed towards the door. She tipped it onto its side to get it through the door to the landing. Gripping the bed by the headboard, she lifted it and slid it down the stairs, adding weight and bulk to the improvised barricade. The men pulled and tugged at the ladders but they wouldn't budge.

'What's going on, Mummy?' Claire was standing in her doorway, rubbing her tired eyes with her tiny hands. A black bear dangled from her tiny hand. 'It's so noisy, Mummy!'

Seeing Claire, made her think of her husband Chris. She looked up at the loft hatch. Chris had panelled out the attic two years earlier and it was his man cave. A drawstring dangled tantalisingly out of reach. Rachel jumped up and felt the cord between her fingers but she couldn't get a grip. She tried again but it was just too high. One more jump. She missed it completely.

'Rachel!' the men screamed.

'Come here, darling,' Rachel said, as calmly as she could. The sound of frantic activity at the bottom of the stairs kept her focused.

'Pull the thing out of the way!'

'It's stuck!'

'Pull it!'

'You pull it if it's so easy!'

'Move!'

'It's jammed!'

'I know it is jammed, Einstein!'

Rachel lifted Claire by the waist. 'Pull the cord for me, sweetheart.' Claire pulled the cord and the hatch opened; a telescopic ladder unfolded automatically. 'Run, run, run, up the ladder.' Rachel pushed Claire gently from behind. She heard wood cracking from the stairs. The men were making progress. Rachel scurried up the ladder, reached the attic and rolled onto her back, her chest heaving in lungs full of air. She got to her feet and pushed the retraction button. A motor whirred and the ladder began to fold up and the hatch closed slowly and silently. It clicked closed and Rachel sighed with relief.

'What is happening, Mummy?'

'Nothing. Don't you worry, darling. Mummy needs to make a phone call.'

Chris spent hours locked up there so that he couldn't be interrupted. The females of the house were never allowed up there. She fastened a sliding bolt home so that the ladder couldn't be lowered from below and then she took out her mobile and dialled 999.

CHAPTER 8

Lloyd pulled the X5 to a halt and turned off the engine. He looked at the neon sign above the door of the nightclub. It glowed electric blue and announced to the world that Paradise was open for business. He shook his head and smirked in the darkness. Paradise, it was not. It was a shithole full of drug takers and drug dealers. Crack sellers mingled hip to hip with crack whores and deals were done for cash or flesh until the early hours of the next day. A few years earlier, it had been acquired by force from a Turkish mob by a local gangster but was now part of the Karpov empire, managed by their enforcer, Jaz. Jaz had shot his boss at the bequest of Viktor Karpov and he took control of the business under the Karpov umbrella. Jaz used Paradise as his base and had an office upstairs.

Lloyd sat quietly for a few minutes, trying to get his pitch straight in his head. He felt sick to his stomach that he had been betrayed to such an extent. Two men he had respected and admired had deceived him in the worst possible way. Their actions would have repercussions all the way up the power tree right to the very top. The evidence that they had gathered would rock the underworld for months, if not years. This would be one of the most important conversations of his life. It would determine how long or short his life may be. He checked his appearance in the mirror and opened the door before climbing out. The bassline of a trance song echoed up the cobbled street and a portent of what was to come showed itself as the heavens opened. The sudden downpour was joined by a flash of lightning, which forked across the sky and a cutting wind blew off the straits. Fast food wrappers blew past like tumbleweed as if they had somewhere important to be. Lloyd dwarfed the two bouncers who were standing on the door and they greeted him with a half nod-half scowl as they stepped aside to let him in. He shook hands with both as a sign of mutual respect. Two more gorillas greeted him inside. Their faces were vaguely familiar to him, his very familiar to them. No one thought to ask him for the entrance fee. Men like Lloyd Jones didn't go to the club to dance.

'Where is Jaz?' Lloyd asked a blond bombshell, who was seated behind some plasti-glass, staring at Facebook on her phone. She glanced up and stopped chewing her gum for a second while she thought about her answer.

'Hold on a minute,' she frowned. 'It is coming to me.' She smiled and then frowned again. 'No, it's gone. My psychic powers have failed me again.' She grinned sarcastically. 'How the hell should I know?'

'Fuck you very much,' Lloyd snapped as he walked away towards the club. He pushed through two sets of heavy fire doors into a wall of sound. The club was bouncing. Powerful lasers pierced the blackness in time to the music and the dance floor was an undulating mass of writhing bodies. Lloyd scanned the bar area but there was no sign of Jaz. He doubled back through one set of doors and headed up a carpeted staircase towards the office. The music became a dull thudding sound as he reached the second floor. The office door was open and he could see Jaz sitting at his desk, wearing a dark suit. His gold jewellery twinkled in the light. He was in deep conversation with another familiar face. Del Makin. He looked thinner than the last time they had met. His hair had been cropped to the scalp, making him look harder, tougher somehow. Lloyd felt his stomach tighten. *Why the fuck was Del Makin talking to Jaz? How the hell does he even know Jaz?* He knocked on the door before stepping inside. Both men looked uncomfortable to see him. Del looked like he was going to throw up again.

'Lloyd Jones, what a pleasant surprise,' Jaz said, standing up and offering his hand. 'You know Del Makin, don't you?'

'We have done a little business together,' Lloyd said, shaking his hand. He threw Del a dark glance as he turned to greet him. 'It's a small world, eh, Del,' he added, squeezing Del's hand a little too tightly. 'How's the family? Is that pretty wife of yours putting out?' Lloyd winked. Del smiled thinly, hate and fear in his eyes.

'She's fine,' Del said, flatly. His discomfort with Lloyd's presence was blindingly obvious. He turned back to the man across the desk. 'Thanks for your time, Jaz. I'll leave you guys to it. I need to get off home anyway. It's very late.'

'Thanks, Del. Have a think about what I said and if you have any questions, call me tomorrow,' Jaz said, shaking hands with Del. Something passed between them. Lloyd spotted it. Something in their eyes. Something that they didn't want him to know. Something secret. 'I'm free any time after one.'

'I will do and thanks again,' Del said, turning for the door. He blanked Lloyd as he left. The door closed and the room fell into an awkward silence.

'It's late for a social visit, Lloyd,' Jaz said, sitting in his chair. His black skin wrinkled at the corners of his eyes. His forehead creased. He loosened his silk tie and straightened the gold sovereigns that he wore on every finger. His knuckles cracked as he did each one in turn. He eyed Lloyd suspiciously. 'I'm glad you came though. It saves me a journey. I was going to come and see you tomorrow.'

'Why?' Lloyd asked bluntly. Jaz was spooked by something. He could sense it. It took a lot to spook a man like Jaz.

'Bad news,' Jaz said, the gravel in his voice more pronounced when he lowered his tone. 'Bad news should never be delivered over the telephone. I think it should be delivered in person, eye to eye.'

'I agree.'

'Good.'

'That is why I'm here. I have some bad news for you too.' The two men locked stares, neither wanted to speak first. 'Well?' Lloyd said, tiring of the standoff. 'Are you going to tell me or what?'

'You first,' Jaz said, fiddling with his rings. 'Mine may change, depending on how bad your news is.'

'Matrix are trying to put a case together to nail us. Not just me, all of us, you included,' Lloyd said, sitting forward. He leaned towards Jaz, his elbows on the desk.

'Really?' Jaz said, chuckling. 'This is news to you?'

'No. But the fact that they have had two of my men recording and filming us for over a year was news to me.'

'Are you joking?' Jaz said, sitting bolt upright in his chair. His mouth was part open. 'Tell me that is a joke?'

'No joke. Matrix busted them last year with a kilo and a shooter. They said that they were looking at a ten stretch and offered them a deal. Information for a walk. I only found out when the prison delivery went tits up and I knew we had a leak.' Lloyd paused to let it sink in. Jaz didn't blink for what seemed like ages. 'I don't know exactly what they gave them but it will be substantial. It will incriminate myself, you, and the Karpovs.'

'When did this come out?'

'I found out tonight and came straight here.'

'Who was it?'

'That doesn't matter. The men involved are done. I've dealt with that side of things.'

'That is something at least,' Jaz muttered. 'They were filming for over a year. How could you not know, Lloyd?'

'I didn't expect my best men to be working for the filth. I got careless I suppose. I trusted them.'

'You should trust no one,' Jaz said, pointing his finger again. 'That is the first rule, the second rule, the only rule that matters.' Lloyd thought that sounded rich coming from a man who shot his best friend to death and was now sitting in his chair. 'I don't know how we square this one, Lloyd.' Jaz put his head in his hands and sighed. He put his palms flat on the desk and shrugged, looking Lloyd in the eyes. 'Viktor is on one since they arrested his top tier management and banged them all up. He was an evil bastard before, now he is way beyond being a bastard. There isn't a word for what he is now.'

'That's why I'm here. I didn't want him to hear it from someone else.'

'I think he might have already heard, Lloyd,' Jaz said, thoughtfully. He shook his head slowly, choosing his next words carefully. 'He has his sources in the force. It all makes sense now.'

'What does?'

'There's a contract out on you.'

'What the fuck are you talking about?'

'Fifty-grand to shoot you dead.'

'Karpov?'

'Of course,' Jaz said with a shrug. 'You owe him money, which is why I couldn't understand why he would want you dead. You don't kill a man until he's paid his debts. He wants you dead now. Dead means silent. I think someone has tipped him off about the Matrix sting. He wants you neutralised in case they turn you too.'

'Who is picking up the contract?' Lloyd asked calmly. 'You, Jaz?'

'Me,' Jaz scoffed. 'If I had picked it up, you would be dead already and you know it.' He fiddled with his rings as he thought about his words. 'Fifty-grand isn't enough to tempt me.' He smiled coldly. 'I don't want to be dragging your big fat arse through the forest for fifty-grand. Fifty-two and I might have done it.'

Lloyd managed a grin although his insides were twisting. 'What do I do?' he asked with a shrug.

'Say goodbye to your loved ones and fuck off abroad somewhere. Go tonight and tell no one where you are heading. Get your men to collect what you're owed and put it into a bank account where you can live off it. Then tell them to go home and keep their heads down. The contract is for you. Your firm are not in any danger as things stand but if they try to carry on where you leave off, I can see it being expanded to include your men.'

'Just like that, Jaz?' Lloyd chuckled. 'I'll get on an Easyjet plane with my bucket and spade and sit on a beach until I'm dribbling and don't know my own name?'

'At least you have the option,' Jaz said, pointing his index finger again. 'I'm giving you the heads up here. We go back and I'm giving you the respect that I think you deserve. Take the chance to run while you can. There are plenty of people in this city who wouldn't think twice about putting a bullet in you for free. Fifty-grand is a life changing sum for the wannabees out there. Someone will take you out and you won't see it coming.'

'It just doesn't sit right, Jaz,' Lloyd said, shaking his head. 'After everything I've done for the Karpovs. It isn't right.'

'You've fucked up, Lloyd.' Jaz shrugged. 'You have let Matrix into your outfit. You have exposed us all and there are consequences for that kind of mistake.'

'When was the contract put out?' Lloyd asked.

'Tonight. That's why I was coming to see you in the morning.'

'Who knows about it?'

'Viktor Karpov, you, and me at the moment but it will be all over North Wales by lunchtime tomorrow. You have the time and the opportunity to get on a plane. Leave while you can. I won't circulate the contract until tomorrow but Karpov might. It will give you time to get yourself as far away as you can.' Jaz stood up and walked to a wall safe. The door was open and he reached inside and took out a wad of notes. He tossed it onto the desk in front of Lloyd. 'That is the door take from tonight. There's over six grand there. That will get you away and keep you going until your boys collect what you're owed.'

'I appreciate the offer, Jaz but I'm okay for cash.'

'Call it a redundancy payment. Take it and disappear.'

Lloyd stood up and picked up the cash. He looked at it and then put it into his inside pocket. Jaz held out his hand. Lloyd looked at his hand and slid out the silenced Berretta. Jaz stepped back; his eyes widened in fear. Lloyd fired three times, knocking Jaz off his feet into his chair. He was dead before Lloyd reached the safe. Inside were six bundles of twenty-pound notes. Lloyd stuffed them into his pockets and smoothed down the material to hide the bulges. He looked at Jaz, a dark patch was spreading between his legs.

'Thanks for the heads up, Jaz,' he muttered beneath his breath. 'Say hello to Big Ron for me. I miss him.'

Lloyd took the silencer off the gun and put it in his pocket. He leaned over the desk and opened the top drawer. A shiny Smith and Wesson was sitting on top of an iPad. Lloyd took the revolver and stuffed it into his sock and then rummaged through the drawers for something long and thin. He found a screwdriver set in the bottom drawer and took the Phillips from the box. He pushed it into the barrel of the Beretta, scratching the rifling and scoring deep grooves into the metal. After a few minutes work, he wiped all the prints from it and carefully put the gun into his jacket. He checked his watch and headed for the door.

As he reached the office door, his mobile rang. He looked at the screen and then answered it.

'Lloyd it's Justin. We've got a problem at Chris's place.'

'I'm having a few problems myself, Justin,' Lloyd said, leaning against the door. The wood vibrated with the baseline from the club. 'What's up?'

'Chris's missus has locked herself in the attic. We can't get to her. I reckon the coppers will be here in no time!'

'Fucking hell,' Lloyd moaned. 'How hard can it be?' he rolled his eyes to the ceiling. 'Use your imagination will you. If you can't get her down, make sure you're not around when the coppers get there.'

'Okay.'

'Justin.'

'What?'

'I'm going to have to disappear for a while. I need that collection list sorted tomorrow. I want every penny owed, understand?'

'What's happened?'

'Doesn't matter, just collect what's owed, okay?'

'Yes, boss. Leave it with me.'

Lloyd hung up and took a deep breath. He opened the door and snapped on the lock. If the door was locked, they may think Jaz had slipped out early and gone home. Lloyd stepped out onto the landing, closing the door behind him. The music became louder as he descended. He pushed through the double doors into the club and looked around. The dance floor was packed with gyrating bodies. There was an empty cider bottle on a shelf to his right. He picked it up and hurled it high towards the middle of the dance floor and then tossed an empty pint glass into the crowd for good measure. Two revellers went down bleeding and the dance floor erupted into a melee.

Lloyd went back through the doors and reached the reception area. The sound of screaming was becoming audible, even over the music.

'It's kicked right off in there,' Lloyd said to the bouncers. 'I'd get in there sharpish if I were you!'

The doormen sprinted in the direction of the dance floor. The blond didn't even look up as he walked out of the nightclub. He knew that it would take hours to sort out the trouble, closing time at least. Jaz wouldn't be disturbed for a long time, probably the next night. Lloyd intended to take his advice and be a long way away by then. He jogged down the steps onto the street and saw what he was looking for. Rainwater was running like tiny rivers along the gutters and disappearing down a grid. Lloyd took the Beretta from his pocket and dropped it through the metal bars and then followed suit with the silencer. They sunk quickly, spiralling towards the thick sludge at the bottom of the drain. Lloyd checked around, looking up and down the street. There was no one around. He jogged along the soaking cobbles towards his vehicle. Lloyd reached his car and opened the door with his remote. The rain became more intense and water trickled down his neck, making him hunch. The sound of footsteps behind him made him turn quickly. Standing in front of him was Del Makin. He was holding a sawn-off Remington with both hands. Lloyd was about to speak when Del pulled the triggers and the shotgun roared. Both barrels hit Lloyd in the chest and blew him backwards off his feet. He slammed into his vehicle and slid down onto the soaking cobbles. The sound of the music began to fade and darkness flooded his mind.

CHAPTER 9

DI Kim West sat back in her chair while Alan went through the legalities. Brian Selby had stopped looking at his feet and he wasn't muttering. Kim had wondered if he had mental health issues but now, he seemed calmer and more aware. There was intelligence in his eyes where before they had been blank. Kim thought about what Alan had said. Maybe he was playing a game. If he was, she would give him ten out of ten for acting. She glanced at Alan. The older he got, the more worn out he looked. Selby's brief looked annoyed at the fact that he had been called back so soon and couldn't go home to his bed.

'I'm sorry that we have had to resume so quickly. We know that it is very late, Brian,' Kim sighed. 'We're all tired but we have new information that we need to discuss with you as a matter of urgency.' She saw something in his expression change. He seemed to steel himself against what was coming. A light came on behind his eyes. 'We've found a body in the woods where you were arrested.'

'A body?' his brief asked, open mouthed. 'Wait a minute. I need to speak to my client in private.'

'I didn't shoot him,' Brian said, matter-of-factly. He folded his arms. The detectives and the lawyer looked stunned. 'I didn't kill him. It was Lloyd Jones that killed him. He made me bury him.'

'Brian don't say anything else at this stage,' his brief tried to interrupt him.

'I'm not stupid,' Brian said, glancing at him. 'I know what I'm saying.'

'I'm advising you to say nothing further until we've spoken in private.'

'Noted.' Brian said, folding his hands together on the table. 'I'm choosing to ignore your advice.' He looked Kim in the eyes. 'Lloyd Jones killed him and he made me help bury him. He said that he would kill my mum if I didn't help. Look what he did to my face,' he added, pointing to his scar.

'Lloyd Jones?' Kim said, writing the name down. She looked at her DI. They both realised that their Matrix operation may have been compromised. 'He's a big guy with a shaven head and tattoos, always wears a suit?'

'That's him,' Brian said, excited. 'Do you know him?'

'Our paths have crossed once or twice.' Kim said, nodding. A knot tightened in her stomach. The information they had gleaned from the men inside Jones's outfit had been priceless. 'Who is the victim, Brian?'

'Stuart,' Brian said, sitting forward. 'Stuart Radcliffe. Lloyd said he was a grass.'

'Stuart Radcliffe,' Kim said, writing the name down. She passed the note to the uniformed officer, who was standing outside the door. She whispered in his ear, 'Get this to Matrix. Chris Cornell may have been exposed too. They need to move on this ASAP.' She tucked her hair behind her ears and sat down. Brian was gawping at her breasts. She noticed his stare and closed her jacket. Brain blushed and looked away. She cleared her throat and looked at Alan. He nodded to continue.

'Tell me what happened in the woods, Brian.' Kim carried on with her questioning.

'I was digging the hole and I thought he was going to kill me right there and then but Lloyd started asking how much the information was worth and he mentioned something about the Drug Squad.' Brian wiped sweat from his brow as if recanting the story was traumatic. 'I didn't have a clue what he was talking about. I thought he was asking me about the Drug Squad, you see but then he shot Stuart twice in the chest. Stuart collapsed and then Lloyd made me help bury him.'

'Why did you think he was going to shoot you?'

'Well, he was pointing the gun at me, you see. I had to dig a big hole first,' Brian said, talking at a hundred miles an hour. 'I thought it was my grave. I thought he was going to shoot me, you see. Stuart must have thought that he was going to shoot me too or he wouldn't have hung around, would he?'

'I wouldn't have thought so,' Kim agreed. She couldn't make sense of Brian's rambling. 'What were you doing there in the first place?'

'I went to dig up my drone.'

'Your drone was buried in the woods?'

'Yes. I buried it to keep it safe.'

'And why was your drone buried in the woods?'

'No comment,' Brian said with a confident nod. He nudged his brief and smiled. 'You see. I know when to shut up and when not to.' The brief and Kim looked at each other baffled. Brian was a mixture of innocent child and naïve adult. 'No comment,' he repeated.

'Okay. We can come back to that,' Kim said. 'You said that Lloyd shot him twice.'

'Yes. I thought he was going to shoot me but he didn't. He shot Stuart. Twice.'

'Stuart also has deep lacerations to his face and neck, Brian.'

'Does he?'

'Yes, he does. How did he get them?' Kim asked. Brain hesitated. 'Tell me what happened?'

'Oh, yes. I remember. We were burying him but he wasn't dead. He was only nearly dead,' Brian said. His eyes flickered upwards just for a second. Kim knew a lie was coming. 'He wasn't dead and he tried to get out, you see? He put his hand out of the soil and grabbed Lloyd by the ankle. I nearly jumped out of my skin. Lloyd was shocked too and he said the f-word and hit him with the entrenching tool. Three times. One, two, three.' Brian demonstrated a stabbing motion with his hands.

'Then what happened?'

'Stuart stopped trying to get out. He was dead this time.'

'And then?'

'He said that he had to go and that I had to finish burying Stuart and that if I didn't do it properly, he would kill my mum. So, I did it. I had no choice.'

'Okay. Go on.'

'That is, it, really,' Brian said with a shrug. 'When I had finished, I left the woods and that's when I was arrested.'

'Why didn't you tell us all this before?'

'I was scared.'

'You were only scared until we found the body,' Kim mused. 'Did you think that we might not find it?'

'I was waiting.'

'Were you waiting for us to find the body?'

'Lloyd Jones is a very dangerous man. I couldn't tell you what he did until I was sure.'

'He is dangerous. What is your connection to him, Brian?'

'What?'

'Why were you in the woods with men like Lloyd Jones and Stuart Radcliffe?'

'They made me go there.'

'Why?

'I told you. I went to dig up the drone.'

'Why did you bury a drone in the woods?'

'No comment.'

'Did you travel there with them?'

'No. I went alone and they followed me.'

'They followed you?'

'Yes.'

'Why did they follow you?'

'To make sure that I dug it up.'

'So, they were concerned about the drone being buried there?'

'Yes.'

'Why?'

'I don't know.'

'I think you do know.'

'They made me go there. I don't know why.'

'I think you built the drone,' Kim said, smiling. Brian blushed. 'We have officers at your home. I think we'll find incriminating evidence linked to that drone. When we do, your part in all this changes. You become complicit in all this.' Kim made a big circle in the air with her finger. 'You will become part of their circle. You understand that, don't you?'

'I haven't done anything wrong. Lloyd Jones shot Stuart and made me bury him.'

'I think you're lying to me,' Kim lowered her voice. 'I think you waited for us to find the body and then you came up with the Lloyd Jones story. If I was going to pass the blame, I would use someone with a track record for violence. Lloyd Jones fits the bill perfectly.'

'I didn't shoot Stuart,' Brian said, offended. He blew air from his lips like a child in a huff. 'As if I could shoot anybody! Where would I get a gun?'

'It isn't hard to get hold of a gun these days.'

'You'll find his footprints there in the woods. It was pouring with rain and the ground was soft and muddy.'

'The rain can destroy more evidence than it creates, Brian but if he was there, we will find traces.'

'He was there. I'm not lying.' He folded his arms across his chest, sulkily.

'So, you say.'

'He smoked a cigarette. I took the butt away from the scene.' Brian said, looking smug. In his mind, he had placed his ace card. 'There will be DNA on it.'

'Where is it?' Kim asked.

'It is in a plastic water bottle in my bag.'

'So, it isn't at the scene any longer, is it?' Kim said, raising her eyebrows. 'You removed a vital piece of evidence.'

'Where else would I have got it from?' Brian mumbled. He hadn't been quite as clever as he thought he had.

'Okay we'll check that too. Your bag is in the lab.'

'And there is a garage across the road,' he added, excitedly.

'And what?'

'There is a CCTV camera there. Stuart and Lloyd were waiting for me near the garage. If it was on, it will show you that I'm telling the truth.'

'Okay, let's leave that there for now,' she said, staring at his neck. 'Where did all the scratches come from, Brian?' Kim pointed to his neck. 'You look like you've been in a scuffle. Who scratched you?'

'Stuart roughed me up.'

'You haven't mentioned anything about that.'

'Haven't I?'

'No.'

'When they made me dig the hole,' Brian said, blushing red. 'I was asking Lloyd not to kill me and Stuart got mad. He grabbed me by the throat. I think.'

'You think?'

'I was scared. It is all a bit of blur to be honest. Can I see my mum?'

'Not tonight, Brian,' Kim said, standing. 'We'll be keeping you in here overnight while we check what you're saying. We'll talk again in the morning. Interview terminated.' She switched off the recorder.

'I'm hungry,' Brian said, stretching and yawning. 'Can I have something to eat?'

Kim opened the door and beckoned a uniformed officer into the room. 'It's late, Brian. The kitchen is closed for the night. You'll be fed in the morning.'

'That isn't fair,' Brian moaned.

Kim looked at him and bit her bottom lip.

'Brian,' Alan interrupted, standing up from the table. 'I can't decide whether this spoilt little boy act is really you or if you're playing a game but let me get one thing straight in your head.' Alan paused and locked eyes with Brian. He looked away immediately. 'You were arrested with blood on you near a murder victim and your explanation as to why you were there is sketchy at best.'

'It is the truth …'

'Shut up!' Alan snapped. 'I haven't finished.' Brian blushed. 'Your explanation implicates one of the island's most dangerous criminals as the murderer. If you're lying to us, you're screwed. You'll go down for a very long time. If you're telling us the truth, Jones will come after you and you're screwed. Either way you're screwed, Brian.' Brian looked at Alan, fear in his eyes. 'Good. I can see you've got the message. I suggest that you sleep on what I've said. If you want us to believe you, then you need to come clean on what you were doing in the woods in the first place. Cut the crap, stop the games, and understand how much shit you are in.' Alan put his palms flat on the table and leaned towards him. 'Do you understand me?'

'Yes,' Brian answered, sulkily.

'Good,' Alan said, nodding. He glared at him once more and then turned and left the room in a hurry. Kim walked with him. They knew that Matrix, the Drug Squad, and Alan's Major Investigation Team would already be reacting to the news that a key informer had been murdered. Stuart Radcliffe was one of two working together and Kim shuddered as she wondered where the other one was.

'I'm going to call a briefing,' Alan said, turning to her. 'I want you to go and call ACC Carlton. I know it's late but he'll blow a fuse if we move on this without his say so.' Kim nodded and peeled away.

'I'll use this office and meet you shortly.'

CHAPTER 10

Rachel Cornell put the phone to her ear and waited for the emergency services to answer. It rang once and then went silent. She looked at the screen, her heart in her mouth as she watched the battery icon flash and the phone died.

'Oh fuck!' she hissed.

'That's a bad word, Mummy,' Claire said, innocently.

'I know it is, baby,' Rachel said, hugging her daughter tightly. 'Sometimes grown-ups say bad words.'

'I know. Daddy says it all the time.'

'Most daddies do, angel.' Rachel said, looking around. Chris had built a man cave. He had a sixty-inch screen attached to a Play Station and a gaming chair. His laptop was on his desk to her left and a small beer fridge hummed quietly to her right. The roof structure was hidden. The rafters and tiles were covered with plasterboard that he had painted white, the floor was oak laminate. She couldn't see anything that could help them out of the situation they were in. They were trapped. The men who had come for them couldn't get into the attic. All she had to do was wait for them to leave. She couldn't call the police but they didn't know that, did they? For all they knew, they could be on their way already. They would have expected her to call the police.

There was no sound from below. The plaster boarding and insulation nullified everything. She was blind to whatever they were doing downstairs. They may have gone already. If they had any sense, they would be well on their way by now. It would be obvious that they could not reach her in the attic. They would realise that and leave.

Rachel went over to the desk, opened the top drawer and looked inside. A packet of menthol cigarettes and a zippo lighter told her what she already knew. He hadn't stopped smoking. She fumbled through a stack of papers, pens and spare cables. A packet of triple-A batteries had split and they rolled around the drawer as she searched for something useful. She closed the drawer and got the whiff of petrol. Was it from the zippo? She opened the drawer again and flicked the lid on the lighter. Thumbing the wheel three times, she knew it was dry. There was no fuel in it. The smell had become stronger. Her heart began to beat faster as she approached the hatch. Tendrils of smoke, tinged grey blue, were climbing between the hinges and the laminate floor. She didn't need to open the hatch to know that they had set fire to their home.

CHAPTER 11

Alan watched as bleary-eyed detectives gathered in the MIT office. There wasn't time to summon a full briefing. This was an emergency gathering of the nightshift. The discovery that the dead body in the woods was Matrix criminal informer, Stuart Radcliffe, had sent shockwaves through the building. Images of the crime scene flickered on the screens behind Alan.

'This is Stuart Radcliffe. He was a CI for Matrix and he was found dead a few hours ago. This man, Brian Selby, was arrested near the scene and he has positively identified Radcliffe as the victim. Radcliffe and another man, Christopher Cornell, were members of an outfit from Holyhead headed up by Lloyd Jones.' He paused as murmurs passed through the gathering of detectives. 'Although only a mid-level target, I can see some of you know the name. He was on the up and heading for the big league. Radcliffe and Cornell were working surveillance for Matrix after being busted in a drug deal last year when Jamie Hollins was sent down. They were arrested with a kilo of cocaine and a firearm and Matrix turned them. We think Lloyd Jones found out that he had a leak and has bubbled them. Brian Selby claims that he witnessed Jones shooting Radcliffe. He said that Lloyd Jones told him after the shooting that he had killed him because Radcliffe was a grass. We need to find Lloyd Jones and we need to find the remaining informant, Christopher Cornell.' DI Kim Davies entered the room. She nodded to him. 'Good timing,' Alan said. 'Finding Chris Cornell is the priority. He may still be alive.'

'The ACC gave the green light. I've already sent a team to his home to bring him in,' Kim said.

'Excellent. I think we should pick up everyone involved in the Matrix sting. If we leave any of Jones's men out there, we risk the chance of them running around making our witnesses disappear.' He looked at Kim. Matrix operations were her call. 'Agreed?'

'Agreed,' she said. 'We'll need uniform and armed response to back us up.'

'How many do you think you'll need?' Alan asked.

'All of them,' Kim answered, sarcastically. 'None of this bunch are going to come in quietly. We'll need everything we've got.'

'Sorry to interrupt, inspector,' a uniformed officer said, poking his head around the door. 'We've just had a report of a shooting outside of Paradise nightclub in Bangor.'

'And?'

'The victim is Lloyd Jones.'

CHAPTER 12

Rachel froze to the spot as she tried not to lose it in front of her daughter. Claire held her hand and clung to Bear, strangely calm as she watched the smoke creeping through the edges of the hatch. The attic would become their tomb if she didn't move quickly. She had no choice but to go down into the house or choke to death and burn.

'We have to go back downstairs.'

'Okay, Mummy.'

'You stay close to me and don't let go of my hand, no matter what, okay?'

'Okay, Mummy,' Claire mumbled. She squeezed Bear harder, as if to pass the message on to him.

Rachel undid the bolt and pressed the release button. The hatch clicked open and the ladders began to extend. A thick cloud of choking smoke billowed through the gap, stinging her eyes and making them water. Her vision was blurred as she walked around the hatch and checked the landing. There was no sign of any intruders there. The orange glow of flames flickered on the far wall, coming from the downstairs.

'Let's go, careful on the steps now,' Rachel said, leading the way. She paused halfway, scanning the bedroom doorways for danger. She could hear the flames crackling and the air was becoming hot. Breathing was becoming more difficult. When Claire reached the bottom step, Rachel picked her up and ran towards the staircase. Her makeshift barricade was still in place but now it was ablaze. The entire hallway was an inferno, the flames creeping quickly up the banister and stair carpet. There was no way down from there. She pushed Claire's head into her shoulder and ran for the bathroom, closing the door behind her. Claire started to cry. She had tried hard not to but the time for being brave had passed. Once the first sob had broken, it was followed by an uncontrollable flow of tears. She felt scared and tired and just wanted to lie down and sleep; she could not comprehend what was going on around her. Rachel grabbed a bath towel and turned on the tap. She soaked it in cold water and then put it over her head, covering Claire.

'Mummy, I don't like it!'

'It will stop the smoke going in your eyes,' Rachel said, opening the door. 'We won't be able to breath otherwise.' The flames were near the top of the stairs, the heat was blistering the paint on the walls. It felt like stepping into an oven. She ducked beneath the smoke and ran across the landing to the spare bedroom. Something exploded downstairs. The house trembled for a few seconds. Rachel put her back to the wall and waited for the vibration to subside. The sound of the downstairs windows shattering spurred her on. She ran to the window and pulled at the handle.

'No, no, no!' she moaned. It wouldn't budge. The window led onto their garage roof. Chris said it was a weak point where burglars would break in. *'Keep it locked and don't leave the key in the lock otherwise you might as well leave the thing open.'* She looked around the room. The bedside table caught her eye. It was small but made from solid wood. She put Claire down and picked it up. 'Stand over there!' Claire stood in the corner. 'Face the wall for a minute!'

'I don't want to!' Claire shouted.

'We don't have time for this, Claire!' Rachel snapped. 'Do it now!' Claire relented and turned away. She hugged Bear tightly to her chest. Rachel thrust the table at the glass as hard as she could. It bounced off and clattered onto the floor. 'No, no, for fuck's sake!'

She picked it up and held it by two legs, one in each hand. Stepping back, she swung it like a baseball bat, keeping hold of it on impact. The glass shattered. She swung it three times to clear the shards and then flattened the edges by stabbing at them with the table-top.

'Come on, sweetheart!' she said, reaching for Claire. She lifted her through the glass and lowered her onto the flat roof. 'Wait there,' she said, coughing and spluttering as she cocked her leg through the window and climbed out. A jagged piece of glass slashed her inner thigh. She gritted her teeth and dropped down next to her daughter, feeling blood running down her thigh. They both sucked in deep gasps of the cold night air. Rachel looked to the road and saw blue flashing lights in the far distance and she wondered how they had known about the fire so quickly.

'Is that the fire engine, Mummy?'

'I think so, darling.' Rachel hoped it was coming their way.

'I knew you would come out this way, Rachel,' a gruff voice said from behind her.

She heard Claire screaming for a second before a crushing blow to the back of her skull switched her lights out.

CHAPTER 13

Kim and Alan arrived at the scene of the shooting and he slowed his vehicle at the police cordon, showing his ID to the uniformed officer who was standing on watch at the crime scene tape. He drove through a gap between two ambulances and navigated his way further up the street. Another marked police car arrived and four officers deployed. Alan parked the Shogun on the pavement behind them and turned the engine off. The street was bathed in flashing blue lights.

'How many ambulances do you need for a shooting?' Kim said, shocked. 'There are way too many for just one incident.'

'There's something else going on here,' Alan agreed.

The first detective on the scene spotted them and headed over. He was accompanied by a uniformed sergeant who looked like he was not far from retirement. The rain had stopped but the cobbles were still wet and the neon signs reflected from them. Kim counted six ambulances and a seventh was just arriving.

'DI Alan Williams?' Alan nodded a silent hello while he assessed the scene. It was chaos. 'DS Sampson from Bangor station. This is Sergeant Evans. We've got a right mess here. This is one for telling the grandkids, I can tell you.'

'I can see there's a lot going on. What have you got for me so far?' Alan asked. He was trying to pinpoint where the shooting had happened.

'We got a call from a cabbie around three-thirty, who says that he witnessed a man being shot as he tried to get into his car,' Sampson explained. Alan noticed that he was wearing a dark fur lined parka and trainers. The new breed of detective. 'The shooter used a sawn-off shotgun. We've got a decent description of him and I've circulated it.'

'And the victim?' Kim asked, looking around.

'A local man from your neck of the woods named, Lloyd Jones, guv,' Sampson said, not realising that they knew his identity already.

'Where is he?'

'He's on his way to Ysbyty Gwynedd,' the uniformed sergeant answered. 'The paramedics treated him here, stopped the bleeding and then took him away. They left about ten minutes ago.'

'He's alive?' Kim asked, surprised.

'He was wearing a vest,' Sampson said with a shrug. 'He's got pellets in both his upper arms, his neck and a couple in his face but he'll live. The vest took the brunt of it.'

'Has he got an armed escort?' Kim asked, concerned.

'Yes,' the sergeant answered. 'When I got here, I patted him down for ID. He was out of it. I found a Smith and Wesson revolver in his sock and a large amount of cash. Forensics are bagging everything now,' He said pointing to a CSI unit, who were parked a way down the street. 'I called in an ARU to escort the ambulance. It was a madhouse here. Apparently, it had kicked off in the nightclub about the same time as Jones was shot and the doormen lost control of the situation. It spilled out onto the street there and all hell broke loose.'

'That's why all the ambulances are here?' Alan said.

'That and the second victim, guv,' Sampson said, pointing to Paradise. Alan and Kim looked at each other.

'Nobody mentioned a second victim,' Alan said.

'We've only just found him, guv. When the nightclub situation had calmed down, one of uniform went looking for the manager. They found a body in the office. Walter Ricks, goes by the name of Jaz. He found him shot dead in his office with three bullets in his chest and the safe empty. I was waiting for you to arrive before going up there myself.'

'Okay, good,' Alan said, walking towards the nightclub. 'Let's go and have a look before forensics get in there.'

The three detectives weaved through the emergency vehicles and entered the club. The foyer looked like a tornado had twisted its way through, broken glasses, bottles, and bar stools were scattered everywhere.

'The cleaners are in for a shock,' Kim said, looking around. She pointed to the ceiling. 'I wonder if those cameras are recording.'

'Surely, they will be,' Sampson said.

'During operating hours, I doubt it very much,' Kim replied. She picked her way through the debris to the double doors and pushed them open using her elbows. 'Jaz and his goons turn a lot of blind eyes in this dump. They'll be on when the place is shut but not while the dealers are trading.'

They walked up the stairs to the office in silence, each one scanning the area for something out of the ordinary. When they reached the office, Sampson passed them some gloves and they put them on before entering the room. The smell of blood and excrement drifted to them.

'That is Jaz,' Kim said. 'No doubt about that.'

'Yes, that's him,' Alan agreed. 'It looks like karma came in here and bit him on the arse.'

'Three to the chest from close range and an empty safe.'

'Jones comes up here, makes him open the safe and then shoots him?' Alan said, with a frown.

'Bit too much of a coincidence to think anyone else did it, isn't it?' Sampson mused. Alan knew why he hadn't been made an MIT detective yet.

'So, Jones shoots Jaz, robs him and then gets shot on the way to his car. His pockets were full of money so whoever shot him wasn't robbing him,' Kim said, shaking her head. 'They just wanted him dead.'

'Must have been personal,' Sampson said, raising his index finger. 'Somebody had it in for him.'

'No shit, Sherlock,' Kim muttered under her breath. Alan raised an eyebrow and grinned. 'Couldn't have happened to a nicer man.'

'How many men are on him at the hospital?' Alan asked.

'Two-armed response and two uniforms,' Sampson answered.

'Good, double it,' Alan ordered. 'As soon as the doctors are sure he's not in danger, I want him out of that hospital and in a cell.'

'Yes, sir,' Sampson said, reaching for his radio. He turned to walk away.

'It's time to round them all up, Kim,' Alan said, turning to her. 'Before they kill each other – and our witnesses.'

'Wouldn't that be a crying shame if they killed each other,' Kim muttered as she walked back towards the stairs. The urge to get out of the nightclub and have a long hot bath was overwhelming.

CHAPTER 14

Rachel woke up with a sickening headache and a sore throat. She felt like she had swallowed powdered glass. Her eyes flickered open and they felt red, raw, and gritty. She could only see blurred outlines. Sounds drifted to her. The sounds of animals in distress. Not random animals – pigs. She could hear them squealing. The cloying odour of animal waste floated on the air, so thick that she could almost taste it. She could sense death all around her. It filled her senses. The memories of the night before drifted back slowly in pieces and she panicked.

'Claire!' she gasped; her voice was hoarse. 'Claire!'

'Mummy!'

'Where are you?'

'Over here, Mummy!'

Rachel tried to rub her eyes but her wrists were tied together. Her vision wouldn't clear. She leant forward and wiped them on her knees. It wasn't perfect but it was better. She turned towards Claire and saw her sitting on the floor nearby, her hands tied behind her back. Black smudges spread beneath her eyes and around her mouth. Next to her was her husband, Chris. His face was swollen and bruised, his lips split and scabbed. Congealed blood clung to his nostrils and top lip. He was gagged but his eyes were open. Tears streaked his face. He was sobbing uncontrollably and he was trying to communicate but she couldn't understand his muffled message. There was something different about his eyes. They looked desperately sad. She thought that he was trying to say sorry but she didn't know why. Nothing that she had experienced that night made sense. The break in was bad enough, the fire worse but this place was the stuff of nightmares.

'Mummy!' Claire called out again. 'I want to go home, Mummy.'

'I know you do, darling. Don't cry. I'll get us out of here and we'll go home soon.'

'Hurry up, Mummy!'

'What the fuck have you done, Chris?' she whispered. Chris read her lips and shook his head and closed his eyes tightly, his body shaking. 'What have you done, you idiot?' she shouted, losing her temper. 'Why is our daughter tied up?' Chris kept his eyes closed but the tears continued to roll from the corners. 'What did you do to them? They burned our house down!' she screamed.

She heard a motor kick into life and the clank of metal on metal. Hooks automatically attached to a large hopper and tilted it towards a huge funnel. It took her seconds to recognise that the hopper was full of pigs, their heads, legs and feet. Claire covered her eyes and began to scream as the hopper was tipped and the stinking contents slopped into the grinder. In her brain, she was asking why anyone would bring them to a place like this and the answer was unthinkable. The sound of the cogs whirring and bone splintering filled the air. A stream of pale pink mince began to fill a hopper below the machine. There was only one reason that they would subject them to seeing this. She knew what they were planning to do. She looked at Chris and shook her head.

'Oh my god, what did you do to them?' she shouted.

'Mummy, stop shouting!' Claire began to sob again.

'What did you do for us to deserve being treated like this?'

'Mummy!' Claire wept. 'Stop it!'

'Shut up a minute, Claire!' Rachel snapped. 'Why are we here, Chris?'

'I can answer that question for you,' Justin approached from behind them. Two men shadowed him. They were big men, their eyes dead like a shark's. There was no empathy in them. Rachel could feel their eyes on her body and they leered at one another. The captives fell silent as they stepped in front of them. Justin had removed his balaclava but still had a black jumpsuit on. Rachel didn't think that the fact that he was showing his face was a good sign. He was no longer hiding his identity. That made her shiver. 'Your husband is a grass, Rachel. Simple.'

'What are you talking about?'

'Tell them it is true, Chris.' Justin kicked him in the midriff. 'Nod your head and tell her that you're a snake.' Chris nodded.

'Don't hurt him like that, you bully!' Rachel hissed. 'I don't care what he has done. His daughter is watching!'

'Daddy!' Claire sobbed. Justin stepped back and smiled coldly.

'Apologies,' Justin said with a grin.

'Thank you. Now tell me what you mean that he is a grass?' Rachel asked, astounded.

'Simple. He is a police informer.'

'What on earth has he informed about that could justify burning down my home and frightening the life out of my daughter?'

'What could he have informed about?' Justin asked, shaking his head. 'Are you joking with me?'

'I don't see any joke here. Nothing about this is funny from where I am sitting.'

'You don't know what we do for a living?'

'Not really no but whatever it is, it cannot warrant this.'

'It does, believe me.'

'He told me that you were importing and exporting.' She looked at Chris but he wouldn't make eye contact with her. 'Is that not true?'

'You've been a little bit flexible with the truth there, haven't you, Chris?' Justin chuckled.

'Whatever he has done, it cannot be that bad. Nothing can justify this,' Rachel challenged him. 'You burnt down our home for god's sake!'

'No matter, you won't be needing it anymore,' Justin said, an evil grin on his face. He gestured towards the meat grinder. Chris began to struggle against his bonds like a madman possessed. A high-pitched mewing came from behind his gag. 'You can thank your husband for this. You see in our business, if you become a police informer then you lose everything. Houses; cars; pets; family are all fair game. That is how it stacks up. The rewards are rich but the penalties for betrayal are high. You had a nice house, nice car, nice clothes, didn't you?'

'Yes but ...'

'Where did you think all the money came from?'

'I still don't understand,' Rachel sighed. She couldn't comprehend what was happening. Had he really just gestured to that mincing machine? 'What has he done that could be so bad?'

'He made a deal with the devil to save himself. Chris decided that your safety, your lives were not as valuable as his liberty. He valued his own freedom as worth more than your life and the life of his own daughter. He's a lowlife snake.'

'What exactly did he do?' she whined. She turned on Chris. 'What the hell did you do?'

'Mummy, stop shouting at Daddy!'

'I'm sorry, darling,' Rachel said in a soothing voice. She took a deep breath and tried to calm herself. 'Please tell me what he has done and how we can fix this.'

'He stabbed us all in the back. He betrayed all of us,' Justin said, shrugging.

'That means nothing to me. Tell me why we are here? I want to know exactly what has led to us being here like this.'

'He tried to branch out on his own behind our backs but the sneaky bastard got caught, didn't he?' Justin said, turning on Chris. 'Didn't you?' Chris nodded that it was true. 'He was busted by the police with a kilo of cocaine and a gun.' Rachel turned and scowled at her husband. He couldn't look her in the eyes anymore. 'They told him that he would get ten years but he decided that he couldn't do the time. He turned informer instead.'

'A kilo of cocaine and a gun, Chris?' Rachel said, incredulous. 'You had a kilo of cocaine and a gun? I told you that I would never have anything to do with drugs. We have a daughter, you idiot!'

'He has been recording us and filming us and passing on the

information to the police, risking your lives every day for fourteen months. He was happy to gamble your wellbeing for his own. What a total selfish bastard, eh?'

'What are you going to do with us?'

'I think the guys behind me have a crush on you.'

'Don't be so vile!'

'It's the way we do things.' He paused to let the intent sink in. He pointed to the machine. 'Once they're done with you, we'll kill Claire, then you, and then eventually him. Watching his family suffer and die is the price he pays, the price you pay too unfortunately.'

'My god, no!' Rachel whispered.

'Mummy, why is he saying bad things?'

'We're just talking, honey,' Rachel said, turning to her daughter. She took a deep breath to calm her. Her voice was faltering. 'We haven't done anything. I didn't even know that he was involved in drugs or I would have left him long ago. You can do what you want to him.' Rachel turned and spat at Chris. 'I don't even know who that man is. He is not the man that I married. Let us go and I'll never speak a word about it to anyone.'

'Hey, Chris!' Justin taunted him. 'How does that feel, bro? Your missus couldn't give a toss what happens to you.' He laughed and looked at Claire, thinking about what she had said. 'Sorry, Rachel. You're a nice lady, wasted on that scumbag over there but it can't be done. We have a job to do.'

'Please! We're innocent in this.'

'Can't be done, I'm afraid.'

'Then let my daughter go. She's a child!'

'It's just the way it is. It can't be stopped now.'

'It can,' a voice said from the shadows. Matt stepped out of the dark corridor to their left. 'Hi, Rachel, hey, Claire.'

'Matt!' Rachel cried out. 'Oh my god, I'm so glad to see you! Help us, please!'

'Uncle Matt!' Claire cried. 'He's saying bad things!'

'Don't you worry, Claire,' Matt said, kneeling to touch her face. 'I'm going to talk to him and everything will be okay.'

'Help us, Matt, please!' Rachel begged.

'Enough is enough. Untie them,' Matt said, turning to the other two men. They looked at Justin. 'Don't look at him for permission! Untie them now.'

They moved towards the captives, doing as he ordered.

'Don't touch them!' Justin snarled. They hesitated. 'If you don't have the stomach for this, then fuck off, Matt and let me get on with the job,' Justin straightened up to his full height. 'You can fuck her first if you want.'

'There's a frightened little girl there. Watch your mouth,' Matt said, ice in his tone.

'Or what?'

'Don't push me, Justin. This is over.'

'Nothing is over. Lloyd gave me an order and I intend to do it. If you don't like it, leave. I'll fuck her twice, one for you, eh?' Justin laughed dryly. The other men grinned. 'What's up, are you losing your edge?'

'How stupid are you, Justin?'

'Not stupid enough to defy Lloyd.'

'Listen to yourself,' Matt said, fronting him up. They stood toe to toe, eye to eye, neither man showed any fear. 'Lloyd Jones is finished.' They stared at each other. 'He's finished.'

'I'd like to see you telling him that to his face.'

'If he was here, he would tell you himself.'

'What are you talking about?'

'The law is all over him. They have been trying to nail him for years and thanks to Stuart and him,' he said, gesturing to Chris, 'they can lift him whenever they want to now. He's finished and when they take him in, you had better believe that we're next on their list.'

'He seemed okay earlier when I spoke to him. He just said that he might have to disappear for a while but he sounded okay.'

'He's not okay. He's finished.'

'Are you sure?'

'I've never been surer. It has all come on top. He's finished and you and me will be top of their list.' Matt could see doubt in Justin's eyes.

'Are you sure about this?'

'I've just heard from a little birdy at police headquarters that they have got fat Brian in the cells and guess what?'

'I'm listening,' Justin said, without flinching an inch.

'The police have found a body in the woods near Berwyn prison and Brian Selby has told them that it is Stuart.'

'What?' Justin stepped back, slightly. 'So, Stuart is dead?'

'Yes, he is dead and Brian has also fingered Lloyd as the killer. He told the police that he watched Lloyd shoot Stuart!'

'What?' Justin took a step back, not quite believing the news. 'Brian told the police that, you're joking?'

'No. I'm not joking. He reckons that he was there when Lloyd shot him,' Matt turned to look at the others. 'Lloyd is going down for good and the only way that he might ever see the light of day again is to cooperate with the police and that means stitching us up.' The men and Justin exchanged concerned glances. 'Now then, we are in this up to our necks already but if you want to add a triple murder to your list of things to give a shit about, then carry on and kill them but put twenty years on your sentence. Killing kids doesn't go down well with juries or inside.' Justin stepped back again. He looked at the floor. 'Or you can untie them and we'll drop the women off at the hospital and then we'll go our separate ways. It's every man for themselves.'

'What about him?'

'We leave him somewhere they'll find him.'

'Hold on a minute, we're not letting that rat go!' Justin snapped.

'Okay,' Matt shrugged. 'Do it your way. Kill him but do it when I've gone because I'm having nothing to do with it. I'm not doing more time for him.'

'What do you mean, more time?'

'If you want to do life for killing a police informer then go ahead but I'm out of here with Rachel and Claire.'

'This is so fucked up!' Justin said, sighing.

'Listen to me.' Matt lowered his voice and stepped closer to the men. 'Lloyd Jones will be banged up for shooting Stuart. He is fucked. We are fucked. All you need to think about now is how fucked do you want to be? Kill any of them and you'll be locked up for good.'

Justin walked away and turned his back. He put his hands on his hips and then on his head.

'He's right. Untie them,' Justin said, quietly.

'Do it now.' Matt encouraged them. The men moved towards Rachel and Claire.

'Thank you, Matt,' Rachel wept. 'Thank you, thank you, thank you.'

'I'll get someone to drop you at the hospital and then you need to go somewhere safe. Somewhere no one can get to you, understand?'

'Not really,' she answered confused. 'Isn't this over? I thought everything would be alright now.'

'Nothing will ever be alright again, Rachel,' Matt said, holding her face in both hands. 'Your husband has turned informer against some very dangerous people. We could try and get him out of the country but the police will be all over us soon. If they catch us, we'll do time. As for him, they'll give him a new identity and hope that he can blend in somewhere new. The people he helps to put away will chase him until he's dead. If they can't get to him then they will come for you, just like tonight. You and Claire are in danger as long as he's breathing.'

Rachel turned and glared at her husband. 'I don't believe that you have done this to me and our daughter. How could you?' Claire was freed and she ran to her mother. The men reluctantly untied Chris. His injuries were so bad that he couldn't move well or stand. He reached out his arms towards his family, tears still streamed down his face.

'I'm so sorry, Rachel,' Chris gasped, as the gag was removed.

'Don't you even think about coming near us!' Rachel shouted. 'I will make sure that you never set eyes on us again.' She turned to Matt. 'Whichever hospital I am going to, make sure he doesn't know where I am, please. I don't want him anywhere near us.'

'Rachel, please!'

'Fuck you, Chris! We're finished.'

'Rachel, I can explain!'

'Explain it to someone who gives a fuck because I don't!' she said, turning to Matt. 'Get me out of this hell hole.'

'Take them to Ysbyty Gwynedd and drop them on the doorstep,' Matt ordered. 'There's always loads of coppers there. They'll snap you up straightaway and look after you.' Rachel hugged him briefly. He ruffled Claire's hair. 'I won't say that I'll see you soon because I won't. Take care of yourselves.'

'Thanks again, Matt.' She looked at her husband. Something inside her broke. 'Please tell me that you won't kill him, will you, Matt?'

'Not tonight. You have my word.'

'Thank you.'

'Go, go, go,' he said with a smile. 'When you've dropped them off, take off. Best if we split up and go our separate ways.' He said to the driver. He nodded and took them away. 'You don't know how lucky you are,' Matt turned to Chris. Chris didn't speak. He had his head in his hands, a broken man.

'We should kill him anyway and make sure the bastard can't testify,' Justin said. 'We can make sure that they don't find the body.'

'They don't need a body anymore, Justin.'

'What?'

'Think it through. They had two informants in our outfit, one is dead. If the other one vanishes, they'll assume he's dead. Body or no body, we're guilty by association. They will charge us all with conspiracy to murder at least and give us life anyway. Unfortunately, the bastard needs to live for us to do less time.'

'This is fucked up.'

'It's over, all over. It's damage limitation time. We need to cut and run.'

'What do we do about the debt list for Lloyd?'

'Forget it,' Matt sighed. 'Where he's going, he won't need it. None of us will. The debts will still be debts whether they are collected tomorrow or not. We all need to run and stay free for as long as is physically possible.'

'What do we do with the rat?'

'I'll dump him in town somewhere quiet,' Matt said, looking at the injured man. 'Someone will call an ambulance. He's no longer our problem. He'll get what's coming to him eventually.'

'Put him into Matt's car,' Justin ordered. 'Good luck.' He held out his hand and Matt shook it. 'Where will you go?'

'I don't know yet. I don't suppose it matters really. They'll catch up with us sooner or later. The airports and ports will be on alert to look out for us. Have you got a bent passport?'

'No.'

'Me neither,' Matt smiled, thinly. 'See you on the other side.' They nodded to one another and walked in different directions. The noise of the pigs squealing reached a crescendo. Matt hoped that he would never have to hear that noise again.

CHAPTER 15

Matt drove the vehicle in silence. Chris was slumped in the passenger seat, staring out of the window. He pulled a packet of cigarettes out of his pocket with a blood-stained hand and put one into his mouth. His fingers were shaking as he lit it. He offered Matt one as an afterthought. Matt shook his head and snorted. Chris shrugged and put them away. His swollen face looked monster-like in the half light.

'Suit yourself,' he mumbled. He opened the window a few inches and exhaled the smoke. It was sucked out of the window into the night. Yellow light strobed inside the car, making their skin look sallow. The roads were quiet. 'Where are you taking me anyway? I could use a drink.'

Matt glanced at him and shook his head again.

'What do you think, we're mates again because I stopped Justin tossing you and your family into the machine?'

'No.'

'Good because I'm not your friend.'

'We go back a long way, Matt,' Chris said, quietly. 'I appreciate what you did for Rachel and Claire.'

'I did it for them, not you.'

'I know that.'

'You're an idiot,' Matt snapped. 'What the fuck did you throw it all away for?'

'I'm not hard like you, Matt,' Chris said, glancing at him He sucked deeply on the menthol, allowing the smoke to escape from his nostrils. 'I wouldn't have lasted a week in the clink. You know I wouldn't. I just couldn't face it. Rachel used to watch *Jeremy Kyle* and she always told me that if her man went to jail, she wouldn't wait for him and he would never see their child again. If I had gone down, she would have run a mile and I would never have seen Claire again.'

'Oh, I see,' Matt scoffed. 'And what the fuck do you think just happened? How did your alternative plan work out for you, Chris?'

'I took a gamble. Put me in the same position again and I would do the same thing.' Matt glared at him. 'What? I'm a coward. I know it. They would have eaten me alive in there. If Stuart had been more careful, no one would have been any the wiser.'

'Until we all got lifted.'

'Lloyd would have been lifted with or without my help. He's a psycho.

I couldn't do time. It is what it is.'

'You would have been protected.'

'Oh really?' Chris scoffed. 'By who?'

'Lloyd has contacts inside. They would have looked after you.'

'No one does anything for nothing in the clink. I wasn't becoming someone's bitch. That was never going to happen. I took the gamble and lost. I can't change it now so fuck it.'

'Don't try and justify what you have done. You're a grass. How many nights have we spent drinking, talking with our families and all the time you were stabbing me in the back? You're a selfish bastard and you've fucked everything up.' He indicated onto the slip road that joined the A55, heading towards Holyhead, accelerating into light traffic. An articulated lorry moved over to let him in and then fell behind.

Chris inhaled the last of the cigarette and flicked it through the window. Matt watched it hit the road in the rear-view mirror, a shower of orange sparks glowed for a second, then faded to nothing. He thought it was ironic. A split second in time and everything can change. One-minute things were okay, the next everything has turned to shit.

'You were right, you know,' Chris said, staring out of the window.

'About what?'

'Killing me and my girls. They would have crucified you for that. All of you.'

'That's the only reason they're alive,' Matt said, looking at him for a second. 'They won't be if the Karpovs get hold of them.'

'You were right about that too.' Matt glanced at him again. 'They will never be safe as long as I'm breathing. Lloyd, Jaz, and the Karpovs will hunt them down. I can't let that happen.' Chris opened the door and unclicked the seatbelt simultaneously and then tossed himself into the night. Matt watched his body bouncing along the asphalt, rolling over and over until the articulated lorry hit him and launched him into the middle lane. His body somersaulted in the air and landed beneath the wheels of a National Express bus. The wind whistled around the car. Matt leaned over and pulled the door closed and then accelerated into the fast lane. Another example of a split second where everything changed in the blink of an eye.

CHAPTER 16

Rachel and Claire were sitting in the back of a BMW. The radio was on and Rhianna was singing about being naked. Claire hadn't asked what had happened to her father or why he wasn't going with them. She sensed that her mother wasn't telling her everything, things that she didn't understand. Rachel would sit her down and explain everything to her one day but it wouldn't be any day soon. He had lost the right to be top priority in their lives the day he picked up a gun and a kilo of cocaine. If that was the world, he had chosen then he could have it but it had put his daughter in danger and that was unforgiveable. There was nothing that he could say, no number of apologies and no gestures of remorse that could take that away. He had crossed a line and there was no way back. She knew something was amiss but hadn't suspected drugs. Importing and exporting. That was what he said he did. When she asked what it was that they imported and exported, he had mumbled something about commodities. It didn't sound like a word he would have used. More likely he had heard somebody else saying it. She doubted he even knew what a commodity was. A chair with a hole in it and a pot that people piss in underneath it.

Her mother had told her that he was as thick as pig shit but that was part of the reason, she had married him. He was easy to manipulate. His brains were in his pants and she had used that to control him. He was like a puppy dog following her around, sniffing at her behind, waiting for some love and affection. She had rationed sex, giving him enough to make it not a chore for her but also kept him wanting her. The sex had been good if she was honest. Good, not spectacular. Her ex had been spectacular but he had been spectacular with two of her best friends too. She knew Chris wasn't the brightest bulb on the tree but she knew he would be faithful. Faithful and trainable. He had made a lot of money, so much that she should have realised it was drugs. In her mind, she had told herself that they were importing and exporting fake designer goods. He had come home with a few pairs of Ugg boots for her the year before and a couple of Hugo Boss shirts for himself and said Lloyd had given them out as a bonus on a good shipment. Drugs had never crossed her mind. In hindsight, she should have known better.

Claire snuggled into her and murmured. She would be asleep in seconds. She could fall asleep on a washing line.

****

Vasily Karpov pulled alongside the BMW. He timed it perfectly as the motorway bridge loomed in the headlights. He steered the Range Rover left into the driver's side of the BMW. The driver was taken completely unawares and the car veered left across the hard shoulder. He tried to brake but it was too late. The BMW hit the massive concrete structure at over sixty miles an hour, forcing the engine block through the dashboard cutting the driver in half, smashing the front seats and pinning Rachel and Claire in the back. The collision was devastating and Rachel was stunned. She only had a second to comprehend what had happened when the petrol tank exploded.

CHAPTER 17
FORTY-EIGHT HOURS LATER

Peter Clough put his wallet, car keys, and phone into his locker. He picked up his comms set and the keys to his wing and headed to the office to see how many of his shift had phoned in sick. Staff shortages and a steep spike in violent incidents had pushed the sick leave through the roof. Built in recent years, HMP Berwyn was already dirty, overcrowded, and unsafe for prisoners and prison guards. He knocked on the security glass window and a fellow officer looked up from his newspaper and let him in.

'You're on a skeleton shift again, Peter.' The officer said, going back to his paper. 'You're two down on the shift. Barnes and Ellis are still sick.' He opened his mouth and pointed inside it with his index finger. 'Bad throat again.'

'They should call them sicknote and sick throat,' Peter moaned. 'How many times can a man get tonsillitis anyway?'

'I don't know why they keep on scheduling them.'

'Me neither. Having said that, I hardly notice when they're not here. Pair of empty-heads.' Peter laughed hoarsely. 'They're a waste of oxygen if I'm honest.'

'That's putting it politely!'

'Anyway, once again, into the fray we go,' Peter said, in a theatrical voice.

'Be careful out there.'

Peter clocked on and made his way to the wing gates. The sound of men's voices echoed from the ancient walls, eight wings packed with prisoners locked up night and day meant the place was a tinder box waiting to be lit. He opened the first gate and stepped inside the buffer zone, locking it behind him. The nightshift officers were filling in their notes, ready to hand over the wing. The landings were filling up. The prisoners were being let out, three cells at a time to collect their breakfast, before having to return with it to their cells to be locked up again. The shortage of officers meant that communal dining had been suspended temporarily, which was causing tension throughout the jail. There had been three attempted drone deliveries in a week and the governor was extremely pissed off. Making the prisoners eat in their cells was his way of punishing them.

'Anything exciting to report?' Peter asked his opposite number from the nightshift.

'The usual shenanigans.' The officer sighed. 'Some bright spark catapulted a package over the wall last night. The dogs were on it straightaway. A couple of mobile phones and some spice. We think it was aimed at the Ahmed crew. They're the only ones thick enough to toss stuff over the wall when we're on lockdown and they're the ones who are the most pissed off about it being intercepted. I've made a report for the governor, apart from that, all is quiet on the Western Front, officer Clough,' he joked. 'Keeping the bastards locked up helps take the pressure off a bit, although this place feels like it's about to explode. Have a good one.'

'Will do,' Peter said with a nod. He unlocked the last gate and stepped onto the landings, waving hello to the officers on the higher tiers. The lower level was quiet, the prisoners already eating their breakfast. Peter walked along the landing towards the single cells. They were used for the senior hierarchy, the prisoners who ran the wings. The officers had the keys but the city's gangsters ran the prison. They always had and always will. If a PO stepped over the line with the hierarchy, their families would be targeted on the outside. They were just as vulnerable as anyone else and bars and barbed wire couldn't stop a powerful criminal's influence beyond the walls. Nothing could. Playing the game kept a fragile peace. Peter reached the cell that he wanted and knocked on the bars before he opened the door.

'Officer Clough,' the prisoner said, as he stepped inside and closed the door behind him. Anthony John was lying on his bunk reading a book. Everyone knew him as AJ. His skin was the deepest black colour that only those from central Africa possess. His eyes were deep brown with intelligence behind them. 'What can I do for you?'

'I have got a problem that I need help with, you owe me one, remember?' Peter said, keeping his voice low. 'You help me and I'll help you. You know how it goes.'

'Tell me what your problem is and I'll think about it,' AJ said, putting his book on the floor. He swung his feet off the bed and sat up. His wiry frame seemed to grow as he stood up. He was seven inches taller than Peter. 'I do owe you one but a man can lose his reputation in here doing favours for a PO,' he said, a wide grin on his face. 'We don't want the landings thinking AJ is a snitch.' He moved closer. 'What's up?'

'Do you remember Lloyd Jones?' Peter said, his voice a whisper. AJ nodded, suspicion in his eyes. 'He's trying to move gear onto the wing and he has set me up. The bastard has my fingerprints on some packets and he's threatening to tell the governor that I'm dealing.'

AJ rubbed his chin. 'I've heard that he is moving stuff on some of the other wings. How does he have your prints?'

'One of his crew in here stitched me up by getting a nonce to show me some old coins. They were in little packets.'

'And now those packets have traces of cocaine in them, yes?' AJ grinned.

'Yes.' Peter leaned closer. AJ lowered his head. 'I need those packets destroyed. They're on this wing somewhere, I know they are. They must be. There's no way that I'm moving gear onto this wing or any other wing, not for Lloyd Jones, or anybody else for that matter.'

'Plenty of screws do,' AJ said, grinning again. 'How else would it get in here?'

'I know what goes on, I'm not stupid but I'm not bent either. Help me to destroy those packets and I don't mind turning a blind eye sometimes, especially in your direction.'

'I don't want Jones trading on the wing. This is my wing.' AJ turned serious, his face like stone. 'You've got yourself a deal. Who is the motherfucker that stitched you up?'

'Jack Howarth, little kiddie-fiddler with glasses.'

'I know him. Leave it with me. If those packets are still on the wing, he'll give them to me. It will be a pleasure to rattle that dirty paedo!' He pointed his bony index finger at Clough. 'Then we're even.'

CHAPTER 18

Alan and Kim walked into the interview room. Brian Selby was sitting behind the table his brief next to him. He didn't look up as the detectives took their places and read out the legalities. As she sat down, Kim straightened her hair above her ears and opened a manila file. Alan undid the buttons on his grey suit jacket. His blue tie was already loosened at the collar.

'Before we start, I have some important news for you,' she said. 'Christopher Cornell was found on the A55, tossed from a car we think. He was hit by a lorry and then thrown under a bus.' Brian looked up then back down very quickly. He looked even fatter in the grey tracksuit that they had given him to wear. The trousers revealed six inches of the crack of his arse when he sat down. Sweat patches had formed beneath the armpits and he was already starting to smell of body odour.

'Is he dead?' Brian glanced at his brief.

'Yes, very,' Kim replied, curtly.

'That's a shame. He was alright with me,' Brian said, unconvincingly. 'Not like the others.'

'His wife and daughter were killed in a car crash the same night and their home was burned to the ground. Do you think these were terrible coincides or were they linked?'

'I don't think my client ...'

'They're not coincidences,' Brian interrupted his brief. 'Bad things happen around Lloyd Jones.' Brian shrugged but his face had gone pale. Alan wanted him scared. He needed him to know that this wasn't a game. 'If they're all dead, Lloyd had something to do with it. I'll guarantee it.'

'Are you ready to tell the truth, Brian?' Alan asked. He nodded but didn't speak or look up. 'For the tape, Brian.'

'Yes,' he muttered.

'Good,' he said, sitting back in her chair. 'What were you doing in the woods on the night Stuart Radcliffe was shot?'

'I went to dig up my drone.'

'You had buried a drone in the woods?'

'Yes.'

'Why?'

'Lloyd Jones made me fly a football over the wall of the prison.'

'A football?' Alan said, frowning.

'He had filled it full of drugs and mobile phones.' Brian sat up and looked at them. He twiddled his fingers, nervously. 'He made me pilot my drone to deliver the football into the exercise yard.'

'So, you attempted to smuggle drugs into the prison?'

'He said that he would hurt my mum if I didn't.'

'So, he threatened you. Forced you to do it?'

'Yes.' Brian pointed to the scar on his face. 'He did this to me with a steak knife because I buried it.'

'Tell us what happened.'

'I flew the ball over the wall and dropped it in the exercise yard but the prison officers were waiting. The delivery was intercepted and I knew that the police would be looking for the pilot along the road so I buried it in the woods and left it there. When I told him that it was still in the woods, he cut my face.'

'Okay,' Kim said, smiling thinly. 'Thank you for being honest with us. Tell me what happened afterwards. Why did you go back with Lloyd Jones and Stuart Radcliffe?'

'I didn't,' Brian mumbled. 'I went alone. Lloyd told me that I had to throw it in the Straits but I didn't want to destroy it, so I moved it.'

'Moved it?' Alan asked.

'I dug it up and then buried it somewhere else where Lloyd couldn't find it.'

'Go on.'

'I don't think they trusted me to throw it in the sea,' Brian said with a shrug. 'They followed me and when I reached the garage on the way back, they were there. That should be on camera,' he added, quickly.

'We have seen that but it doesn't show Lloyd,' Kim confirmed. 'What happened in the woods?'

'I dug up my bag and showed them the drone inside. That was when Lloyd pulled out a gun.' Brian paused and swallowed hard, his eyes becoming watery. 'He told me to keep digging. I thought he was going to shoot me and bury me in the hole because I hadn't done what he asked.'

'What was Stuart Radcliffe doing?' Kim asked.

'He was shouting at me. I was asking Lloyd not to shoot me, you see. I was nervous and frightened and I ramble when I get nervous. I think I was getting on his nerves.'

'Go on.'

'I kept on digging and when it was done, that's when Lloyd started asking how much the Drug Squad had paid for the information. I thought he was asking me but he was talking to Stuart. Then he shot him.'

'Then what?' Alan encouraged him. 'Take your time.'

'Then he made me help to bury him so we used all the dirt and old leaves and stuff. Then Stuart tried to get out of the grave, he wasn't dead.

So, Lloyd stabbed the spade into the ground, three times.' He made the action as he explained. 'And then he stayed dead.'

'Then what?'

'We buried him again, properly. Lloyd said he would feed my mum to the pigs if I didn't.'

Kim and Alan exchanged glances. 'What pigs?'

'What?' Brian blushed. He looked at his hands.

'You said that he threatened to feed your mum to the pigs,' Kim pushed. 'What pigs?'

'I don't know,' Brain lied. 'He just said it.'

'Where does Lloyd Jones have pigs?' Alan pushed.

'I don't know,' Brian said, looking at the floor.

'You're lying again,' Kim snapped. Brian jumped.

'I'm not lying.'

'Then explain yourself!'

'He has shares in a farm that has an illegal abattoir.'

'An illegal abattoir?'

'It's in Caergeiliog somewhere. They ship the meat abroad,' Brian said, looking from Alan to Kim to his brief. 'I overheard them talking about it. So, when he said he would feed my mum to the pigs, I believed him.'

'Well, you would, wouldn't you?' Kim said, sitting back. She watched his eyes. She couldn't tell if this was a fantasy or reality.

'They have done it before, you know,' Brian added.

'Done what?' Alan asked, coolly.

'Fed people to the pigs,' Brian said, conspiratorially. 'I heard them talking about some brothers, once. They killed them and fed them to the pigs.'

'Can you remember their names?' Kim asked.

'Wats or Wicks.' He closed his eyes. 'Wicks it was.'

'Okay, we'll consider that,' Kim said, looking at Alan. He nodded. 'When did Stuart attack you?' Kim changed tack.

'Stuart?'

'Yes. You said he attacked you.'

'I'm not sure,' Brian mumbled. 'When I was digging the hole. He kept shouting at me, then he grabbed my throat.'

'You didn't mention that when you were talking us through it,' Kim said, staring into his eyes. He looked up and then down again. 'So, you and Lloyd buried Stuart and left the woods together?'

'No,' Brian blurted. 'He left me there and told me to make sure the grave was hidden with leaves and stuff. So, I did what he said and then I left and that was when I was arrested.'

'Okay, Brian,' Kim said, smiling. 'That's all we need for now.'

'Really?'

'Really,' she said, watching his expression closely. 'We need to ask Lloyd Jones what his side of the story is before we make any decisions.'

'Will you tell him what I've said?' Brian asked, quietly. 'I mean everything?'

'We'll see what he has to say and take it from there.' She watched him for long seconds but he didn't speak. 'If you have told us the truth, there won't be any problem will there?' Brian shook his head almost imperceptibly. 'Good. Interview terminated.'

Brian looked pale and frightened as they stood up and left the room.

CHAPTER 19

Lloyd Jones was handcuffed to his hospital bed. He had been moved to HMP Berwyn and was recuperating on the hospital wing. He was isolated from the other patients in a secure room. His brief had arrived half an hour earlier in anticipation of an initial interview with DI Kim Davies and DI Alan Williams. He heard the key turning in the lock and the door creaked open. Kim and Alan stepped inside and for a moment, her perfume masked the overpowering stink of antiseptic and sweaty men but it was soon overwhelmed.

'Good afternoon, detectives,' Jacob Graff said, standing up to greet them. His dark, silk suit was tailored perfectly and his silver hair was gelled back from his forehead. Highly polished brogues reflected the surroundings on the toe. His face looked younger than his sixty-five years but the liver spots on his hands and his turkey neck gave the game away. 'I trust Anglesey's finest are in good fettle.'

'I see you're still defending the island's lowlife,' Alan countered. He undid the button on his dark blue suit jacket.

'Shall we dispense with the horseshit and get on with it?' Kim said, a sarcastic grin on her face.

'She's a feisty one, this one,' Jacob said, winking at Lloyd. Lloyd didn't look impressed. 'We'll have to be on our best game with her around.' Lloyd shifted uncomfortably on the bed. He was propped up with pillows behind him. His right hand was heavily bandaged and there were a dozen dark purple entry holes on his neck and lower face. Some of the larger holes had been stitched. He eyed the detectives with suspicion but there was also a glint in his eyes as if he was excited.

'We've come to speak to you about a few matters, so I need to remind you that you're under caution,' Alan began. 'Let's start with how you ended up here.'

Lloyd looked at Jacob and Jacob nodded that it was okay to answer the question.

'I was shot by Del Makin,' Lloyd said, sitting up further. 'Sorry, Derrick Makin. He lives in Rhoscolyn Village.'

'Do you have an address?' Kim asked, her eyebrows raised in surprise. She hadn't expected him to give them a name.

'Refail Farm somewhere. I can't remember the number but you're the detectives. I'm sure it won't take you long to find him.'

'You're sure it was him?' Alan asked.

'Oh, yes, one hundred percent. He stood in front of me as clear as you are now, no mask, no balaclava, nothing,' Lloyd said, smiling. 'He probably didn't expect me to survive to identify him, still, you have to admire his balls, don't you?' he looked at Kim. 'Excuse the language.'

'I've heard much worse,' she replied, curtly. 'Do you know why he shot you?'

Jacob nodded again.

'Because I'm an eyewitness.'

'To what?' Alan asked, frowning.

'The murder of Jaz.'

'Makin shot Jaz?' Alan asked, shocked.

'Yes.'

'You saw him shoot Jaz?' Kim asked, shaking her head.

'Not exactly.' Lloyd shrugged. 'I heard him shoot Jaz. Then I saw him leaving his office.'

'Tell us what happened, exactly,' Alan asked, sitting back.

'I was there on business,' Lloyd said, cheerily. 'I parked up the motor, walked into the club, said hello to the bouncers and the miserable bitch on the till and then I looked into the club to see if he was at the bar,' he paused. 'He wasn't there so I figured that he would probably be in his office. As I got to the first-floor landing, I thought that I heard something. Three times. Like a spitting noise.' He looked from one to the other to see if they were following him. The detectives looked taken aback. 'The next thing I know, Del Makin was coming down the stairs, white as a sheet, he was. I said hello and shook his hand but he made some excuse for being in a hurry and legged it down the stairs. Of course, when I got to the office, Jaz was as dead as a dodo. Makin must have shot him just minutes before I arrived.' He could see the doubt on their faces. 'Ask the bouncers, they will verify that he arrived before me and left in a hurry, I'm sure.' He paused and feigned sorrow. 'I always liked Jaz. He was old school. Don't get me wrong, he was no angel but we got on, you know?'

'Your pockets were stuffed full of cash and the safe was empty,' Kim said, rolling her eyes. 'You liked him enough to steal his money while he was still warm?'

'What can I say,' Lloyd sighed. 'It was a moment of weakness. There was my old friend Jaz, shot to death and all that cash was lying around. It was an opportunist crime but a crime, nonetheless. I hold my hands up. I took the money.'

'Very gallant of you,' Kim said, sarcastically. 'So, you took the money and then what?'

'I went back to the car. As I approached it, Makin shot me with both barrels.'